Only The Leaves Whispering

Only The Leaves Whispering

The Hundred Book 1

Jim Ellis

Copyright (C) 2020 Jim Ellis
Layout design and Copyright (C) 2020 by Next Chapter
Published 2020 by Magnum Opus – A Next Chapter Imprint
Edited by Lorna Read
Cover art by Cover Mint
This book is a work of fiction. Names, characters, places, and incidents are the product of the author's imagination or are used fictitiously. Any resemblance to actual events, locales, or persons, living or dead, is purely coincidental.
All rights reserved. No part of this book may be reproduced or transmitted in any form or by any means, electronic or mechanical, including photocopying, recording, or by any information storage and retrieval system, without the author's permission.

Acknowledgements

Thanks to Sally McElwain for her encouragement. And many thanks to my Good Lady Jeannette for her patience and support

Go, bid the soldiers shoot.
Shakespeare, Hamlet, act 5 sc. 2,1.

Chapter One

He was born in 1849 in Westburn, a tough seaport on the River Clyde on the West Coast of Scotland. Jock MacNeil's family were Highlanders, Catholics from the island of Barra. When he was thirteen, his mother died, and a few weeks later, in despair, his father, a blacksmith by trade, killed himself.

With both parents dead, Jock MacNeil worried that he'd fall into the care of Irish priests and nuns who ran the local Catholic orphanage. His dislike of God's Messengers started in primary school when, one Friday afternoon during a period of religious instruction, he'd bungled the answer to the question, "Who made you?" from Sister Mary Ann, a bruiser Irish nun in charge of the class.

Gripped by funk, he lowered his head and said nothing, though the answer rang inside his head: "God made me to know Him and love Him in this world and forever in the next."

Sister Mary Ann dragged him from his seat to the storage cupboard.

"Yer a wee devil, MacNeil. For yer dumb insolence, ye'll stay in the dark cupboard until Ah tell ye to come out."

Jock cried and struggled in Sister Mary Ann's iron grip, and his right hand hit her face. The Sister slapped him about the ears.

A tear-stained, sullen Jock blinked as he came into the light of the empty classroom. Sister Mary Ann, threatening in her black habit stood by her desk, arms folded, petted lower lip and lantern jaw jutting beyond the tip of her nose.

Only The Leaves Whispering

"Well, MacNeil, are ye ready to say yer sorry for yer bad behaviour?"

Jock said nothing, just turned on his heel and fled the classroom.

"You've been cryin'," his mother said when he came home.

He told her, and later, mentioned to his father what had happened. The parents thought it best to let the incident blow over.

"Ye'll be fine on Monday," his father said. "That old bat will have forgotten all about it."

Sister Mary Ann said nothing on Monday, but the incident was far from over. Sister Mary Ann meant to crush the spirit out of young MacNeil.

Father Seamus Riordan appeared half an hour before the class went for the mid-day meal. The class rose as one and saluted the priest.

"Good morning, Father Riordan."

The boys sat down, folded their arms and sat up straight. The priest dragged Jock from his seat.

"Sister Mary Ann, fetch me the cane."

"Are ye ready, boy, to say yer sorry to the Good Sister?"

Silence.

"Answer me, boy."

Silence.

"I know fine well yer not Irish, but that's no excuse. Yer one of them Scotch Catholics, an insolent brat."

Father Riordan cuffed Jock, leaving the mark of his hand on his right cheek. He grabbed Jock by the back of the neck and pushed his head down until the boy's buttocks stuck out. The cane whistled as the priest whipped it against Jock's arse. Six brutal lashes, a pause, and three more added for good measure.

"Ah'll be back tomorrow to hear ye tell Sister Mary Ann yer sorry."

A humiliated Jock skipped afternoon class and limped home.

Jock's bare arse was crisscrossed by angry red welts and mottled patches of bruised blood. His trousers had protected the flesh from breaking.

"Who did that to ye?" his mother said.

"Father Riordan. He said Ah wis insolent. Ah never said anything when he told me Ah had to say sorry to Sister Mary Ann. Called me a Scotch brat."

"That man is no Father. He's a thug. A tinker in a dog collar."

Mrs MacNeil got her son ready for bed and, with buttocks bared, had him lie on top of the bed. She prepared a mustard paste and flannel patches cut from an old nightdress, and spread the mustard paste with a knife on the flannel patches and laid them on the welts and bruises. His mother fashioned a primitive bandage from an old muslin curtain, firm enough to hold the flannel patches in place, which she wrapped around Jock's middle,.

The boy didn't want to go to bed so early in the day, so his mother let him rest on a wooden settle lying on his side.

When Jock's father came home from the forge, he was furious when he saw what had happened to his son.

"Ah'll see to that damned priest in the morning," he threatened.

Jock's father didn't have to wait until the next day to deal with Riordan. The family had not long finished the evening meal when a black-coated figure opened the front door and walked into the apartment.

"Ah'm Father Riordan, here to see about that son of yours."

Jock's father rose, closed the space between him the priest and whipped off his wide-brimmed hat with the round crown, forcing the brim into the priest's hand.

"Did ye forget to knock? Have ye no fuckin' manners? Ye'll take yer hat off when ye come to this house."

Riordan scowled, his face contorted by rage. He'd grown used to a deferential, subservient flock.

"Stay where ye are, Riordan. There's no chair for ye here. Say yer piece."

Riordan had a well-fed body. He was a sybarite leading a hungry flock. A fat man who worshipped his belly. He shifted his stance, repositioned his blackthorn stick and rested his weight on it, composing himself for a counter-attack. Catching his breath, Riordan had a good look around the room. He pointed the blackthorn at a picture frame hanging on the wall.

"And what might that be?"

Jock's father gazed at the gold frame, a rectangle measuring two foot by a foot and a half, holding a piece of heavy blue silk, with an eagle and badges embroidered in gold thread. The raptor sat on a narrow plinth, with the name *Waterloo* embossed on the front, mounted on the regimental name: *The Royal Scots Greys.* Beneath it, the regimental motto: *Nemo Me Impune Lacessit.*

"Ah, the Latin. An edicated man are ye, MacNeil?" a smirking Riordan intoned.

"Ma old regiment. Captured an Eagle at Waterloo when they beat the French. Ah acquired ma trade in the Greys. Farrier Sergeant, ten years service. Aye, Riordan. You heed the Latin: 'Nobody Touches Me With Impunity; Second to None'."

"How can you, MacNeil, a Catholic, have served in the British Army after what they did in Ireland?"

"That's fightin' talk, mister. Yer no up to a scrap. Yer big, but yer a fat man, good for nuthin' but sittin' on yer arse and stuffin' yer face. Ah'm Scots and British. There's no Irish in me.

Rage got the better of Riordan. He waved the blackthorn and made to smash the shaft on the edge of the kitchen table. Instead, he dashed the point on the floor. Jock's father got an arm lock on Riordan, and the stick fell from his hand. He prodded the priest in the belly with the blackthorn, edging him out the door of the apartment.

"Get out, and don't come back here. Ye'll no see ma son again in yer damned school. Ah'll be sendin' him to the Protestant school. Away and take yerself back over the water."

* * *

After the deaths of their parents, Jock's younger brother and sister, too young to attend school, were taken into care. They were made wards of the local Catholic orphanage run by Irish Clergy and Nuns. A kindly Protestant neighbour, a blacksmith, helped Jock stay clear of

God's Messengers. He took him in, keeping Jock at secondary school for a few months and gave him a job in the forge as an apprentice blacksmith and farrier. This man's goodness was Jock's sole experience of Christian charity. But, after some months, he knew that these arrangements could not last. Jock took up space in an overcrowded tenement flat; he was a drain on the meagre resources of the blacksmith, his wife, and their four children. So he went to sea.

The blacksmith did the best that he could for Jock. He gave him five shillings from his savings to start the journey and a small, well-thumbed, leather-bound King James Bible. For a time, Jock turned to the Good Book, but the way Christians actually behaved quickly drove him from it.

Some men fail in the struggle with circumstances and other men fight on. Jock MacNeil was a fighter. He went to sea to escape a dire Westburn slum and stay clear of Irish priests and nuns. He wanted no truck with the Messengers of God.

Jock signed on the schooner *Jane Brown* as galley boy. She carried general cargo between British and Irish ports. He came aboard wearing a Tam O' Shanter, a shabby, heavy black jacket from his father's wardrobe. Below the coat he wore an ill-fitting waistcoat too big for him, and a heavy grey flannel shirt. Jock's legs and feet were protected by black woollen trousers, and second-hand, rugged hobnailed boots. His bundle carried his mother's good blue linen shawl, a change of clothing and a spare pair of used brogans made on a straight last. The cobbler told him the brogans would take to the shape of his feet. He dreaded wearing them. A plaid in the MacNeil tartan for foul weather at the top of the bundle protected his concertina. Jock's job was to assist the cook.

Jock's berth on the *Jane Brown* was the crew's glory hole. The sleeping quarters and living area for the crew. A boy among tough men, he refused to be brought down, perhaps by a closet pederast. With a sharp blade in his belt, he kept to himself. Cast adrift from shore, a youth not yet out of childhood, living among hard seafaring men, Jock matured beyond his years.

Only The Leaves Whispering

The cook's habits disgusted the young Scot. He was a piss-artist and a habitual nose picker, rolling bogies in his fingers and flicking balls of snot about the galley. His fingernails had permanent crescents of dirt; he never washed his hands after visiting the head. When he'd finished cutting meat or preparing fish and potatoes, he'd wipe his hands on his grubby apron.

Jock chose his meals and, when he had the opportunity, cooked for himself.

"Whit's wrang wi' you?" The cook said. "Don't like mah cookin'?"

"Ah like mah food clean."

"Well, fuck you, MacNeil. Yer nuthin' but a wee shite."

One day, well in his cups, this disgusting Glaswegian blew his nose into the hem of his apron. Jock left the galley and puked over the windward side of the schooner.

On the second voyage, the schooner, bound for Sligo, heaved and twisted through heavy seas in St George's Channel. The cook, going through the motions of cleaning up after breakfast and preparing for the mid-day meal, honked over the galley deck and passed out. He was a fat man, and Jock could not move him. He left the galley and ran into the Bosun.

"Skylarking, are we?"

"No, Mr Driscoll. The cook's sick."

The Bosun entered the galley.

"For Christ's sake, he's fuckin' drunk an' he's covered the place in his puke. Ah'll get him to his bunk to sleep it off. Can you cope here, lad?"

"Ah'll clean up. Dried peas and boiled mutton at dinner-time. Ah'll get it ready."

"Ah'll send the Steward. Help you with the evening meal."

The Captain sacked the cook when the ship docked in Sligo. He sent for Jock.

"Ah'm rating you cook. A galley boy is joining the ship tomorrow. His name is Liam Fallon. He'll assist you. You can ask the Steward for help."

Jock and the new hand cleaned the galley, scouring and polishing the coppers, pots, cutlery and crockery. They soon pleased the crew, providing clean, wholesome ship's food, a welcome improvement on salt meats and hard biscuits.

The Captain, a former Royal Navy Master's Mate, took a greater interest in the workings of the galley. He knew that greens and root vegetables in the diet kept the crew healthy and instructed the young Scot to obtain and serve them two or three times a week. He told Jock to buy cheaper cuts of mutton, pork and beef, to be served once, and infrequently twice a week. Jock and his assistant learned to make soft tack, a relief from hardtack: soft bread served with butter twice a week.

But the Steward, bristling with resentment at Jock's promotion, stayed drunker than usual and gave no assistance to the galley.

Jock knew about looking after sick and injured horses. He'd been well-taught by his father, a blacksmith. The Steward, a dedicated toper, was often too drunk to deal with sick or hurt crewmen. The Captain cut the Steward's wages. He had Jock treat sick and injured crew, and increased his pay. Poisonous rage and a desire for revenge at the loss of face consumed the Steward.

The young men kept contact with him to the minimum required for the good of the ship.

The Steward craved revenge and could not wait until his temper cooled. He decided to mark Liam Fallon first, a sweet enough youth. He'd humiliate the lad and, with luck, ruin him.

The Steward waited until first light and watched Jock leave the galley.

Jock had left Liam preparing thick barley and mutton broth for the mid-day meal. He went for'ard to the hutch set in a few square feet of space, where the Captain and the mate kept a brood of eight hens and a rooster. Jock's hand explored among the straw, feathers and clucking birds until he found half a dozen eggs, placing them in a clean dish towel for safe passage to the galley. The Captain and the mate liked fried eggs and bacon for breakfast.

Only The Leaves Whispering

The locked door surprised Jock. He unlocked the door and entered the galley to find the Steward pinning the young Irish boy face-down on the chopping block with his right arm. The Steward held his erect member in his left hand, forcing it into Liam Fallon's backside.

"Be still, ya wee cunt. Ye'll love it when Ah get it up ye. Ye'll be wantin' it a' the time."

The Steward, determined to sink his dick, did not hear Jock enter. He laid the eggs safe by the coal-fired range, withdrew the sharp blade from his belt and slashed the Steward across both cheeks of his bare arse. The Steward screamed and staggered back, clutching his cut backside with both hands. He turned on Jock and screamed louder, and louder still, a tortured wailing, when he saw his fingers and hands sticky with blood. The Steward's swollen member shrank back into its foreskin.

Liam, sobbing, collapsed on the galley deck.

"Yer a fuckin' Papish bastard, MacNeil," the Steward screamed. "Ah'll get ye! Some night Ah'll come fur ye. Ye'll be sorry ye ever met me."

Jock brained him with a rolling pin, and the Steward fell unconscious on the galley deck.

The Bosun, alerted by the commotion, burst through the galley door.

"Whit the fuck is goin' on here?" He glanced around the galley. "Ah see whit's happened. The fuckin' Steward is at it again."

The Bosun picked up Liam.

"Are ye all right, son? Did he get tae ye?"

"No. Jock stopped him. Thanks be to God, and Saint Patrick."

"Jock, look after the lad. Ah'll take care of this twat. Mind now, the skipper, the mate and the crew'll be wantin' breakfast. Ah'm hungry masel'."

Word spread among the men. The crew had a new respect for Jock, and they were embarrassed and worried for the young Irish boy in the galley. They liked the improved feeding and saw that Jock MacNeil would help a shipmate and could look after himself.

Jim Ellis

"Everything all right, Jock?" the sailmaker said, the day after the incident.

"We're fine thanks, Mr Fleming. Is the Steward in irons? Ah've no' set eyes on him."

"Ah heard there was an accident. The Steward fell overboard. The Bosun might have gi'ed him a wee nudge."

"My God!" Jock said.

Fleming reckoned Jock and his Irish assistant needed something to take their minds off the Steward's capers.

"Tell ye what, Jock. Tomorrow in the afternoon. Come and see me. Bring the Irish lad. Ah'll teach yez tae make and mend. Add wee touches. Keep yer kit smart and in good repair."

The sailmaker, an old RN hand, taught the boys the rudiments of sewing damaged seams and torn clothing, replacing lost buttons, darning and washing clothes in saltwater.

"Rinse yer clothes in rainwater if ye get the chance, or freshwater when the ship's in port," Fleming said. "And keep yerself clean. Better salt on yer body when yer dry than bein' clatty an' stinkin'."

Later, he had Jock bring more of his kit.

"Let's get yer breeks and jackets fitting. Ye look like a midget inside kit that's too big."

Jock and Liam were the smartest, cleanest, saltiest crewmen of the *Jane Brown* when they had a run ashore in British and Irish ports.

After some months at sea, Jock suffered injuries when he fell into the hold of the *Jane Brown*. Two sailors carried him to the premises of James Gunn, retired Naval Surgeon of Westburn.

Surgeon Gunn examined Jock.

"Galley Boy, are you, on the *Jane Brown*?"

"Yes, sir. Can you get me back to her soon? She sails for Ireland on the evening tide."

"Only if you want to kill yourself. Torn ligaments in your right leg, bruised ribs and that nasty cut on your left arm wants suturing. You need to rest. You'll be here for a week or two."

Only The Leaves Whispering

James Gunn treated Jock, bound his cracked ribs and leg, painted arnica on the bruising and sutured the cut to his arm, then had him put to bed.

"I'll tell you when you can get up."

"But Ah've little money."

"Don't worry about that, son. My practice is charity. I survive on donations. When you're well, you can help in the kitchen."

"Very happy, sir. By the way, Ah wis rated cook when the Captain sacked the cook for getting' fu'.

"Ah, you mean he got drunk?"

Jock nodded.

While Jock convalesced, Surgeon Gunn got to know him and discovered that he had been responsible for dealing with the cuts and bruises of life on the *Jane Brown*.

"The Steward wis a drunken-arse bandit. He went over the side. The Captain found out that Ah'd treated sick horses, and asked me to take it on."

"Good God. Cooking, treating horses, and now looking after sailors, and you only a lad."

"Ah've no' hurt anybody yet."

"Well, I'm going to teach you to treat cuts, bruises, suturing, sprains, dosing with medicine. You can see how I set a broken bone. When you rejoin the schooner, you'll know more."

Jock worked in the kitchen in the mornings, and in the afternoons James Gunn added polish to Jock's medical and nursing skills.

James Gunn donated a generous medical chest to Jock before he returned to the *Jane Brown*.

"Look after yourself, Jock. Think about joining the Royal Navy. You'd make a grand Loblolly Boy. You'd be helping the surgeons look after the sick."

"It's the Confederate Navy I'd like to join, sir."

They shook hands, and James Gunn grinned.

"You're a wild fellow, Jock, wanting that. Fighting for a foreign power. Some would say you'd be fighting to preserve slavery."

"Not me, Mr Gunn. What Ah'm against is the War of Northern Aggression. The Yankees invading the Southern States. Anyway, Mr Gunn, Ah treat people as Ah find them. Ah believe we're a' Jock Tamson's Bairns,"

"I understand, but not everyone will agree with you. The American Navy might hang you for piracy if you're captured. You'd be better off in the Royal Navy. Fight for your own country, son."

"Well, Mr Gunn, Ah'm British, and Ah'll no' fight against ma country. But Ah'm a Scot wi' an understandin' of how Southerners feel about the Yankee invasion."

Jock was literate and poor, and he scrounged newspapers. His romantic streak blossomed, strengthened by reports of the Civil War in the *Westburn Gazette* and the Irish papers. He devoured articles about the fighting at Fort Sumter, the First Manassas, and word of Lee and Jackson, Jeb Stuart, and Beauregard. Jock would talk to anyone who'd listen about Southern rights to secede from the Union. Jock, young and single-minded, was, from the start, for the South. He consumed news of the war. He believed that the War for Southern Independence was a struggle between David and Goliath. Southerners resisted just like his Highland ancestors, whose turncoat leaders drove them from the land after the collapse of the Forty-five.

Jock had listened to his father sitting by the fireside telling stories of island life. Barra was not threatened by clearance. But islanders knew of the Clearance taking place elsewhere in the Highlands, and Highlanders moving to the Americas.

The beauty of the land in the hamlet of Balanabodach by Loch Obe hid the interior of houses with earthen floors, families sleeping by the peat fire. The monotonous diet of thick broths, gruel and porridge, with occasional treats of fish and meat. A frugal life at the smithy supplemented by fishing and crofting, light-years from Kisimul Castle, the seat of the Clan MacNeil of Barra.

Poverty drove Jock's father and mother out of Barra. They left the island in 1848 before the landlord, during a potato famine, cleared the island in the 1850s.

Only The Leaves Whispering

Jock's parents brought poverty with them from Barra to Westburn. The father worked hard at the smithy, but from time to time hardship dogged the family. Hard knocks had left Jock feeling powerless but had deepened his sympathy for the South, standing up to the Yankee invader.

Gazing on blockade runners anchored in the River Clyde, he wanted to believe the rumours sweeping Westburn. Confederate warships were on the stocks of local shipyards.

Chapter Two

In 1862, the *Jane Brown* landed a cargo of hides from Dublin at Liverpool, and the fulfilment of boyhood dreams, of crossing the ocean and fighting for the South, lay within Jock's grasp. Across the Mersey in Birkenhead, a ship, launched in May, was fitting out at John Laird Sons and Company. The wiseacres on the docks said that she was a Confederate Cruiser. It did not take Jock long make enquiries and approach David Herbert Llewellyn, the Assistant Surgeon.

On first sight, Jock respected Llewellyn and he, in turn, liked Jock, who told a small lie, a venial sin. Jock said that he was sixteen, to convince Llewellyn that he was old enough to join the crew.

The Surgeon, an Englishman of Welsh extraction, was a tall, elegantly dressed man in his mid-twenties. In the days he spent standing by the ship, without the benefit of a uniform, Llewellyn seemed tall, clad in a slim-fitting frock coat and tight trousers fastened underneath the instep of his boots. Later, the impression of height was strengthened by his Confederate naval uniform. Lewellyn's face was stiff, and his long side-whiskers added years to a smooth complexion. Still, a smile played at the corners of his mouth, suggesting an underlying kindness of character. Jock could read and write, and he counted quickly, and Llewellyn admired his elegant penmanship. The lad's control of the pointed steel nib impressed the Assistant Surgeon: swift movements of the pen creating an open, flowing beautiful script of contrasting thick and thin strokes.

Only The Leaves Whispering

There was an incisive streak in David Herbert Llewellyn, a talent to improvise for the good of the ship. He took Jock around the ship. A workman approached and asked for help with a nasty gash on the heel of his hand.

"Alright, MacNeil. I'm going to clean the wound, and you show me what you can do with the needle. Then dress the wound."

In the unfinished sickbay, Llewellyn cleaned the wound. He watched as Jock inserted five sutures, neatly tied, then applying the Black Ointment, a drawing salve, finally covering the wound in lint and a tidy bandage.

Jock had survived Llewellyn's scrutiny.

He signed an affidavit that he had served aboard the schooner *Jane Brown* as Galley Boy and Cook. The document confirmed that he'd looked after the injured crew. Jock understood that the ship would sail as a man of war for the Confederate States of America. Ship's articles would be signed when the vessel left British territorial waters, and he would be rated Loblolly Boy.

The password '290' allowed him on board. He presented it to the watchman at the yard gate and the sailor stationed at the gangway. Lewellyn had said that he was confident that Mr MacNeil would do very well, so Jock jumped ship and brought his kit aboard.

But Jock could never refer to the vessel as The Ship, as others did. For him, she was always *Alabama*.

Jock was one of twenty hands on board, seamen and former Royal Navy men, many of them belonging to the Reserve. At first, Jock had little to do and, being level-headed, he explored the ship. At midday, chewing on hardtack and cheese, Jock would leave *Alabama* and walk to the other side of the fitting-out berth for a complete view.

Alabama was the most beautiful ship Jock had ever set eyes on. She was a fighting ship, a screw steamer of one thousand, one hundred tons, barque-rigged for long-distance cruising. The expert craftsmen who'd built *Alabama* said the best materials had been used. Nine months on the stocks and the fitting-out had given the South the best that British art and craft could build. For Jock, she was better than any vessel to come from a Royal Navy Dockyard. Jock loved the way she lay in the water, laden with stores and bunkers, a sleek, menacing Confederate Man of War.

Jock, a solitary boy, an orphan, desired to belong to her and was very happy when some of the crew, and workmen from the yard, invited him to a run ashore. Walking to the Liverpool ferry, observed by Federal spies, the men sang *Dixie*, and Jock MacNeil knew that he was one of them.

* * *

Jock's first duty on board was hardly naval, but he was willing to please. A party of elegant ladies and sober gentlemen came on board just before the ship, decorated with flags and bunting, left her berth, edging into the Mersey for a 'trial'. Llewellyn had volunteered Jock to wait on the visitors, seeing the visit as an opportunity for Jock to shine.

Jock, on deck in a smart white jacket and black trousers, conscious of his polished black shoes, glad that his rough hands were hidden by white gloves, moved quietly among the visitors with a silver tray bearing glasses of Champagne. Waiting tables at lunch in the saloon, he showed off his mastery of French Service learned aboard the *Jane Brown*. The deft movement of fork and spoon in his right hand, bringing food from the serving dish to the plate, impressed more than one guest. Llewellyn, seated at table, caught Jock's eye and winked approvingly.

Jock discreetly assisted the disembarkation of the guests returning to Birkenhead on a tug. *Alabama* then set a course south for a secluded bay on the island of Anglesey to embark more crew. Jock was surprised to see the new seamen had wives and girlfriends with them. While the crewmen and their women were paid an advance on their men's wages and fed and watered, two Ladies of the Night worked the ship.

Women were still a mystery to Jock, and an ugly rash of acne sapped his confidence. But, he was maddened by tumescence and, like many boys of his age, tormented while he slept. A hag, a parody of the girls he longed for, haunted his dreams. This phantom woman stoked his

Only The Leaves Whispering

desire until she vanished in nocturnal emissions that left him both gratified and ashamed when he woke.

One of the tarts who'd come aboard fired up his desire: thickening figure and sagging breasts, kohl-blacked eyes, rouged lips, and decaying teeth. Perversely, the whore's gin-soaked breath drew him on, and he had to go with her. Jock sought compassion, wanted a caress or a warmhearted touch. He lay with her in the sickbay, gorged with her sweat and cheap perfume. His hands probed her soiled underclothing. She whispered to Jock, "Take off my drawers." But she forbade him to kiss her or murmur endearments. Jock entered her. A thrust or two, and he was done, his deflowering over.

"That'll be five shillins. But seein' it's yer first time, I'll charge ye two and sixpence."

Llewellyn saw Jock escort the tart off the ship. He collared an embarrassed Loblolly Boy.

"Come and see me, Jock. A consultation. I want to make sure you don't have the pox."

* * *

The ship hove to in the North Channel off the North coast of Ireland, holding her own in a choppy sea. Jock, glad of the oilskin jacket issued to him, stood aft and watched the fishing boat approach and, under the skilful hand of her helmsman, touch alongside. Spray fell on Jock, and the wind tugged at his Tam O'Shanter just as he clamped his hand over it. A hand on his shoulder startled him.

"How are you, MacNeil?"

"Very well, Mr Low, sir."

Jock was surprised that Lieutenant John Low, returned from service in the CSS *Florida*, knew his name and bothered to notice him. Low's reputation preceded him aboard. An Aberdeen man who'd settled in the South and gone to a Georgia Cavalry Regiment before transferring to the Confederate Navy, he was known as Fearless John Low.

"You sailed on the *Fingal*, Mr Low?"

"So I did, son. A fine ship. An iron-hulled screw steamer. A foul night when we left Westburn, worse than this evening. Well down the Firth we ran down and sunk a brig. Austrian, I heard she was."

There were Scots, some of them Westburnians, that sailed on *Fingal*. Jock felt an affinity with these men who'd risked attack by the US Navy and brought her safely to Savannah.

Ahead to the northwest was Malin Head. On the port side, the Irish coast and the Giant's Causeway; on the starboard side to the east, a blurred line on the horizon, Scotland and the Mull of Kintyre. Deep in the Firth of Clyde was Westburn and home. Jock had a premonition that he'd never see again the town that he loved for the memory of his family and despised for its hatred of Catholics. He felt shame, too, for the brother and sister he'd abandoned to the care of nuns and priests. Jock could not stop the sob, and his shoulders shuddered involuntarily. The new-minted Confederate sailor whimpered, the wee boy that he was.

Then Jock got control of himself and dried his eyes on the sleeve of his oilskin jacket. He felt Lieutenant Low's hand on his shoulder, gentler this time.

"How old are you, son?"

"Sixteen, sir," Jock said stoutly.

"Aye, right enough, sixteen going on fourteen more like it."

The Confederate Agent disembarked and fetched onto the deck of the fishing boat. Hands flew aloft, and the ship made sail. Under Jock's feet, the hull came alive and he grinned as Low smiled, satisfied that they were underway.

There was a palpable sense of danger on board: the war was now touching Jock directly as the ship went out into the Atlantic to evade Federal warships. The USS *Tuscarora* was searching for *Alabama* in British waters and would have sunk her had she found her. Sailing under British colours was a ruse. Still, the Red Duster, the ensign of the British Merchant Marine, was no protection from the guns of the US Navy. They sailed past Tory Island, heading south, far off from the west coast of Ireland. Jock looked forward to fair weather. He wondered

Only The Leaves Whispering

what would change when Commander Semmes and his officers joined the ship.

Clearing Western Approaches, there were days of smooth sailing. The miles rolled away in the ship's wake. Jock brimmed with happiness, the worry of the pox forgotten as he capered aloft with the younger hands, surprised to discover that he was unafraid of heights.

The tops could be reached through the Lubber's Hole, an approach scorned by experienced hands. Jock used the Lubber's Hole the first time he went aloft.

"Once through the Lubber's Hole is enough, Jock," a leading topman said. "Next time, follow me."

After that, he made the final approach to the top climbing the underside of an overhanging rope at an angle of 45 degrees.

Jock felt he'd taken an important step, strengthening his status as a Man of War's Man. And he stowed and inventoried medical stores that had come aboard. His careful penmanship and attention to detail pleased Assistant Surgeon Llewellyn, confirming that it was a wise decision to bring Jock MacNeil on board.

One morning, after a few days at sea, Jock made a pot of coffee for Llewellyn and served him. He liked it black and strong.

"Thanks, Jock." Llewellyn reached across Jock in the confined space of the sickbay and brought another mug to the small table. He filled it and turned the handle towards Jock. "Join me. Try black coffee, and for heaven's sake, sit down."

They sipped the coffee, Jock nervously, for he was used to tea and a formal relationship with his officer.

"You're all right, MacNeil. You don't have the pox, but next time take yourself in hand. I suppose that was your cherry gone?"

Jock's face crimsoned. "Yes, sir, Thank you. Mr Llewellyn."

"You've made a good impression on Mr Low. He liked the way you waited on the guests when we left the Mersey. He's seen you flying aloft with the younger hands. He asked me to transfer you to the deck."

Llewellyn waited, letting the news sink in. "Well, Jock?"

"I like it here, sir. If it's up to me, I'd as soon be your Loblolly Boy."

He poured coffee into Jock's mug. "Then here it is, Jock.

* * *

Alabama anchored a mile off Terceira in the Azores. Her tenders, the *Agrippina* and the *Baha*, anchored nearby. They carried ordinance, stores and *Alabama's* officers.

On 24th August 1862, Jock stood in the ranks of the crews from the three ships, mustered on the deck of *Alabama* as the officers in full dress uniforms came aboard. Captain Semmes boarded last. A small-made man, but a commanding figure in his grey uniform, Semmes mounted a gun carriage and read himself in, his commission from President Jefferson Davies granting him the power to take command of the cruiser.

The reading-in completed, a scratch band from the crews of the three ships played *Dixie*, as the Quartermaster hauled down British colours. Jock's light but breaking voice joined the singing.

"I wish I was in the land of cotton…"

A signal cannon fired. The commissioning pennant rose on the mizzen gaff, stretching her length in the breeze. The splendid new battle ensign at the top of the mainmast snapped in the wind.

The ship was now The Confederate States Steamer, *Alabama*. Her motto was engraved on the bronze of the great wheel: *Aide-toi et Dieu t'aidera*; God helps those who help themselves.

Captain Semmes urged the men to support the Southern Cause. To tempt waverers, he promised signing-on money, double wages, paid in gold, and prize money awarded by the Confederate Congress for all destroyed Federal ships.

The British hands cheered the captain, and Jock was among the first of the eighty-three to sign on. Service aboard promised to be a far remove from the wretched state on board *Jane Brown*. Swallowing the lump in his throat, he watched the ink drying on his signature. The Loblolly Boy loved *Alabama* as only a once rootless orphan could. At last he was a Scots volunteer, a sailor in the Confederate Navy, serving

Only The Leaves Whispering

The Cause, defending the South. He was a proud Man of War's Man aboard its most excellent ship.

Jock loved the game of cat and mouse that Semmes played with the Yankee Navy. *Alabama* was everywhere and nowhere: a phantom feared by the Federals. He gave himself to the comradeship of working the ship: bunkering, taking on stores. Jock's keen sight helped him to be accepted as a lookout. He capered aloft with the young top-men; shared in the excitement when boarding parties rowed the ship's boats to take possession of Federal merchant ships.

Life aboard was not all duty and discipline. In fair weather during quiet spells, day workers stood down, watch-keepers at their station and the watch below standing by for orders to shift sails, a red sun on the horizon slipping through cerise and slate-blue clouds. A breeze going for'ard as the ship made her wind, sailing fine through a calm sea. Captain Semmes' permission given for dancing on the foc'sle.

Aboard *Alabama* were fiddlers, a mandolin, an alto horn, a bugle, Northumbrian Small Pipes and a banjo. The musicians invited Jock to play his concertina, brought with him in his bundle when he left *Jane Brown* to join *Alabama*.

The crew loved the hornpipe. It could be danced in a small space and did not require a partner. Many of the sailors, being former Royal Navy men, requested *Lord Nelson's Hornpipe* and *Trafalgar Hornpipe*. And they sang, the voices carried aft to the delight of the watch on the quarterdeck.

They had two favourites. One was *Spanish Ladies*:

Farewell and adieu to you, Spanish ladies,
Farewell and adieu to you, ladies of Spain;
For we have received orders
For to sail to old England,
But we hope in a short time to see you again.

British Tars was the other:

Come all you bold young sailors,
A warning take by me
and never leave your happy home
to sail the raging sea.

But the sailors all knew *Dixie*, and to a man stood at attention while they sang the final song of the evening.

Jock knew he belonged to the ship. A Man of War's Man.

The singing and dancing over, Jock sat on up for'ard with Davy White, a young wardroom steward.

"Davy, you're the first black man Ah've met."

Davy turned his gaze from the sea and smiled.

"You ain't the first white man Ah've met, but you the first one Ah'd call mah friend."

Davy White had been the body slave of a Delaware man, who'd come aboard from a prize, the US schooner *Tonawanda*, bound for Europe on 9th October 1862. Captain Semmes had set him free, and he'd enlisted as wardroom mess steward.

"Ah remember you takin' them officer's dress boots off that brigantine. You sure look after them, dustin' and polishin'."

Jock laughed. "Fine boots. Glad Ah stole them. First footwear Ah ever had that fitted me."

The young friends sat a while. Davy rose and went to the water butt and brought back a beaker-full. He offered it to Jock; he took a good swallow.

"Thanks, Davy, Ah needed that."

"That's what Ah thought."

Davy drained the beaker and returned it to the butt. He resumed his seat beside Jock.

"Ah felt it would be alright on the ship that day after you spoke to me."

Jock had approached Davy on deck soon after he came on board.

"Ah'm the Loblolly Boy, Jock MacNeil. Ah work for Assistant Surgeon Llewellyn."

Only The Leaves Whispering

Jock had offered his hand to the young black man and, after a moment's hesitation, Davy shook hands.

"Davy White, Wardroom Mess Steward. It's all new to me. Ah'm tryin' hard to learn fast."

"Ah was cook on a British schooner, the *Jane Brown*, before Ah joined the Confederate Navy. Ah know a few tricks about preparin' for meals and servin' tables. Happy to share with you."

Davy gave Jock a quizzical stare, then he grinned.

"That's a grand offer, Jock. Ah thank you kindly."

The boys sealed their bargain with a handshake.

The wind got up, and the officer of the watch sent hands aloft to shorten sail. The slap of feet on the deck and the officer's cries hurrying the crew to the sails brought the boys back to the present.

"Hard being a slave, Davey?"

"The Master treated me well enough. Ah'm from Delaware, a Union state that kept me a slave. An' Ah thought the Yankees was against slavery. But it was Captain Semmes, a Southern man and a Confederate Officer, who freed me."

"Glad to hear that, Davy. Captain Semmes is an excellent officer."

"He sure is. You know, Ah gets paid the same wages as the white stewards. Ah'm glad to belong to the ship. But Jock, never go down and deep into Dixie. Lots of my people down south. Ah heard some of them has a hard time of it. Glad Ah never was sent down there."

* * *

On 11th January 1863, the US Navy blockading fleet was hove to off the Texas coast near Galveston. Lookouts hailed the decks: a sail just over the horizon. USS *Hatteras* was ordered to intercept the chase.

CSS *Alabama* sailed closer to the shore and drew on the *Hatteras*. Aboard *Alabama*, now eighteen miles west of Galveston, the Master's Mate, George T Fulham, a Briton, ordered 'beat to quarters'. Rapid drum rolls called the crew, and the ship cleared for action. Jock MacNeil, Loblolly Boy, hurried to his place in the orlop below decks.

At dusk, after four hours of pursuit, *Hatteras* had closed within hailing distance of the unidentified vessel. Commander Blake of *Hatteras* demanded the identity of the chase.

Alabama flew the White Ensign of the Royal Navy.

"Her Britannic Majesty's Ship *Petrel*," replied Fulham, falling back on a stratagem of war, the *ruse de guerre.*

Blake ordered one of *Hatteras's* boats to inspect the vessel.

Fulham raised a speaking trumpet and hailed *Hatteras* again.

"HMS *Petrel*," then louder, "Confederate States Steamer, *Alabama.*"

At the same time, Captain Semmes ordered the White Ensign struck, and the Stars and Bars raised.

Alabama opened fire. Shot from her guns smashed the hull of the *Hatteras* and set her on fire. Six-foot gashes to the ship's hull let in the sea. The Federals returned fire at forty yards. From the quarterdeck of *Alabama*, volleys of rifle fire and pistol shots rained down on the Yankee sailors.

A quarter of an hour of fighting and *Hatteras* fired a lee gun, then another, and another still. Jock MacNeil heard cheering and knew that the Federals had struck. No wounded had come below, so Llewellyn sent Jock on deck in time to see *Hatteras* sink.

The young Scot saw the Federal ship disturb the surface of the Gulf waters, the blazing hull slipping below the waves. Her boilers collapsed, and a burst of steam ruptured a sea stained by coal dust, oil and swirling debris. He shuddered at the thought of Yankee sailors trapped inside the hull. Fulham's voice cut through *Alabama's* cheering hands. He gave the order to cease fire.

The Confederate ship suffered minor damage: a hit on the smokestack and a sailor injured on the cheek. *Hatteras* had not crippled the cruiser. Jock helped injured and wounded Federals to board the ship. Shortly after the action, Captain Semmes sent for Jock.

The smell of gun smoke and powder added to Jock's excitement. He walked aft with his officer, Assistant Surgeon Llewellyn, through the jubilant ship's officers and crew to the Captain's quarters. Jock had made his duty in the sickbay, but a part of him wondered had he been

Only The Leaves Whispering

on deck, would he have failed his obligation, given in to cowardice and crept away from danger?

Jock was surprised that Captain wanted to see him.

"This is Jock MacNeil, the Scots Loblolly Boy, sir," Llewellyn said.

Jock stood straight and saluted; with fingers clenched and forefinger half-curled, he touched and knuckled his forehead with the first knuckle. "Sir."

"You know that Midshipman Hollister is ill?" Semmes said. "He has the ague."

Jock respected the Captain, amazed that a Catholic commanded *Alabama* and that aboard the ship, no one gave a damn about Jock's own Catholicism.

Llewellyn nudged Jock.

"Yes, sir," Jock said.

Midshipman Hollister, the youngest ship's officer and youngest son of a Maryland family, doted on by loving parents, old friends of Semmes, had joined *Alabama* in Terceira in the Azores, when Captain Semmes took command.

"I want him well," Semmes said. "He must live."

Jock had spent the last week nursing the Midshipman – at eighteen, four years older than himself – through a severe fever, poulticing a painful crop of boils. Jock believed the Midshipman would die, for neither Llewellyn nor the Ship's Surgeon could identify the illness or bring down his temperature. Day by day, Hollister gasped and spluttered, choking on a hard, barking cough. He'd fall back on his bunk rubbing his chest to ease the pain of congested lungs.

Llewellyn, having reached a decision, turned to the Captain. "Mr Hollister has severe pneumonia."

"Might Midshipman Hollister live if we can put him ashore?" Semmes asked.

"He might, sir," Llewellyn said.

"Mr MacNeil," Semmes said, "I would be obliged if you would take Mr Hollister ashore to a doctor, and I ask that you stand by and attend to him. I won't have the Midshipman in the care of a sailor. You have looked after him. You are a responsible young man, among the best of the crew. Take him to Silas B. Merriweather, a good Southern Man, a retired Naval Surgeon, and friend from my years of service in the Union Navy. Help Mr Hollister live. There's a fishing boat alongside. Her skipper will take you into Galveston."

Jock realised that Semmes wanted more than obedience from him. He wanted Jock's loyalty. On the Atlantic crossing, the Captain had done no more than pass the occasional remark to Jock, who was surprised that Semmes knew he existed. Still, Mr Low, Fourth Lieutenant, a fellow Scot, had spoken well of him. Captain Semmes had decided that Jock was the right man for the job.

* * *

It hurt the young Scot to leave *Alabama*. Semmes' solicitude softened the blow, but the praise added to his torment and did not assuage his feelings of rejection.

The sinking of USS *Hatteras* had been Jock's proudest moment, the Confederate victory wiping out Yankee taunts that Rebels were only good for preying on unarmed merchantmen. Now, nine months aboard his beloved ship was ending.

Llewellyn nudged Jock.

"Yes, sir. Very happy, sir, to attend to Mr Hollister."

"Thank you, Mr MacNeil. When he is well, Mr Hollister will help you find another Confederate ship."

Later, in the sickbay, Llewellyn handed Jock a 0.36 Navy Colt revolver, snug in a shoulder holster.

"You know how to use this?" Llewellyn said

"Yes, sir," Jock said. "Mr Howells, Marine Officer, taught me."

Silence filled the sickbay. Jock sensed that he'd never meet Llewellyn again and knew Llewellyn felt the same.

Llewellyn placed both hands on Jock's shoulders, steadying him, an older brother. "Take care ashore, Jock."

"Do my best, sir."

Jock turned away.

Only The Leaves Whispering

The Bosun drove the two sailors lowering the sick Midshipman, lashed in a Bosun's chair, into the fishing boat. Mr Low left the quarterdeck and shook Jock's hand.

"A pleasure to sail with you, Mr MacNeil."

"Thank you, sir."

Jock returned Low's salute.

Hands reached out and touched his shoulder; gruff, hoarse whispers of sailors: "Good luck, Jock." "Sorry, you're leaving the ship, lad." "Yer a lucky healer, son."

As Jock was about to leave the ship, Davy White came on deck from the wardroom, making his way through the group of sailors.

"Ah just heard you were goin' into Galveston with Mr Hollister. Ah'm real sorry you're leavin' the ship, Jock."

"Me too, Davy, we're good friends. Ah hope we'll meet again."

"Yes, but it'll have to be aboard the ship. Ah'm stayin' on *Alabama* until the end. However it turns out."

Jock fixed his cap securely and tugged his pea-jacket closer. *Alabama* was getting underway, and hands hurried aloft making sail. He turned aft and saluted the quarterdeck. Captain Semmes returned his salute and waved farewell. Jock followed his kit over the side into the fishing boat.

His sea legs good, Jock swayed with the fishing boat as she rose and fell in the Gulf swell. He'd had five months at sea on the South's grandest cruiser, enjoying good pay and conditions, stirred by the memory of Semmes raising the Confederate colours at Terceira. He was proud to have belonged to the Confederate Navy, a volunteer aboard its most glorious ship.

Jock stared at the widening gap of choppy sea between *Alabama* and the fishing boat. His eyes cut the dark, and he watched for landfall. He expected no welcome from Galveston.

The sleeping Hollister, roped snug to a chair, barely moved in the heavy swell. Jock tugged the oilskin cover up to Hollister's chin to keep him dry from the spray coming aboard. He had given his word to Semmes, and he would keep it. He was a sadder but more resilient boy as he turned aft and looked for *Alabama's* running lights, but they had vanished.

Lewellyn gave Jock responsibility to treat minor injuries, the warp and weft of life on a Man of War at sea. The young Scot liked the respect of sailors and officers when he'd applied arnica to their bruises and abrasions. The crew preferred Jock's neat suturing.

One day, after a storm, Tom Cuddy, the Gunner from Charleston, North Carolina, was dashed by a wave against the eight-inch smooth-bore gun and nursed a rough, bleeding cut to his forearm.

He had asked for Jock, telling the Surgeon,

"Well, Mr Lewellyn, you'll be busy with them poxed-up sinners with the Ladies of the Night, or good men fallen ill. Let the Loblolly Boy stitch me up. Jock's a fine lad."

Jock remembered the incident now as he stood for'ard, while the swift-sailing fishing boat closed with the quay near the East Beach. Men came forward to catch mooring lines thrown by fishermen as she came alongside.

He felt grim as he stepped ashore at Galveston but put on a brave face. Jock cut a smart figure in his dress blues. He was proud of the flat black cap with the ribbon he'd embroidered with the words CSS *Alabama* in gold thread. He was chuffed with the well-polished officer's dress boots that he had taken from the brigantine *Baron de Castine*; a prize released on bond. The boots were kit he could never have afforded and were the first footwear he'd ever owned that actually fitted. Yet, despite his swagger and smart dress, Jock felt bleak. He remained proud to have served aboard *Alabama*; pleased that he was a Man of War's Man. But the discharge from the Confederate Navy, leaving the ship and coming ashore, brought doubts about his fitness to serve The Cause.

Jock asked a man on the quay the way to the Merriweather house. He refused to let his sour first impressions of the battle-damaged town depress him and cheered up, thinking about the additions to the kit in his seabag. He was better off and more smartly dressed. He had packed his concertina along with the small case of surgical instruments and

Only The Leaves Whispering

medicines that Llewellyn gave him. The weighted money belt loaded with Captain Semmes' sovereigns lent him security. And Jock was fond of the grey officer's jacket Semmes had presented to him, that lay folded and packed in his kit.

He pressed his arm against the comforting bulge of the 0.36 Navy Colt revolver snug in its shoulder holster.

Having received directions, Jock hired a carter and had Hollister made comfortable on top, covered with a blanket and a tarp. They left the port, heading south-west for the Merriweather house. He walked beside the carter, taking mental note of the route.

After a walk lasting a good forty-five minutes, the carter stopped in a quiet, dusty, un-metalled street.

"That's Doc Merriweather's place."

He pointed to a spacious, low-built white house with a broad porch on all sides, one wing of which was brightly lit, the rest dim.

The carter waited while Jock opened the gate of the white-painted fence and mounted the stairs to the front porch. He rapped the knuckles of his right hand on the door, waited a minute and rapped again.

An irate man called from the back of the house,

"All right, all right. I'm comin'. What the hell's your hurry?"

The door burst open. A big man filled the space. Silhouetted by the lamp in the hall, he seemed even larger than he was. He placed his hands on his hips and gazed down at Jock, weighing him up.

"And who might you be, young feller?"

Jock, elegant in his dress blues and the naval cap, came to attention and gave Merriweather a smart salute.

"Good evening, sir. Jock MacNeil, Loblolly Boy, late of Confederate States Ship, *Alabama*. Captain Semmes sent me. I have a sick midshipman in the cart. This letter is for you, sir, from Captain Semmes."

Jock handed the sealed cream envelope to Merriweather.

"Come into the light, Mr MacNeil, while I read this."

Jock removed his cap and came into the hall.

Merriweather turned over the envelope and fingered it to make sure that Semmes' wax seal was intact, then opened the letter and read it.

Jim Ellis

As the man perused the contents, Jock weighed up Doc Merriweather. He was a tall man with a cadaverous face, the skin of which was tight from overwork. His shirt, crushed and far from brilliant white, was worn open at the neck, sleeves rolled past the elbow, exposing blood-stained hands and arms. A thick white cotton, blood-blotched apron covered Merriweather's trousers. His elastic-sided boots hadn't seen black polish for some time.

"Hmm… hmm," Merriweather grunted as he read, then put the letter back in the envelope and shoved it in his trouser pocket and regarded Jock once more.

"You're a Scotchman," he said.

"Yes, sir!" Jock said, cap held behind his back, standing at ease in the hall of the Merriweather house.

"You'll be a Presbyterian?" Merriweather said.

"No, sir! My family is from Barra. I'm a Catholic."

"So you're a Teague. Good. That's what the great Dean Swift called the poor Irish. I'm a Papist myself. Many's the time I attended Mass with Captain Semmes. We'll get along fine."

Jock paid off the carter and Merriweather assisted Jock to bed Hollister in an airy room. The fishing boat captain had mentioned to Jock that Merriweather had turned much of his home over to the care of wounded Confederate and Federal soldiers.

"What the Hell are you doing in the Confederate Navy, son? I never expected to meet a Scots sailor fighting for the South," Merriweather said, while Jock was settling Hollister.

"I volunteered. *Alabama*'s packed with British seamen and Royal Navy reservists, all volunteers."

"What will you do now that *Alabama*'s at sea," Merriweather said.

"Captain Semmes asked me to stay by Mr Hollister."

"I could use someone with your experience, Mr MacNeil."

"Captain Semmes' duty, sir, but I'm to look after Mr Hollister. Then I can help you."

Merriweather looked at the letter again and nodded.

"You should go home."

Only The Leaves Whispering

"No, sir. Ah'm for The Cause. Ah'm a Man of War's Man, happy aboard *Alabama*. After Galveston, Ah'll try to find another Confederate blue water ship."

"I like your spunk, son.

* * *

The next morning, Doc Merriweather conducted a detailed examination of Hollister. He concurred with Llewellyn's diagnosis; the young man had pneumonia. All the classic signs were there: laboured, painful breathing from an infection-filled lung; fever; costive; thirst; skin hot to the touch; flushed face; head and limb pains; painful coughing; and an expectorant that was meagre, and then profuse and bloody.

Doc Merriweather showed Jock round the property. They walked past vegetable plots.

"This is set up like a market garden, but nothing is for sale. I feed the sick and wounded, both Federal and Confederate. Some Galveston hardheads didn't like that I care for Federals. Told 'em it was that way or no way. I'm a doctor."

"What happens to the Federals when they leave you?" Jock said.

"Prison, God help them. Maybe Andersonville."

They walked on.

"I'm from Virginia, but I got a liking for Texas during the Mexican War. When I left the Federal Navy, I settled in Galveston. Then my wife died. As for me, well, I am self-sufficient. I add to the rations the Government supply. It's nothing great. But I'm glad I kept the place since this cursed war broke out. My quarters are small, on the west wing. A sitting room, bedroom, a small kitchen where I take my meals. And there's the privy and washroom. The rest of the house I use to treat wounded soldiers and the sick. My man looks after me. There he is. Let's go over."

Doc Merriweather stopped and stared at the trees behind the house. He shook his head.

"All this damned killing. I've lost family. My son, a Lieutenant in the Navy, killed at the Battle of Memphis. My brother came out of

Jim Ellis

retirement and volunteered for the Navy. Commander of a gunboat blown up at Sabine Pass."

They walked to where the cabbage and cauliflower grew. A thick-set, middle-aged black man of medium height laid down his hoe on seeing them approach. He removed a wide-brimmed, ancient, grey Stetson and dabbed at his brow with a grey neckerchief.

"Good morning Doctor," the man said.

"Good morning, Ben. Meet Jock MacNeil, out of the Confederate Navy, a Scotchman. He'll be with us a while, looking after a sick midshipman. Jock, meet Benjamin Houston, my friend and associate."

Benjamin and Jock shook hands.

"Glad to make your acquaintance, Mr MacNeil."

"Likewise, Mr Houston."

"Ben knows everything about looking after hogs and chickens," Doc Merriweather said. "We have them back there." Doc Merriweather pointed to the edge of his property. "Together, we look after the place."

Ben grinned. "Ah've been called the Hog Doctor. Say, young man. We can be friends. Call me Ben, and Ah'll call you Jock?"

"Why thank you, Ben. Very kind of you."

Dock Merriweather and Jock walked back to the main house.

"Is Ben your slave, sir?"

"No, son, he is not. I won't have slaves here. Ben's a free man, born free. We left the Federal Navy at the same time. We've been good friends for many years."

"I had a black friend aboard *Alabama*, Davy White. We got on well. He came aboard from a Yankee schooner, the *Tonawanda*, body slave of a Delaware man on passage to Europe."

"Poor young man. A slave from a Union state," Doc Merriweather said.

"Captain Semmes set him free, and he enlisted as wardroom mess steward. Paid him the same wages as white waiters. Davy was a good steward. Everyone liked him. He said he was better off in the Confederate Navy."

"I like that," Doc Merriweather said. "Bravo, Raphael Semmes."

Only The Leaves Whispering

Jock had more to say. "When *Alabama* sank *Hatteras*, Yankee sailors died. That's war. But Raphael Semmes was no killer. When Ah wis aboard, *Alabama* captured ships, and Captain Semmes destroyed a lot of them. But he released some ships on bond, and paroled prisoners to a bonded ship for release at the next port."

"That sounds like the fine officer I served with."

Doc Merriweather's days were taken up looking after wounded and sick soldiers billeted in his establishment, survivors of the fighting around the town. He also treated natives of Galveston. He had little time to spare for Midshipman Hollister.

"Now, about Midshipman Hollister. You'll look after him, Jock, but under my supervision."

"Yes, sir."

And so Jock got Midshipman Hollister's recovery underway. First, he dealt with the reduction of the crop of boils, eliminating them with regular soap and sugar poulticing. A deep-rooted furuncle hung on. Jock dry cupped it with a small glass, creating a vacuum that sucked out pus and blood. Jock probed with tweezers and removed white shards of the root, then cleaned and dressed the gory hole.

By the third week, Hollister was recuperating: coughing and spitting reduced and his breathing more comfortable. But he remained weak and kept to his bed. Jock worked at relieving the Midshipman's pain. He bound the infected lung with a large linseed poultice, covering the poultice lint with a piece of oiled silk. While the pain was intense, Jock changed the dressings every three hours. He dosed Hollister with laudanum brought from *Alabama*. The opiate reduced Hollister's pain and coughing. Jock cooled the feverish Hollister by body-sponging him with tepid water.

"Good job, Jock," Merriweather said. "But he's still costive. Let's get his bowels working."

Jock had the Midshipman eat grits and drink hot water soon after waking, but they had limited effect. Evacuations came after a dose of cream of tartar. Jock now concentrated on a diet to return the Midshipman to health, walking into Galveston for milk and scraps of meat

Jim Ellis

and bones for the stockpot. He obtained eggs from the Doc's chickens and the makings of nourishing broth from his vegetable garden. Jock made loblolly, a Navy cure-all; a thick porridge fortified with chopped meat and vegetables, and backed up by doses of whiskey. Silas Merriweather approved.

Hollister said little, giving the impression that he resented having Jock, a mere Loblolly Boy, looking after him.

"You owe your life to that young Scotchman," Merriweather said, sternly. "The flannel that he bought, wear it next to your skin until you're well."

Later, Hollister received orders that, when recovered, he was to report for duty at the Pensacola Naval Base. He'd been under Doc Merriweather and Jock's care for two months.

By then, he had come to accept Jock. "I never thanked you properly, Jock, for bringing me ashore," he said. "You saved my life."

"Captain's duty, Mr Hollister."

"Why don't you come with me, Jock? I'll do what I can to get you sea duty. There's work for us across the Gulf at Pensacola. It's what I'd like myself."

But at that point in the war, there was little chance of appointment to a bluewater ship. Jock had an honourable discharge, and still felt he belonged to *Alabama*. He wanted deep sea, not shore duties in a naval base, or crewing an improvised man of war.

"Very kind, Mr Hollister. I'd like to think about it."

* * *

Doc Merriweather called Jock to his study after they'd attended to patients. He asked the young Scot to stay.

"You have a good heart and caring hands for the sick and the suffering. You have the beginnings of an education. Tend the sick and the wounded with me. Enough soldiers and sailors want the killing."

Merriweather paused.

"I'm a Southern man, and I know your liking for The Cause, but we're going to lose this bloody war. I've told you about my son, a

Only The Leaves Whispering

Lieutenant in the Navy, killed at the Battle of Memphis. My brother, a Commander of a gunboat blown up at Sabine Pass. Putting the Southern men back together to rebuild the South, that would be noble work. Goddammit, boy! In time, you'd become a doctor. I'll help you."

It was a generous offer, and Jock wanted to think about it. He'd hardly been out of the Merriweather household since he arrived, so he asked Doc Merriweather for leave to visit Galveston town.

Early that afternoon, Jock rode into Galveston on one of Doc Merriweather's horses. He was smart in his Confederate Navy uniform, his cap with the *Alabama* ribbon, dress blues and pea-jacket. He wanted to re-enlist in the Confederate Navy, but settled for finding out if ship work was available. Jock was cautious in a city packed with victorious and rowdy Confederate troops. He carried a shoulder holster and .36 Colt Navy revolver.

Major General John B. Magruder had retaken Galveston for the South. The scarred streets and damaged houses depressed the young Scot. But citizens and soldiers greeted Jock warmly, cheering him up.

A man, delighted to meet a foreign naval volunteer who was now working with Doc Merriweather, invited him to dine with his family.

"Ah'm Thomas Bean, Ah work around the harbour. Do a bit of fishin'. Sometimes Ah crew one of the fishin' boats. Call me Tom, young feller."

Tom Bean had been to the war as a deckhand aboard a blockade runner coming from Cuba, but came ashore when he was wounded by gunfire from an attacking Yankee schooner.

"We got the cargo into Galveston. Made some money on that run. Splinters in mah right leg. The thigh is weak. No more war capers for me."

Jock entered the four-roomed wooden house with a deep porch, flower garden to the front, and, he supposed, vegetables growing in the backyard. The living room had simple, homemade solid oak furniture: a settle, a table and six chairs and two benches with patchwork cushions against the wall near the empty fireplace. The floor was scrubbed pine boards. He met the family, the wife, Mildred, a kind, mousy woman, and a boy of twelve, Bill, and Ann aged ten. They smiled and sat next to Jock at the table.

The meal was delicious. Fried Black Drum fillets dressed with a butter and lemon sauce. Fried potatoes and beans, homemade sourdough bread, coffee.

"Tom caught the Black Drum early this mornin'. I got the butter from a dairyman," Mrs Bean said. "The lemons, Tom grows outback."

And Jock told his story.

Bill stared wide-eyed at Jock. "You really served on *Alabama*? When I'm fifteen, Ah'll try for the Confederate Navy."

Jock smiled. "Ah hope the war'll be over and won by that time, and you won't have to go. You stay home with your wee sister and your mum and dad."

Mildred Bean smiled and touched Jock's arm. "Thank you, Mr Mac-Neil."

The family walked Jock to his horse. They shook hands.

"A pleasure meetin' you, son, Tom said. "We're right proud of you servin' in our Navy, and workin' with Doc Merriweather."

"Go on now," Mildred said to her son and daughter. She handed the boy a good-sized jar wrapped in muslin. Together, Bill and Ann presented the pot to Jock.

"Orange marmalade. Homemade. A couple of orange trees outback," Tom said. "Doc Merriweather likes Mildred's marmalade."

* * *

Galveston was not an essential port for Confederate blue water ships; a change from the days when it was the main base for the Republic of Texas Navy. In 1863, blockade runners sailed from the port laden with cotton, and ships from the Caribbean and Cuba brought in weapons, munitions and trade goods. Jock considered finding a berth, serving on deck, or in catering as the steward. But Jock recognised that the Federal Navy would run an ever-tightening blockade. He risked capture and deportation sailing on a blockade runner.

Only The Leaves Whispering

Later that afternoon, as he rode further into Galveston, a chill breeze cutting the afternoon warmth, Jock saw an unconscious man slumped in the dirt. He turned the horse into the lane where the man lay.

"Stay out of that, *Alabama!*" a carter yelled, having seen Jock's hat, the band embroidered with the ship's name in gold thread. "Nuthin' but a drunk Injun."

Jock's job aboard *Alabama* was to help the surgeons and attend to the injured, sick and wounded sailors. He retained a strong sense of responsibility and compassion so he ignored the carter's warning.

He knew assailants might be nearby, but he quelled his fear. He'd been nine months aboard a warship, four months standing by and five at sea. The young Scot had never fought. Jock felt sweat trickle down his back and dampness in his armpits as he unholstered the Colt.

A slouch hat with a CSA badge and feathers in the band lay in the dirt beside a prostrate Indian. His grey uniform jacket and army trousers said he was a Confederate soldier.

Jock lifted his head: he was about eighteen or nineteen and had been clubbed about the head and shoulders. The head wounds would need suturing and dressing.

The Indian came round and jerked back in fright when he saw Jock's lightly tanned, freckled face. He looked concussed.

"You'll be all right," Jock said, "Let me help you. What's your name? Tell me what happened?"

Jock looked into the Indian's unfocused eyes. The man moaned from the pain of the beatings that he had been given and touched his bruised head with a careful hand. He was so concussed that he could not speak. Jock's Scots accent had calmed him, but he was groggy, and could not stand without support.

It wasn't hard to work out what had happened. Southern men, who had no time for blacks and little concern for Indians, had beaten up this Confederate Indian soldier. Jock had rejected this way of thinking when he had met Davy White aboard *Alabama*, holding to the old Scots belief that we are all Jock Tamson's bairns – that we are all the same. The Scots belief had helped Jock cement his friendship with Ben,

Doc Merriweather's associate. He believed that we all belong to shared humanity. And for Jock MacNeil, a careless Catholic, it meant we are all the children of God.

"Trust me, keep calm," Jock said. "I'm going to take you to Doctor Merriweather. He'll treat you."

Jock heaved the man up until he lay on his belly across the saddle. "Hold on," Jock said. "Grab the saddle horn with your left hand."

Jock got his left foot in the stirrup and mounted the horse, sitting behind the saddle.

An elegant Doc Merriweather came through the front door, dressed for an evening at home: matching charcoal grey waistcoat and trousers, polished boots and a red silk cravat folded loosely at the collar of his brilliant white shirt.

His face clouded with rage when he saw Jock supporting the swaying Indian with long hair, a bloody face and blood-stained clothing. Merriweather did not care for the colourful patchwork of Confederate uniform and personal tribal adornments.

"For God's sake, Jock. I just sat down to read and now more damned work. We have enough to do without you bring me a drunk Indian."

"No, sir! This man's concussed, not drunk. He's an Indian for sure, and he's a Confederate soldier."

"I hope he ain't wearing no Goddamned breechclout. What do you know about him?"

"Nothing. The Indian is in a bad way. Couldn't speak."

"Sick, goin' to be sick," the Indian said.

Doc Merriweather called for a basin and a maid brought one. The Indian knelt over it, rested his hands on the rim and emptied his stomach of his last meal. Then he suffered a bout of the dry heaves.

A few minutes later, Doc Merriweather was called to attend to a mother who'd brought her injured son for emergency treatment. His plan for an evening's reading vanished.

"Get him into that side room of yours, Jock. Clean him up. Find out who he is. I'll have a look at him later on."

Only The Leaves Whispering

Jock sat the Indian on the edge of his bed. He removed his jacket and shirt, revealing the man's bruised torso.

"Water please," the Indian croaked.

"Sit still," Jock said.

He returned with a jug of cold water and a glass. He fed the Indian sips of water, then refilled the glass and handed it back to him.

"Drink slowly. I don't want you to be sick again. I'll be back in a minute."

Jock returned with a basin of warm water, a towel and face cloth folded across his right forearm, and a small bar of soap in his pocket.

"If you can talk, tell me who you are."

"I'm Jim. Cherokee Jim. Down from Oklahoma to buy horses. Wanted to have a look at Galveston. I left the troop for a couple of hours. They'll be gone now, thinking I've deserted. White men beat me with clubs and kicked me. They got my money and a pistol. Stole my horse and carbine."

"Hmm. I'm Jock MacNeil. Call me, Jock. Can I call you Jim?"

"Yes, call me, Jim."

Jock washed and dried his face and neck, then bathed and dried his torso, which was dirty and sweaty from the days on the trail. There were several large bruises on his ribs but none seemed broken.

"Some of your ribs might be cracked."

His stomach had been kicked hard and was covered by a large bruise. Jock fetched arnica from the medicine chest and applied it to the bruising.

"That'll help the pain. How's your backside?"

"Sore, from the kicking."

"Right. I'll get to that later."

Jock worried about the Indian's head wound, which was leaking blood on to his neck and face. He helped the Indian to a chair and had him sit up straight and put the towel around his shoulders. He examined the scalp and whistled through his teeth when he saw the wound, four to five inches long and swollen. It wanted suturing. The skull might be fractured. Jock changed the water in the basin and washed

Jim Ellis

around the wound. He got iodine, surgical scissors and a razor and soap out of the medical kit he'd brought from *Alabama*.

"Sit still. I'm going to cut the hair around the wound and shave the scalp." Jock tried to suppress a grin. "You'll have a tonsure, just like a monk. Doc Merriweather needs to have a good look at you. I'm putting iodine on the wound. It'll hurt."

Doc Merriweather returned, sleeves rolled up, drying his hands on a small towel. He looked at the Indian, scrutinised the bruises, then felt around the scalp wound. The doctor ran an exploring hand across the skull. He caught the man under the chin with his fingertips and looked long and hard into the patient's dilated eyes.

"Well done, Jock. Good job on the bruising and the head wound. He's concussed alright, so he'll be with us for a while. The head will need maybe ten sutures."

Doc Merriweather felt around the Indian's rib cage.

"Now, let's get a binding him. Give him support. I think a couple of his ribs are cracked. And bejeezus, I'm as busy as hell back there."

"Well, sir, I can do it. He's my first head injury. But I sutured the wounds and cuts of *Alabama*'s crew. Back in Westburn, I learned from a retired Royal Navy Surgeon, and at sea on the *Jane Brown*, I sutured injured sailors. I can bind his ribs. On *Alabama*, Dr Lewellyn stood by me."

The Indian's face turned grey under his copper complexion. His dilated eyes added to the mask of anxiety. He raised himself on the arms of the chair.

"You're going to let a boy sew up my head and strap my ribs? Oh, no!"

Doc Merriweather pressed the Indian back into the chair.

"Damn you, Chief, or whatever the hell they call you. That boy saved your worthless life, bringing you to me. Now he's going to put that head wound right, and bind your cracked ribs."

Doc Merriweather watched Jock complete two of the ten sutures. The Indian sat rigid as the suture needle passed through his scalp.

"Good. You know what you're doing. I'll look in later."

Only The Leaves Whispering

* * *

With Midshipman Hollister recovered and back in the Navy at Pensacola, Jock spent his days assisting Doc Merriweather, treating wounded and injured Confederate and Federal soldiers. When he had time, he worked with Cherokee Jim, now well on the way to recovery and thinking about returning to the Rifles. The pair of them took care of Doc Merriweather's horses. Jock attended to smithing and health, Jim dealt with grooming and feeding the animals. They looked after heavy household chores, their work together strengthening their friendship.

The new friends learned about each other's past.

"I was always for the South," Jock said. "On the Clyde, everyone said the yards were building ships for the Confederacy. I borrowed or lifted newspapers to follow the war."

The Federal Government had sent troops to move the Cherokee on to the Trail of Tears for Oklahoma, Indian Territory. Jim's family belonged to the band that hid out in the Snowbird Mountains in North Carolina.

"Ah've no' heard of the Trail of Tears," Jock said. "It must have been grim."

"Stand Watie had already moved to Oklahoma. A lot of Cherokee died walking about a thousand miles to get there.

"The whites coveted our land and badgered the State and US Governments to push out the Cherokee," Jim said. "Georgians trespassed on tribal property. Prospectors discovered gold at the Dholenga Georgia Gold Rush of 1829. Over time, Federal Government moved out Muskogee, Chickasaw, Seminole, Chocktaw and Ponca. The Cherokee moved in 1838.

"The family, my mother, father and two sisters and I, kept to the Snowbird Mountains, away from Federal soldiers sent to drive out the Cherokee. We didn't get caught up in the move west on the Trail of Tears to Indian Territory."

Jim grinned and gave his hands an awkward rubbing.

"My dad calls me Te-Nuh-La-He. My mother, too. That's my Cherokee name. It means Jim, more or less. I like Jim. It's what I got called in school, and it's what my sisters call me. When this war is over, I'll go back home to the Snow Bird Mountains."

For Jim, the choice between fighting for or against the Federal Government was an easy one. He joined the South. William Holland Thomas, a Carolinian who'd helped the Cherokee Snow Bird, raised Thomas's Legion to serve with the Army of Northern Virginia. Jim thought about enlisting, but headed west to the Cherokee lands in Oklahoma Territory and enlisted instead with Colonel Stand Watie in the Cherokee Mounted Rifles.

Jock told Jim about the death of his parents.

"My family came from the island of Barra, in the Western Isles. My mother died of diphtheria. A few weeks later, the police found my father's body in the dock. They said it was an accident, but I think he lost his mind and killed himself. That left me an orphaned apprentice blacksmith and farrier with a young brother and sister."

But Jock liked his newfound friend well enough to reveal the tender-hearted side of his character. He shared with Jim his cherished memories of childhood. Days of laughter shared with poor Irish neighbours; the barefoot children playing; the busy hawkers and wifies wrapped in tartan shawls; the warm sense of belonging to the Old Vennel. Jock's voice thickened when he spoke about the happy times, with his mother full of life, his father making money at the forge, and they, a loving family. Jock fondly recalled family walks after Sunday Mass in the quiet streets of the affluent West End. But Jock, always honest with those he liked, suffered lingering guilt about having surrendered his brother and sister to the nuns and priests of a Catholic orphanage. That sin would haunt the rest of his life.

"On the *Jane Brown*, the cook was a drunk, so I learnt to cook, and because I knew about helping sick horses, the captain had me tend sick and injured sailors. *Jane Brown* was a ship of hard knocks. I learnt to fight my corner. One day in the dock, I fell into the hold."

"What happened?"

Only The Leaves Whispering

"The schooner sailed for Cork. Surgeon James Gunn, from the Royal Navy, looked after me. He taught me to clean and dress wounds and bruises and to use the cautery and the suture needle. James Gunn told me that spirits made an injury clean."

But Jock could not let go of the Confederate Navy. The memory of *Alabama* moored in the fitting-out berth in Birkenhead was etched in his mind.

"She was beautiful. Ah had to do it. Ah jumped ship. Took mah kit out of the *Jane Brown* and joined the Confederate Navy. Ah felt Ah'd done something worthwhile."

"Worthwhile, Jock?"

"Yes, Jim: worthwhile. Ah felt Ah belonged to *Alabama* even before she sailed. Workin' aboard her as she fitted out. The runs ashore with shipmates. And the months at sea, raidin' Yankee ships. Ah loved the ship. Ah'm a Man of War's Man."

For several days after work, the friends argued about leaving Galveston, and the Merriweather establishment.

Chapter Three

The boys worked the forge, Jim pumping the bellows keeping the heart of the fire at white heat while Jock buried the horseshoe in the pale centre of the coals and flying sparks singed their thick leather aprons. They inhaled the smoky leather fumes but resisted sneezing. When the colour of the shoe matched the pale red hue of the coals, Jock withdrew the shoe. He held it tight in the tongs and beat it to shape on the anvil to fit the animal's hoof. Jock plunged the horseshoe into the tub of water. There was a sizzle of cooling steel and a cloud of steam vanished into the rafters of the smithy.

"That's eight shoes ready," Jock said. "I've nails here."

The animals' coats shone from the careful grooming.

"Got really good at this grooming with the Rifles," Jim said.

Jock grinned.

"My father taught me back in Westburn. He had me working at the forge from when I was eleven. I loved it. I went there after school and every Saturday."

Doc Merriweather's two horses stood, attached to a hitching post, outside the smithy door. Three hooves on each animal needed new shoes. Jock had removed the worn shoes and prepared the hooves.

"Two spares," Jim said.

"Come in handy," Jock said.

The horses trusted Jock, but Jim held the bridles and whispered to the animals while Jock went from limb to limb of the black gelding,

Only The Leaves Whispering

bending each lower leg between his knees, catching hold of the hoof, hammer in hand, driving the nails home. He then worked on the chestnut mare.

The boys rested, ate bread and cheese, drank cold coffee.

"Give 'em another rub down?" Jim suggested.

"Let's do that."

Jock grinned across the withers of the black gelding at Cherokee Jim, his new friend. Jim rested his arms on the chestnut mare's rump.

"I need to get back up there, to Colonel Watie and the Rifles," Jim said. "Comin' with me?"

"Doc Merriweather can use ma help caring for the sick and wounded. Ah could study medicine and, in time, become a proper doctor."

"True enough, Jock, workin' with Doc Merriweather. Is that what you want, though – to become a doctor? What about The Cause?"

"A doctor, Jim? With the war an' all, it's a faraway dream. Ah'm doing good work here in Galveston meantime. But Ah'm not a soldier, Jim. Ah'm a sailor."

"It was our fate to meet. I came from the Snow Bird Mountains in the Carolinas, and you sailed across the ocean, landing in Galveston. It was meant to be, Jock."

Jock guessed what was coming next: Jim telling him again that if he wanted to be part of The Cause, he had to fight.

"You're for The Cause. You're not sure about doctorin', and you can't be a sailor if you're workin' for the Doc. So what're you going to do?"

Jock was scared by the thought of joining a fighting regiment, but would not admit it to Jim, who carried on.

"You can do good work with Colonel Watie's men. There are a lot of fellers like me up in Oklahoma, Jock. Indians – Choctaw, Osage, Seminole. To a man, loyal Confederate soldiers. You might run into Missouri Bushwhackers. Old Rebels. Fearsome hard men."

"Oh, I don't know, Jim. Sometimes I wish I was still serving on *Alabama*."

Jim Ellis

"You can ride, you know about horses, an' you learned to shoot real well when you was in the Navy. An' I'm tellin' you, your doctorin'd be useful right now, up there with the Colonel and the Rifles."

Guilt about his passive role in the war as Loblolly Boy aboard *Alabama* haunted Jock, and he smothered his fear and doubt about going to Oklahoma with Jim.

Jock decided to test himself and enlist in the Cherokee Mounted Rifles, Confederate States Army. Jock would again support The Cause and take a direct part in the fight against the Yankees and the war of Northern Aggression.

Jock knew about the clash of armies up North, and elsewhere in the South, but the magnitude of the fighting puzzled the young Scot. He was used to the brotherhood of Man of War's Men.

Jim described the guerrilla war being fought in Oklahoma Territory: raiding, ambushing Yankee forces and supplies. He drew Jock in. The smaller fighting units with flexible discipline, the chance to improvise and assume greater personal responsibility.

The friends prepared to leave Galveston. Jock had monies paid by Captain Semmes when he signed off *Alabama*. He bought a black mare, harness, saddlebags, saddle, and riding boots that fitted.

"Ah'm keepin' the officer's dress boots good," he said to Jim.

Jock still had the .36 Colt pistol. He carried the Colt in a shoulder holster. A Confederate soldier crippled by wounds sold Jock a Hawken gun taken from a Yankee sharpshooter in Northern Virginia.

Jock bankrolled Jim to a new personal kit.

"Get lariats," Jim said. "A good rope is a handy thing to have. I'll show you how to use it."

Doc Merriweather gave Jock and Jim a slicker each and a pair of woollen blankets. Jim welcomed the saddle and the pinto pony Doc Merriweather gave him. The doctor handed them each a Navy Colt revolver, and a Sharps Carbine for Jim. The Doc had a shotgun for Jock. He held up the weapon for inspection.

"I sawed it off. Jim's advice. You go up against Yankees and a blast from one barrel will stop one dead in his tracks. Be more useful to you."

Only The Leaves Whispering

Jock blanched at the thought of fighting so close up. He was scared in his stomach that he'd let Jim down on his first contact with Yankees.

"Time to put that sailor's cap away, Jock," Doc Merriweather said. "You're joining the Cherokee Mounted Rifles. Take this. Protect you from the sun."

Doc Merriweather removed a wide-brimmed hat from a hatbox and handed it to Jock. He stuffed the sailor's cap into his bundle and put on the hat. The brim shaded his eyes from the glare of the morning sun.

"I like it. Very kind, sir. Thank you."

Doc Merriweather handed Jock a metal badge bearing the letters CSA; Confederate States Army.

"I got this in the town off one of the veterans. Pin it to the crown of your hat, just like Jim has, once you're in the Rifles."

"Thank you, sir."

The doctor picked up a long, slender cloth bundle. He unwrapped a curved sabre. He'd meant to give the weapon to his son, John Merriweather, when he joined the Confederate Navy. But the son insisted his father keep the blade, a memento of his time in the blue water Federal Navy.

The longer the young Scot had stayed at the Doc's establishment, the more the Doc had come to regard him as an adoptive son.

Doc Merriweather thought about Jock's future. He had meant to guide and encourage young MacNeil towards a career in medicine. He had the makings of an excellent physician and, in time, perhaps a surgeon.

But Jock was determined to enlist in the Confederate Army.

Well, the Doc would see to it that the boy was well equipped and armed.

"My Mameluke sword. A Marines Major gave it to me when I was in the Yankee Navy and saved his leg after we beat the Mexicans at Mulege."

Jock let the weight of the blade and scabbard settle in his left hand. He unsheathed the weapon and gripped the hilt, felt the ivory embedded in it. His fingers caressed the V-shaped blade.

Jim Ellis

"Careful, son. That blade has a razor edge."

Jock examined the turned cross piece and admired the ornate engravings on the blade. He sheathed the sword and fastened it to the saddle horn.

"You know how to use a sword, Jock?"

"Yes, sir, Lieutenant Beckett Howells, Marines, showed me when I served with him on *Alabama*."

"You're well connected, son. Howells is Jefferson Davies' brother-in-law."

"He's a loyal friend to Captain Semmes."

"Practice with the sabre. Get ready for what's ahead of you in the Confederate Army. Make your arms and upper body strong. Keep the sabre by you for when your guns are empty, and you're fighting. Used right, you'll cut a man in half."

Jock sent up a silent prayer that he'd find the courage to be a good soldier.

The boys had mounted, ready to leave. Doc Merriweather offered them a hand.

"You boys look after yourselves. Try not to get yourselves killed by damned Yankees. Anything happens up there, you come back down here."

Jim swept off his hat in a gallant salute, his long black hair waving in the breeze. He turned away on his pinto pony.

Jock, reining in the black mare, doffed his new hat.

"You're very kind, sir."

The boys rode out of Silas Merriweather's yard to the causeway linking the port of Galveston to the Texas shore. They turned north for Oklahoma and the five-hundred-odd miles to the Confederate forces, commanded by Colonel Stand Watie.

"Reckon we'll make twenty-five to thirty miles a day," Jim said. "Take us about three weeks to get there."

Jock, the well-travelled seafarer, familiar with the geography of the British Isles, was curious about their journey.

"What's the country like where we're going?"

Only The Leaves Whispering

"We get to East Texas before we ford the Red River. Well, it'll be gettin' hot. We'll be keeping away from settlements. Alligators, bears and snakes for neighbours.

"Well, as sure as hell I want to be well back from them."

"Most animals will keep out of the way. But if we run into a bear or a 'gator, get away from them."

"Snakes. I hate snakes," Jock said.

"Snakes stay away from people," Jim said.

"There are dangerous snakes out there. Vipers, rattlers, cotton-mouths and copper heads. Sleeping out, we'll make a circle of our lariats and put them around us. Snakes won't cross it."

"You believe that?"

"Well, Jock, so far the rope trick has worked for me and the fellers in the Rifles."

"If you say so, Jim. I hope you're right."

Jim, an old hand on the trail, a seasoned campaigner, grinned.

"Stop worrying, Jock."

So the new friends rode across the causeway linking Galveston to the Texas shore. They set a pace their mounts could cope with for the day on the trail. From time to time, they rested the horses by dismounting and walking beside their mounts. But it was still hard riding. Jim guided them through the backcountry, avoiding settlements and the aggressive Conscription Officers pursuing army dodgers and deserters.

"Don't want to get captured and sent to some outfit in Tennessee or Virginia," Jim said.

They crossed the prairie soon after leaving Galveston. On the open range, they saw longhorn steers and a few elderly cowhands. The young men had gone to the war.

They cantered through subtropical East Texas into a land of rolling hills and forests, keeping a course for the Red River.

Late afternoon, the day's riding over, the boys made camp. Jock hobbled the mounts, rubbed them down and fed them. Jock made time each evening to practice with the sabre, building up his strength, and skill. Soon enough, he'd need the sword for the fighting. He kindled the campfire and made biscuits and coffee while Jim hunted small game for the pot. Before turning in, they talked about the war.

The journey north was a happy time. They spent pleasant evenings sharing food, camping out.

These were the days of hope for the young Scot and his Cherokee friend; boys, with their heads full of the romance of CSS *Alabama*, of the Mounted Rifles, the Southern Cavaliers, and the hard-riding Missouri Boys. They longed for news of Confederate triumphs.

They had no opportunity to bathe. The dirt, sweat and grime of the trail invaded their clothing and their bodies.

"After a while, you don't notice," Jim said, sniffing at his armpit. "You'll have gotten used to the stink."

* * *

South of Hugo settlement, early morning; they had been on the trail for close to the three weeks Jim had estimated. The friends crossed the Red River to Oklahoma by a rope ferry pulled hand over hand by the ferrymen.

"We need a bath," Jock said.

Jim shrugged, less concerned about hygiene than Jock, who had absorbed the standards of cleanliness required aboard *Alabama* and brought them ashore.

"We can wash when we get to the Rifles."

Somewhere between the settlements of Hugo and Antlers, canteens empty, and, after a fruitless search for clean water, Jim suggested approaching a house or a ranch and asking permission to fill canteens.

"That's a fine-lookin' place," Jim said, pointing to a white house at the end of an avenue of Prairie Fire Crabapple trees. "We'll ask at the kitchen door."

They rode along the avenue of trees, reining in their mounts in front of the house. A tall man emerged from the house, shut the door and stood between two of the Corinthian columns supporting the portico. He wore a wide-brimmed Panama hat, wide-sleeved loose-fitting

Only The Leaves Whispering

shirt caught at the wrists, white britches and tight-fitted, well-polished black boots. His right hand rested on the butt of a Colt Cavalry pistol tucked into the red silk sash binding his waist. He came down one stair and looked down on Jock and Jim.

"Afternoon, boys. How do y'all?"

Jock doffed his wide-brimmed hat. "Tired and weary, sir."

"Yes, sir, we are worn out," Jim said. "Wondered if we could fill our canteens?"

"Where you boys headed?"

"Been ridin' from Galveston," Jim said. "Came over the Red River, sir, at the ferry. Goin' back to the Rifles."

"You one of them Cherokee fightin' with Stand Watie?"

"Yes, sir."

"That's good. And you, young man? You're not from these parts."

Jock blushed, uncomfortable under the man's piercing eyes that were weighing them up. The man eased the pistol up from his waistband.

"Ah'm from Scotland, sir. Westburn, a port on the west coast."

"Scotland, eh? What the hell brought you down here?"

"Jock's with the Good Ol' Rebels, sir," Jim said.

"You pissin' on me, young man?"

Jim eased his carbine halfway out from the saddle holster.

"I'm not given to pissin'. My friend is a Confederate Navy man. A volunteer, on the cruiser *Alabama*. Assistant Surgeon's Loblolly Boy. You got a busted arm, boils, carbuncles or deep cuts, Jock MacNeil can fix 'em, mister. He's come to join the Rifles."

"Willie, you come on outa them bushes. These boys are alright."

A tall, well-built black man emerged from a clump of green dressed in a blue work shirt and tan cord pants tucked into well-made black mule-eared boots. A broad-brimmed black hat shaded his eyes. He came towards them, and the soles of his boots crushed the grass. He cradled a Spencer seven-shot repeating carbine on his right arm.

"We don't take no chances, boys," the man said. "It's not the first time Confederate or Federal deserters have come to rob an' kill us.

50

But we ain't yet had none o' them Redlegs or Jayhawker vermin outta Kansas."

"Good afternoon, boys. I'm Willie Sullivan," the black man said. He held out his right hand.

Jim grabbed the hand first and shook it.

"I'm Cherokee Jim. People call me Jim, Mr Sullivan."

Jock shook hands with Willie. "I'm Jock MacNeil, Mr Sullivan."

"Glad to know you, boys. My friends call me Willie. Just you boys call me Willie."

"I'm Peter O'Leary," the man said. "Y'all, call me Pete."

Pete O'Leary shook hands with Jock and Jim.

Pete O'Leary was in his late thirties, about six foot tall, slim build, wiry, whipcord muscles. A firm jawline free of dewlaps, blue eyes, fair to red hair, fitting for a man of Irish blood.

"Ah got a likin' for the West when I was in the Army in the Mexican War. Ah was done with goin' to war when it was over. Ah'm a Southern man from Tennessee, but Ah don't hold with slavery. It's an abomination. That's why I settled in Oklahoma Territory. Willie's free, and so is his wife, Miss Sally, and their children, Harriet and James. There are no slaves here. Willie and me been friends for a long time."

"Pete O'Leary's my best friend," Willie said.

"I like that, Mr O'Leary," Jim said.

"Me too," Jock said.

"Now, boys, ya'll call me Pete. But if ya'll prefer it, Mr Pete."

Pete invited the boys to dine.

"Tonight, we're goin' to Willie's cottage. His wife, Miss Sally, is making chicken, and we're all goin'. What do you think, Willie?"

"You boys are welcome at our table."

Jock and Jim dismounted and walked their mounts to the cabin where temporary labour stayed. Pete showed them where to fill their canteens and told them to get feed from the stable for the horses.

"When you've rubbed down, fed and watered them, you can wash your clothes in the wash house. You have clean garments to wear tonight?"

Only The Leaves Whispering

"We do, Mr Pete," Jock said.

"And if you don't mind me tellin' you," Pete said, "you boys need a bath. You can clean up in the wash house. Ah'll see to gettin' you some hot water."

* * *

The boys dressed for the evening meal as best they could. Jim had washed his efforts at a Confederate uniform, which he'd left drying on the washing line. He changed into a clean grey wool shirt, brightened by his red neckerchief, and black worsted trousers. His long black hair hung below his shoulders. He'd cleaned his boots.

Jock wore his one white shirt tucked into the trousers of his Navy dress blues. His blue sailor's scarf, he'd tied in a loose knot below his neck, the ends spread across the front of his shirt. Over this neat arrangement, the young Scot wore the Confederate Naval Officer's steel grey round jacket. And he changed from his riding boots to naval officer's dress boots.

Jock and Jim had tucked Navy Colt pistols into their waistbands.

Willie Sullivan met them at the door to his cottage.

"Why the Colts, boys?"

The boys shrugged.

"Well, Willie," Jim said. "Mr Pete told us you had to be ready for deserters or Jayhawker raiders out of Kansas.

"Yes, Willie," Jock said. "We came ready."

"I thank you for the thought. Keep your Colts. You boys are looking real smart. Come on in."

Everyone was present, and the introductions were polite. Firm handshakes all round from Miss Sally, Estella, Pete's wife, and their two children, and greetings of "How do, ya'll?"

Meeting the O'Leary children, Rebecca and Robert, Jock thought about his brother and sister stuck in a Catholic convent back in Westburn. Guilt stung him.

After five minutes, Jim was half in love with Harriet Sullivan, a lovely girl of sixteen. A sweet damsel in her lilac gingham, empire line cut dress, white stockings and small shoes. Her long hair was caught in a blue ribbon behind her head and a little mob cap sat on the crown of her head, more modest than the frilly ornaments usual in the South. Her small glasses magnified her large, beautiful dark eyes, fringed by long eyelashes.

"Oh, sweet Jesus," Jim whispered.

She held out her hand, and he clasped it. He wanted to take it to his lips and kiss her long fingers. He knew he could not.

"How do, Miss Harriet?" Jim said.

The company dined on fried chicken, sweet potatoes and greens. For dessert, they had buttermilk biscuits with honey.

"Nice honey and biscuits, ma'am," Jock said to Miss Sally.

"Thank you, Jock. Estella is wonderful with her bees. That's why the honey is so good."

"You have bees, ma'am?"

"Why, yes, Jock, Twelve hives," Estella said. "I love my bees. They are fine, clever little creatures."

"I'm sure you are right, ma'am," Jock said.

After dinner, they moved to the parlour. Willie poured small glasses of port for Miss Sally and Estella. The younger O'Leary and Sullivan children sat quietly, turning the pages of two illustrated books. Willie unstoppered a crystal decanter and filled four delicate crystal glasses with sipping whiskey.

"O'Leary and Sullivan whiskey. Smooth liquor. Pete has a still back in the woods. We make a jug or two every couple of months."

"Mr Pete, Willie, would it be alright if we asked how you met?" Jim asked.

Willie nodded to Pete and had a sip of whiskey.

"We can do that," Pete said. "We go back some years."

Peter told the story of how he needed close assistance in overseeing the property. The perfect solution would be a husband and wife, the wife to support Pete's wife, Estella, in domestic arrangements. He drove his two-horse wagon into Newlin, across the state line in Texas, for supplies and to find a suitable couple who were looking for work.

Only The Leaves Whispering

Walking the well-tramped, rutted earth streets of Newlin, he saw a miserable-looking black family surrounded by their shabby bundles, resting in the shade of a Catholic Church.

The woman sat on a well-made wooden toolbox. Pete reckoned they were a free black family fallen on hard times. The woman was beautiful, maybe twenty. She held the hand of a solemn little girl, about three years old. The woman dried the child's eyes with a soiled white rag. Pete walked on to a general store and bought candy.

The little girl put her arms around her mother as he approached. Pete doffed his wide-brimmed Panama hat.

"Good afternoon, ma'am, and to you, sir."

The father frowned.

The child hid her face in her mother's bosom. But Pete, a father himself, wise to the ways of shy children, had prepared.

"What's your daughter's name, ma'am?"

"She's called Harriet, sir."

"That's a nice name, ma'am."

Pete withdrew from his coat pocket a stick of candy wrapped in striped paper.

"With your permission, ma'am."

"Thank you, sir. Go on, Harriet. The gentleman has a stick of candy for you."

Peter O'Leary explained that he was looking for a skilled man to help him at the ranch, and for a woman to assist his wife to look after their new house.

"Ah'm Peter O'Leary. May Ah ask your names?"

"Ah'm Sally, sir."

"Ah'm Willie Sullivan, sir.

Ah'm a carpenter. Ah work real well with wood, and mendin' fences, buildin' cabins. Ah'm good with plants and crops, sir," Willie said. "Ah've worked on farms and ranches with hogs and cows. And Ah'm quick at learnin' new things. Miss Sally is clever with sewin' and knittin'. She's a fine cook, makes the best fried chicken, sweet potatoes and biscuits, sir."

Jim Ellis

There was a gap in the conversation, and Pete O'Leary sensed that Willie had something more to say.

"We are free, sir. Neither Sally or me have ever been slaves."

"Delighted to hear that. I have nothing to do with slavery."

Willie's father, a skilled carpenter, had been freed by his master, an act of manumission.

"We lived in Kentucky. I was my father's apprentice. My mother died in childbirth. After my father passed, I moved around the state, a jobbing carpenter. I made a decent living."

"What about you, Miss Sally?

"Born free, sir, in Tennesee. I had a white mother, but I never met her. Don't know a thing about my natural father. A coloured family in Kentucky raised me. They were my real family."

Willie had met Sally when he was repairing a prosperous house. Sally worked there as an indentured serving girl.

"My family needed money, so I raised it by going into service for four years."

"We wanted to be together," Willie said. "I paid over what was owed."

The couple had come west in pursuit of a better life. Pete tried to imagine how they'd lived. No doubt much of the time from hand to mouth.

"Can you read and write?"

"Our readin' is tolerable, but we need to work at our writin', sir," Sally said.

"My wife can help with your writing. You're just the kind of folks Ah'm lookin' for. I'll pay good wages. You'll have your cottage on the ranch. Well, what do you think, Mr Sullivan?"

Neither Sally nor Willie had to think about it. Pete O'Leary's kindness and unexpected goodness raised their hopes.

"Sir, Ah'm worried Willie might have to go away to find work. Maybe up North to a city or a port. That'd be cruel for Harriet. We're a southern family, Mr O'Leary. We ain't married, proper. But we're together."

Only The Leaves Whispering

"It's a fine offer, Mr O'Leary," Willie Sullivan said. "We're happy to work for you."

They shook hands, cementing the agreement.

"Good. I'm glad you're coming with me.

"Miss Sally, Willie, if you want to marry, a priest is a friend of the family. Ah'll speak to him next time he visits."

"Thank you, sir," Willie said.

Pete reckoned the Sullivans had no place to stay the night and had little money.

"Willie, here's an advance on wages. Find a place to stay tonight."

He handed Willie several folded dollar bills.

"Thank you, sir,"

"Can you meet me at Roland's Hotel with your stuff first thing in the morning?"

Pete O'Leary found them waiting at the door of the hotel, their meagre belongings at their feet. Willie had the toolbox by his side. The stable boy brought the wagon, loaded with goods for the ranch, to the hotel entrance.

"Thank you, young man," Pete said. "You wouldn't say no to a dollar?"

The young black man grinned. "No, sir. Thank you kindly."

Pete showed the Sullivans where to stow their belongings.

"There's room for two upfront. Ah've arranged space in the back where Miss Sally and Harriet can rest. We'll be at my place in a couple of days by late afternoon."

"That's fine, sir," Willie said.

"Thank you, sir," Miss Sally said.

Peter O'Leary knew nothing about these two people and their child. But he liked the look of them. The man was handsome and well-spoken, intelligent and the girl was beautiful. She cared for the man, and the child adored her.

Pete decided to buy clothing for Willie, Sally and Harriet.

"Willie, Sally is goin' to help me at the store. You'll look after Harriet and the wagon?"

Jim Ellis

"Yes, sir."

"Don't follow me, Miss Sally. Walk beside me."

"Yes, sir."

They stood outside a clothing shop that sold simple dress clothes, workwear and field clothes. Pete ran through a list of hats, clothing and footwear needed for Sally, Willie and Harriet. Sally pointed to the items in the window she was sure would fit. Pete entered, made the purchase and had the store clerk deliver to the wagon at the hotel.

"Can you send the parcels right away please?"

"Yes, sir."

Pete folded two dollar bills into the clerk's hand.

"Are you happy with what we have, Sally?"

"That's perfect, sir. Thank you. Our garments and footwear just wore out."

Pete pointed in the shop window to an elegant pair of black leather evening pumps. Pete's wife liked stylish shoes, of which she had several pairs. He figured Sally would, too and could stand a treat.

"Would you like to have a pair to wear for when the day's work is finished?"

"Oh, sir, Ah don't know what to say. It'll be alright, Mr O'Leary?"

"Miss Sally, of course, it'll be alright."

Pete took Miss Sally into the shop, and they stood by the counter. After a few minutes, a second store clerk came out from the back shop.

"You can't bring that Nigger woman in here."

"Ah'm sorry, Mr O'Leary. Ah'll leave, sir," Miss Sally said. "Don't want to cause no trouble."

Pete took her arm and turned her to face the counter.

"Miss Sally, you've nothing to be sorry for."

Pete pulled the Colt pistol from his waistband and laid it on the counter.

"You, sir, are goin' to bring those black pumps to this lady." Pete turned to Sally. "Miss Sally, what size shoe fit you?"

"Smaller, sir, than the pair in the window."

Only The Leaves Whispering

Pete laid his hand on the butt of the pistol. "Boy, get them shoes and fit them on Miss Sally."

They walked out of the store. Miss Sally clasped the shoebox to her bosom.

"Oh, Mr Pete, sir, Ah'm so sorry for any trouble."

"No trouble, Miss Sally. We're friends. That moron was rude. Ah ain't havin' it. You and Willie and Harriet, we're goin' to be good friends. Point of fact, Miss Sally, Ah see you now as good friends.

"And that's how we met, boys," Pete said.

"It's a true story, and a good one," Willie said. "You like it?"

"Very much," Jock said.

"Sure do, Willie," Jim said.

Estella and Sally smiled.

The company moved to the small parlour and sat down.

"How about you boys tell us how your stories and how you met?" Willie suggested.

And so Jock told his story. Orphaned, but a good smith and farrier. Seagoing on the *Jane Brown*, enlisting on *Alabama*.

"The best thing I ever did, volunteering. Proud to belong to *Alabama*. I was sad to leave her, but in Galveston I met Jim, and I'm with him now for the Cherokee Mounted Rifles."

Jim told his story, about being beaten senseless by Texas civilians and robbed and how Jock took him to Doc Merriweather and saved him from certain death.

Pete O'Leary told them how he prospered after leaving the army at the end of the Mexican war. He made his money through cattle ranching in West Texas. His coffers filled and he married Estella, who came from a Mexican family long established in Texas. He moved his family across the Red River to Oklahoma, to the region that became known as Little Dixie. The nearest settlement was Antlers, a good day and a half away by wagon and horseback. He hired Americans and Choctaws willing to work with free blacks and Mexicans. Pete's business grew, buying and selling cotton, breeding horses. Pete worked towards self-sufficiency for much of the food needed for the household.

Jim Ellis

The conversation moved to the war.

"As I told you," Pete said, "I'm for the South, but I had enough of war when down in Mexico. Damned war touches everything. My father is sixty-five. He's riding with Nathan Bedford Forrest's Tennessee Cavalry."

Pete O'Leary supported the Confederate war effort. At the start of the war, he made money funding a couple of blockade runners bringing rifles, and ammunition into Galveston from Cuba for the Confederate Army. The hold of the blockade runners had a corner for a discreet cargo of selected luxuries shipped north to Virginia and sold to Southern ladies. He bought Confederate War Bonds but, worried about an uncertain future, he arranged for the purchase of gold in Great Britain and left it there.

"I supported the South. But I brought in some luxuries, for the ladies. I made a good profit on that. I got to think about my responsibilities after the war.

"I heard Bobby Lee freed his slaves back in '62. He hated slavery," Pete said. "But he looked first to Virginia, his home state. Need more like him."

"Mama, can we have music?" Miss Harriet asked.

Miss Sally looked at Willie. He nodded his head.

"Harriet, you have the gift, knowing just what we need."

Miss Sally sat at the spinet. Willie sent Robert to fetch his fiddle.

"C'mon, Jock. Go on, get that concertina thing," Jim said.

Jock came back with his concertina. The company had never seen one.

"What the hell is that, Jock?" Pete said. "Never seen nothin' like it."

"It's a concertina. It's played in Scotland, and I heard it played in Ireland when I sailed to Cork on the schooner *Jane Brown*."

"Hell and damnation, Jock," Pete O'Leary said. "For a young feller, you sure get around."

"Jock says his fingers are stiff," Jim said. "He's only played it a couple of times since he left *Alabama*. But he plays well and sings real good."

Only The Leaves Whispering

Sally played *My Darlin'* on the spinnet and sang in a deep, honeyed voice.

"*I see my Darlin' in the rainy April sadness.*
I see my Darlin' in the leaves that fall..."

"Fine singin', ma'am, Jim said. "You have a real sweet voice."
"It's lovely, Miss Sally," Jock said.
"Why thank you, boys. Thank y'all."
"Pa," Miss Harriet said, "play with Mama. A happy tune."
Miss Sally and Willie struck up *Rose of Alabama*. Concentrating on the song, Willie coaxed a deep tone from the fiddle, complementing Miss Sally's deft rendering of the melody on the spinet.
"Let's hear you play, son," Willie said.
And Jock played.
Miss Sally sang the lyrics.

"*Away from Mississippi's vale*
With my ole hat there for a sail
I crossed upon a cotton bale
To the Rose of Alabamy."

The company joined in the chorus.

"*Oh brown Rosie*
Rose of Alabamy,
The sweet tobacco posey
Is the Rose of Alabamy."

Miss Sally and Willie, with Jock following, played several favourite songs. *Sweet Betsy From Pike, Buffalo Gals, Lorena,* and *Bonnie Blue Flag.*
Willie played the introduction to the *Cavalier Waltz*, and Miss Sally improvised on the melody. Jock picked up the tune on the concertina.

Jim Ellis

Pete led his wife to the small space for dancing and the children clapped. Miss Harriet looked at Jim and, for a moment, hung her head. Jim wanted to dance with her, but he was cautious, worried that Willie might object to a full blood Cherokee dancing with his daughter. Miss Harriet raised her head and looked again at Jim.

Jim approached Willie, who'd been watching these adolescent manoeuvres with a grin creasing his face.

"Have I your permission, sir?"

"Go right ahead, son. If Harriet says yes, it's all right."

"Miss Harriet, will you dance with me?"

"Yes, I will, Mr Cherokee Jim. I declare I feared I'd die waiting for you to ask."

Jim held out his right arm, crooked at the elbow. Miss Harriet rose and laid her right hand on Jim's arm.

* * *

The next morning, after breakfast was finished, Jock and Jim were ready to leave and head north.

"Thank you, Mr Pete, and Willie, for all your kind hospitality," Jock said.

"Thank y'all for bein' such fine guests," Pete said. "But sit down a while more, boys."

Pete poured coffee into everyone's cups.

"Willie and me, we have a proposal. It'll delay your return to the Rifles, but you'd be helpin' the Confederate war effort."

Pete and Willie explained what they had in mind.

"Fencin' needs to be nailed and repaired," Pete said. "And there's work, too, around the ranch with the horses, and the farm's tools to be inspected. Ah intend clearing land to plant cotton. Export it on a blockade runner. With the money, load another blockade runner in Britain with medical supplies, ether, chloroform, morphine for the Confederate Army. Ah'll make a little money from carrying some items for the ladies. But the ship has to run the Yankee blockade. So there's a risk."

The boys stayed a month, Jock at the forge, shoeing horses and repairing ploughs and tools, while Jim worked the land and rebuilt the fences.

Day by day, they relished the domesticity of Pete's ranch. Jock, a Man of War's Man content with the sailor's life, and now used to the rough life on the trail, had last savoured sparse home comforts when his mother was alive. Jim's home life had ceased when he left his family in the Snowbird Mountains and rode west to Oklahoma to enlist with Stand Watie. Now, they had clean beds and regular wholesome meals. The boys felt honoured to be invited to dine every week with the Sullivans and the O'Learys. They dressed as best they could.

Miss Harriet, drawn to Jim, often brought breakfasts of fried eggs, hash, biscuits and coffee to the cottage where they bunked. Jim watched for Harriet and rushed to open the door when she appeared.

Harriet cooked well, and she was proud of her skill. When she'd been working in the kitchen, she let the boys know with her warm smile.

"This morning, I made breakfast. I changed it. There's ham and steak instead of hash, and honey biscuits, too."

"Thank you, Miss Harriet," Jim said. "We are well pleased."

Jim would return the tray and the dishes to the kitchen just to see Miss Harriet again.

The days when they worked the forge, she brought biscuits and lemonade and honey from Miss Estella's bees.

"Come and sit outside, rest and cool down."

Jim loved to sit beside Harriet. He just had to be with her. Jim was worried that she might not care for him. But when she laughed or touched his hand, he knew the joy of first love.

Jock wandered off, leaving them alone together.

Mature beyond his years in applying his workman's skills and medical knowledge, Jock knew nothing of young ladies. His sole contact with the fair sex had been that first coupling with a trollop, a lady of the night working *Alabama* when the ship lay anchored off Angelsey, taking on crew.

Jim Ellis

"Miss Harriet's a nice person, but she's just a girl, Jim," he told his friend.

"She ain't just any girl. Miss Harriet's special. There's no one like her."

Jim adored Harriet's proud walk and her quiet good manners. That she was a trifle prim made her more adorable.

"I never saw a girl with glasses until I met Miss Harriet. The glasses magnify her wonderful brown eyes and long eyelashes."

And he cared even more for Miss Harriet when she removed the frame to polish the lenses.

"Oh, Jim, you're blurred," she'd say. "I'll put my glasses on. I want to see you nice and sharp."

* * *

As the boys settled into a routine, Pete approached Jock with a new problem.

"Hogs – wild hogs. A horny old boar's wandering about the border of the ranch," Willie said. "Big feller. Keeps tryin' to get in and mount the breeding sows."

Jock waited and said nothing, having no experience of hogs, domesticated or wild.

"I've seen you target shootin' with that Hawken Gun, Jock," Pete said. "You shoot well –

better than either Willie or me. Think you could kill that old boar?"

"I get close enough, Mr Pete, I'll kill him. One shot."

"You sure about that, son? He's a dangerous old hog. You miss, and the hog charges. You'll maybe end up dead."

"I can do it, Mr Pete."

"That's good, son. We'll have ham and pork from the old fellow. Wild boar. Real gamey in the mouth. Tastes different."

"Will the old boar come with his herd?"

"He'll come alone, Jock. Solitary animals, feral boars. We call a bunch of wild hogs a sower, not a herd. A tough old sow leads the sower. Smell anything from five miles."

Only The Leaves Whispering

A sower of about twenty had come through the ranch the previous autumn.

"Near wrecked Miss Sally's garden. We chased 'em off near Estella's hives. Killed a dozen hogs. Year-old sow can have a litter of four to six young," Willie said. "Years ago, Spaniards released hogs into the wild. Nothin' but trouble for ranchers and farmers."

"They outbreed the hunters who are killin' them," Pete said. "After one litter, they can have another in about three months."

"Smart critters, hogs," Willie said. "Smarter than most dogs. Be downwind when you're ready to kill that old feller."

"And he'll be fast," Pete said. "Go like lightning when wounded and furious. Seen one hog run about five hundred yards in twenty seconds. Don't want to trail a wounded boar. It has to be a clean kill."

Jock was confident that with the Hawken Gun, a frontier weapon, he was up to the job. The rifle had a thirty-six-inch-long barrel for sighting on the target across an iron blade sight, accurate to four hundred yards. That felt like a safe distance. But if he missed with the first shot, could he reload in time?

He'd practised reloading, adding black powder paper cartridge, percussion cap and the .54 ball, ramming it home and sighting on a target and firing again. He'd reloaded in twenty seconds. But he could not risk taking precious seconds for another shot if the first one missed and an enraged and wounded animal weighing perhaps five hundred pounds was charging at him. Reloading was out.

Jock tried to project confidence he did not feel.

"Mr Pete, Willie, the Hawken is accurate to four hundred yards, but I want to get the boar in close. The weapon has double triggers. The first trigger is a set trigger. Hammer doesn't fall but sets the second trigger, the hair-trigger. A touch on it and the Hawken fires."

"How close, son?"

"About eighty yards, Mr Pete. I'll kill him with one shot through his brain."

Willie beckoned Jock.

"Come on, son, want to show you somethin' about hogs. Help you get your thinkin' clear for this shootin' job."

Willie walked Jock to the pigpen and the hut where the animals sheltered. Jock had passed the enclosure at a distance and heard the pigs grunting, but had not been drawn to the swine, thinking them dirty and capable of eating anything. What he saw surprised him. The place was clean and the food troughs, too, scoured by one of the hands each day after feeding. Willie pointed to the field a few yards away.

"If a farm hog's dirty, it's been made that way by damned filthy farmers. We let 'em loose in there most days, but not when the weather's bad. Give the old hogs a happy life 'fore we slaughter 'em. Got to remember, Jock, it's business."

A group of young sows came across when Willie called. They crowded around him, and he ruffled the hairs on the back of their heads and the animals grunted happily.

"Go on, Jock, pat the small one. If she lies down, you give her belly gentle strokes."

Jock stroked the animal's head, and he was sure the sow grinned at him. She lay down and looked up at him, and Jock obliged, stroking her soft underside. The sow's contented grunting moved Jock.

"She's just an old pet. Her name's Emily. The children are fond of her. We'll never slaughter Emily. Used to have her in the house, but she was gettin' too big. Emily is a fine, clean and intelligent creature."

Willie got Emily to stand, and she looked at them as he pointed out the locations of her vital parts. The heart and lungs right behind the shoulders.

"This old boar, he's not like Emily. He's dirty and tough. He's no pet. Can't ever tame him. But he's smart. Weigh maybe four or five hundred pounds. Wild hogs destroy everything. It's a hard fight keeping them down, but you need to kill this old feller for us."

"I'll kill him with the Hawken Gun. One shot'll do it."

"Hog comes after you, he'll kill you. Shoot him in the heart and lungs if he's broadside on, and he's dead. And there's the brain protected by his thick skull, strong as boilerplate. The ball has to go right through and into the brain."

"Thank you, Willie. Ah'll see to the Hawken Gun."

Jock cleaned and oiled the Hawken Gun, taking care that the rifling was as new. He charged the weapon with 90 grains of black powder and patched the .54 ball with a piece of old but fine linen, got from Miss Sally, for a well-rifled shot with smashing power.

Willie meant to draw the hog to the killing ground at dawn, when the light would provide a good view of the boar approaching, sunlight at his back. Next morning before sun-up, Pete had a hand in securing a terrified sow in heat to a stake in a clearing frequented by the boar. Nearby, Willie buried several pounds of corn in a shallow hole. A sow in heat and tasty corn; double attractions for the old fellow.

Jock and Pete had prepared a firing position, digging a hollow a foot deep with a close-packed earth mound to the front. Pete brought his seven-shot Spencer repeating rifle, a man-killer with the punch of a .52 calibre bullet. If Jock missed his first shot up close, Pete would riddle the animal with rounds from the Spencer.

"He's dangerous," Pete said. "Kill him with the first shot."

"With respect, sir, you don't need that Spencer. I'll kill this boar."

Pete compressed his lips and shook his head.

"Sometimes it can go wrong. The Spencer's just insurance."

Pete looked at the sawed-off shotgun slung from Jock's left shoulder. Jock caught Pete's stare. He guessed then that Pete was testing his courage and marksmanship.

"My insurance, Mr Pete. Two barrels loaded with buckshot. I made two linen cartridges, each with six balls, and a good powder charge. Jim helped me. A cannon at close range."

"How close?"

"If it comes to it, I'll fire when I can see his eyes."

Jock lay in the prone position, legs spread for stability. The boar came out of a thicket, vanished for a moment in a wisp of early morning mist, then reappeared, caught in the sun. Pete and Jock were downwind of a light morning breeze. The animal sniffed, caught the over-

Jim Ellis

powering smell of the bait and the heat of the sow. He came forward slowly.

The animal grew larger as Jock watched him across the blade sights of the Hawken Gun. When the boar passed eighty yards, Jock steadied, aimed and fired.

The boar went down, got up, unsteady on his short legs, but soon regained balance. Blood leaked from the head wound gouged by the ball. Jock had hit the animal, but the round had not entered its brain.

The wounded creature, confused by the man smell, by the heat of the tethered sow and the bait, charged the firing position, blood streaming from the head wound.

Jock meant to kill the boar, to prove himself before Pete had to save him by dropping the animal in a volley of rounds from the Spencer.

He rose from behind the earth mound, dropped the Hawken Gun and grabbed the shotgun. Jock's bladder emptied, and he felt a warm flood of piss soaking his small clothes as he stepped over the rim of the earth pile. Screaming defiance to mask his fear, he ran at the boar, now thirty yards out and moving fast.

"Jock, get out of the fuckin' way. Let me shoot."

He stopped, sighted the shotgun and at fifteen yards he caught the animal's stink and looked into its eyes, at its bloodstained face and sharp tusks. Jock fired one barrel and the six balls, hitting the creature as one, destroyed the boar's right eye and ear. It dropped to its front knees. Jock moved forward about five yards. He fired the second barrel and the weight of six more balls carried away the left side of the boar's head, ruining the brain. The animal fell on its side.

Jock lost control, and his bowels voided. His stench hit him. He fell to his knees and vomited.

"That was a damned fool thing to do. You're lucky to be alive."

"Ah said ah'd kill him, Mr Pete. Ah'm sorry for taking three shots to finish him."

"Well, I like a man who keeps his word. You have guts, young feller."

Pete held his nose as he propelled Jock to the wash-house to clean up.

67

Only The Leaves Whispering

"Scrub up in there," Pete said. "Throw out them soiled clothes for burning. I'll have Jim fetch clean kit. I'll replace the clothing that's been burned."

* * *

After the near-fiasco of killing the boar, Pete, keen to bolster Jock's confidence, sent him ranch hands with minor injuries. He sutured cuts, applied arnica to bruises and applied soap and sugar poultices to infected wounds, and to one woman with a carbuncle erupting in several openings, discharging pus. His healing hands and kind remarks generated a well of goodwill.

Jock had guts and had been brave in killing the boar, but was worried that he was more a healer than a fighter.

Pete understood what troubled the young Scot.

"You can do good healing out there in the field," Pete said. "Believe me, Jock, the Cherokee Mounted Rifles need men like you. That'd be good service for the South."

"It's up to me. Am I a protector or a warrior? Ah'll find out when Ah get to the Rifles."

Pete knew that the young Scot could do good healing work in the field, but perhaps he didn't want that kind of service. It was an issue only Jock could resolve once he joined the Rifles.

Willie came to the bunkhouse and gave the boys a small flask of sipping whiskey.

"It's a man's drink, so take it slow and easy. Get the smoky taste. You deserve it after labouring at the forge and ploughing the land. Come on over for supper when you're ready."

A dram or two loosened Jim's tongue.

"I could stay here forever, what with Miss Harriet an' all. It's a paradise. White and coloured folks, Mexicans and Indians. We all gettin' along."

"Ah'll find it hard to leave," Jock put in. "Never been better treated in my life. Here, we're all God's children, Jock Tamson's Bairns. Ah'll tell you about that later."

Jim Ellis

"This is the Indian Territory," Jim said. "Ah'm Cherokee and a Southern man. But Ah wish all the South followed the O'Learys and the Sullivans."

The boys knew it would be a hard leave-taking, but they felt they had a duty to join Stand Watie's Command. Jim felt the weight of his people driven on to the Trail of Tears.

Jock was attached to the Southern cause, seeing a people invaded by a more substantial northern neighbour, just like the English invasions of Scotland. He'd begun his service for the South aboard *Alabama* and meant to continue in the Cherokee Mounted Rifles.

* * *

"Ah'll say farewell, Miss Harriet" Jim said. "Ah have to go back to The Rifles."

Jock, embarrassed by the emotion in Jim's voice, looked into the middle distance.

Harriet gazed at Jim, who was mounted now. Her eyes shone. Jim's eyes stung from threatening salty tears. She reached for his hand.

Jim bent low from the saddle and kissed her on the cheek.

"Ah'll come back to see you, Miss Harriet. Ah do care for you."

"Oh, Mr Cherokee Jim, you'd better come back for me, for Ah do love you."

Harriet pulled Jim's head down, ducked under the brim of his slouch hat and kissed him on the lips. Then she walked back to the cottage, her hands covering her face, tears spilling from under her glasses, dripping through her open fingers.

Willie and Pete came forward and shook hands.

"You boys look after yourselves up there," Pete said. He handed Jim an envelope. "Give this to the Colonel. We're acquainted. It tells him you've been helping the war effort with Willie and me."

"Boys, take care. Watch for them Blue Bellies, Kansas Red Legs, and Jayhawkers," Willie said. "Try not to get killed. And Jim, come back soon. Don't break Miss Harriet's heart."

"Yes, sir," Jim said.

Only The Leaves Whispering

Ranch hands and a few of their womenfolk gathered, forming a loose knot beside Pete, Willie and their families.

Estella and Miss Sally detached themselves from family and ranch hands and stood beside the mounts. The boys fidgeted with the reins and shoved their boots into the stirrups until stopped by the boot heels, their uneasiness detracting from the martial appearance created by the weapons they carried.

"Jock, Jim. I beg you, stay with us," Miss Estella said. "You've become family. We shall miss you."

Miss Sally wiped her eyes with her crisp white apron.

"Haven't you done enough fighting for the South, Mr Cherokee Jim? Three years with The Rifles and you only eighteen."

"I signed the paper, Ma'am. I'm a Confederate soldier. I have to go back."

"And you, Jock MacNeil, a Scot, telling us you're sixteen, and I know fine well you be only fourteen or fifteen. The South can't want more from you than your service on *Alabama*."

A red-faced Jock squirmed in his saddle.

"Begging your pardon, Miss Sally, but I gave my word to Jim. I'm going with him to join The Rifles."

The boys raised their slouch hats in farewell. The O'Learys, the Sullivans, the ranch hands and their womenfolk waved. But they stayed quiet.

Jock and Jim, hats on, rode side by side, their mounts' hooves falling silently on the sandy path. The rhythmic creak of leather and the chink of saddle and harness metal broke the stillness as the boys rode along the avenue past the Prairie Fire Crab Apple trees.

Chapter Four

Early the next morning, the friends made their way to the camp of the Cherokee Mounted Rifles near Gainesville.

They rode close to the headquarters and stopped. Jock trotted ahead of Jim and brought his mount to a sudden halt. He looked at the distant garrison and tried to bury his fear of having to fight.

Jim cantered up beside his friend and stopped.

"Don't worry, my friend."

Easy for him to say. Jim had proved he could fight, going into battle at Elk Horn Tavern, in Arkansas, in March 1861. Southern Cherokees captured a battery of guns and turned them on the Yankees. Outnumbered, they had to pull back. Stand Watie showed his talent for soldiering by protecting the retreat of Confederate forces from the field.

Jim, at sixteen, fought at Oak Hills in August 1861. Stand Watie's leadership brought victory to the Rifles, giving the South control of Indian Territory.

"Colonel was a hero after Oak Hills," Jim said.

Jim, battle-hardened by December 26, 1861, had been in the van of cavalry at Chustenahlah that pushed Federal Indian troops, led by Opothleyahola, and Jayhawkers out of Indian Territory and into Kansas. Later, he fought at Wilson's Creek and Cowskin Prairie.

Jock murmured a half-forgotten *Our Father* and several *Hail Marys*, praying that he would not let Jim down when he met the Yankees in battle for the first time.

Only The Leaves Whispering

Jim sensed his friend's anxiety. He wanted Jock to share his pride in belonging to the Cherokee Mounted Rifles. They were a rough old bunch of Horse Soldiers, peerless guerilla fighters and raiders whose war cries and Rebel Yells scared Yankees shitless.

Jock's face turned pale as they closed with the lines of Stand Watie's command. For a long minute, he thought about turning his mount around and going back to the O'Leary Ranch. He swallowed sour bile rising in his throat. His tongue clicked on the dry roof of his mouth.

Jim gazed at Jock's wan face. The friends again reined in their mounts and stared into the garrison headquarters. Jim grabbed Jock's shoulder.

"I'm with you, Jock. There's fighting men over there. You'll be all right."

* * *

"Well, you're back," Stand Watie said. "Thought you'd deserted the Rifles, Jim. You're looking cleaner. What have you been up to?"

Most of the men in the Rifles were from Oklahoma, Indian Territory. The Colonel took a particular interest in Jim, a young volunteer who'd ridden from the Snowbird Mountains to enlist in the Rifles.

"No desertion, Colonel, sir. I got beaten up in Galveston by Texans, white men. You'll recall, sir, that the Company Commander ordered us down there to buy horses."

"Yes, Jim. What happened?"

"Concussion, sir. Real bad. My friend here, Jock MacNeil, took care of me. He brought me to Doc Merriweather. Two of them, they made me well."

Jock studied Colonel Stand Watie. He was a man in his late fifties, about middle height. He had long grey hair streaked with black locks. The Colonel dressed in a three-quarter double-breasted grey uniform coat. The garment was decorated with gold buttons and elaborate gold decoration above the sleeve cuffs. Around his waist, he wore the yellow silk sash of the Confederate Cavalry. A sword belt with cross strap rested above the sash, the sword harness empty. On the right side hung

Jim Ellis

a leather cartridge box, a black leather holster for a cavalry pistol, grip out on the left side for a fast cross draw. The coat was open at the neck, showing a bright white shirt and a folded black silk tie. The two gold stars of Lieutenant Colonel adorned the coat collar. He wore matching uniform trousers with a yellow stripe down the outside leg. Still, Jock's eyes popped when he saw that the Colonel's pants were not tucked into knee-high cavalry boots, but covered to the knee by long deerskin moccasins.

Stand Watie caught Jock's long stare.

"You're surprised I'm wearing moccasins, young man? Well, let me tell you, I'm an Indian, an' I like 'em. They're kind to my tired feet."

Jock blushed, his face crimson. Under the crown of his slouch hat, sweat ran into his hair.

Stand Watie weighed up Jock MacNeil, who was mounted on a beautiful black mare. The youth was well-armed: Hawken gun slung across his back, a sawed-off shotgun holstered to the saddle horn, and on the other side hung a sheathed Mameluke Sabre. A holstered Colt Navy revolver rested at his side and a .36 Colt was in a shoulder holster. Jock sat more comfortable in the saddle as his blushes subsided.

"You're packin' hardware, young man. Know how to use it?"

"Yes, sir."

"And that handsome sabre?"

"Ah can look after myself, Colonel. Ah'm from the Confederate Navy."

"Good."

The wooden box attached to the saddlebags caught the Colonel's eye.

"And that box?"

"A made-up Confederate Navy medical kit. I sailed as Loblolly Boy aboard the Confederate Ship, *Alabama*."

"What the hell is a Loblolly Boy?"

"I worked with *Alabama's* Assistant Surgeon, Dr David Herbert Lewellyn. He's British, like me. I looked after sick and injured sailors. He gave me the medical kit."

Only The Leaves Whispering

"What else can you do?"

"He can handle horses, sir."

Jock held up his right hand, palm out.

"I can speak for myself, Jim,"

Jock explained that he'd been a farrier and blacksmith, working for his father and a neighbour back in Scotland. He explained that while serving as ship's cook aboard the schooner *Jane Brown*, he had learned to dress wounds and treat minor injuries.

"A Royal Navy Surgeon taught me when Ah was under his care."

"Hmmm."

"The *Jane Brown* docked in Liverpool with a cargo of hides from Dublin. That's when I took my chance to join the Confederate Navy."

"I like Scots, son. Some of 'em married Cherokee women. Made 'em real men. Might have a drop or two of Scots blood myself." Stand Watie grinned. "Tell me, son. You're from a faraway place. How'd you arrive here?"

He mentioned that he'd been honourably turned ashore in Galveston with a sick midshipman.

"Ah nursed the midshipman back to health and fit for Navy duty. When I met Jim, he told me about the Trail of Tears. The Lairds exiled my people from Barra. My family had lived there for a long time. But poverty drove my family away before they were chased out. I know how the Cherokee felt. I decided to come with Jim and enlist."

"But why?"

"Why not, sir? Ah came for the South, sir. Ah'm here for Dixie."

"We have smiths, farriers and fighting men. What I need are men to take better care of injured and wounded soldiers." Stand Watie paused and stroked his chin. "Alright son, I'll accept your enlistment in the Rifles. We're allies of the Confederacy. You'll be servin' the Cherokee Nation and the South."

Stand Watie paused and stroked his chin a while. He directed Jock's gaze to the flagpole outside his tent. Jock looked up at the banner. The body of the flag bore a red stripe top and bottom separated by a white stripe, the words *Cherokee Braves* in red letters in the centre of the white stripe and a red star in the centre for the Cherokee Nation. The blue canton with eleven white stars in a circle, representing the South, surrounded by five red stars, symbols of the Five Civilised Tribes.

"That's the battle flag of the First Cherokee Mounted Rifles. You'll be ridin' under it. How do you feel about that?"

"Ah feel alright about it."

"Stand Watie considered Jock again. "Work with my excellent surgeon, Walter Thompson Adair."

"I came to fight, sir. I respectfully request to join Jim's company. After any trouble, I can work with the Surgeon."

"You're a sassy feller." Colonel Watie smothered a grin with his right hand. "All right, young Jock MacNeil, you have yourself an arrangement. I'll get the papers ready. Come to my quarters after supper to sign."

"Yes, sir."

"Mr MacNeil, you'll get all the fighting you can handle and then some."

"Yes, sir! Thank you, Colonel."

* * *

A Lieutenant on the Colonel's staff handed the boys over to a Cherokee Sergeant, a mixed-blood. The Sergeant, a taciturn fellow, took them to tented quarters.

He was unlike any Sergeant Jock had ever seen. He wore a straw hat with a paper rosette of Confederate colours tucked into the red silk hatband. Long black hair rested on the nape of his neck. Over a blue-black, crisscrossed checked shirt with round collar, he wore a grey civilian jacket that hung to his hips, with Black Sergeant's Chevrons sewn on the sleeves. His blue worsted trousers were tucked into stout black mule-eared boots. A black leather belt with a CSA buckle held up his pants. Two holsters, Navy Colt revolvers butt-forward for a quick cross draw, hung from the belt. At his back, tucked behind the belt was a sheathed Bowie knife with a two-foot blade and a guard handle.

"Now that you've had a good look at me, Ah'm Sergeant Buster Parris," he told the awe-struck Jock.

"I'm Cherokee with a bit of white an' some Nigger in there, too. Ma great-grandmother was a Black Cherokee. Ah'm proud to have a bit of African in me." He paused and levelled a hard gaze at the boys.

He turned to Jock.

"You happy about that?"

"Ah'm fine with that. Jim's a full blood Cherokee, and we're best friends. How do you feel about me, a Highlander, with a touch of the Viking?"

A grin split the Sergeant's face.

"You boys are in my squad. You'll be all right. Come on."

Jock glanced at Buster Parris' face as they walked to the Squad area. High cheekbones and a broad nose, almond-shaped dark eyes. He was Cherokee all right. Creases at the corners of his mouth suggested a man who smiled, and Jock noted the laughter wrinkles at the edges of his eyes. Jock thought Buster Parris' gruff manner hid a good man.

Jock had no idea what to expect on entering the Rifles' camp. Influenced by Naval discipline and the seafarers' fetish for cleanliness aboard *Alabama* – officers in grey uniforms, the crew dressed in their smart working kit, and Royal Navy dress blues – he anticipated well turned out soldiers in grey and butternut uniforms. Jock could not resist staring at men who were clothed in a medley of Confederate uniforms, warrior buckskins, and civilian clothing. Somewhere on their person, each man wore an item identifying him as a Confederate soldier. A few had CSA cap badges, or wore belts with a CSA buckle. Here and there were a few men dressed in a mixture of clothing they'd brought with them when enlisting, over time adding a badged forage cap, or a slouch hat, uniform trousers or round shell jackets. On that first day, Jock did not see one man in the Rifles in Confederate field uniform.

"We're the bottom of the Confederate supply chain," Sergeant Parris said. "Kit and supplies meant for us often go to white regiments. Ain't fair. But we fight with what we have.

Jim Ellis

"There's an issue of kit in the afternoon. Bits and pieces that our people have gathered. Some of it scavenged from dead Federal troops. Might be a few things from the Confederacy. You boys are well set but, if I was you, I'd get as much as I could carry. Might be months before there's another issue."

The Sergeant pulled out a notebook and jotted down a list. "Make sure you get your hands on as much of this as you can."

He handed the list to Jim who read over it: socks, small clothes, canteen, cartridge box, two coats, shoes, a washcloth and towel, hat, knapsack, shirts. Personal items: a razor, Bible, small mirror.

The Sergeant gripped Jock by the shoulder and turned him to gaze at the body of the camp, to view tents and shabby soldiers working at their duty.

"You'll see strange things here. Men with old Kentucky Long Rifles, or armed with huntin' rifles. Might see a Brown Bess. There's Enfield Rifles, everyone packin' Bowie knives or Arkansaw Toothpicks, pistols an' sawed-off shotguns. We got some weapons that belong in a museum."

The Sergeant coughed and cleared his throat, and spat a blob of phlegm. He ground the viscous yellow-green mess into the soil with the heel of his boot. His grip on Jock's shoulder tightened.

"You're thinkin', son, we don't look much, you bein' from the Confederate Navy an' all. But we ain't shy when it comes to fightin' Yankees. We'd follow the Colonel through stone walls."

"Yes, Sergeant, sir," Jock said. "Ah'm glad to be here."

Sergeant Parris looked at Jock and shook his head.

"Sergeant Parris, Ah can give you medicine, clear up that cough."

"Surgeon tried that. Didn't work."

"How about cupping?"

"Never heard of it. Quackery, sure enough. The Surgeon tried more than once to cure me with medicine. You know more than him? Oh, go to Hell, son."

Sergeant Parris' irritation over Jock's suggestion caused another bout of coughing, and he bent over, hands on knees, spitting thick, foul

Only The Leaves Whispering

phlegm. Threads of a green-yellow mess clung to his lips and chin. He wiped away the offending filth.

"Sergeant Parris," Jim said, "listen to Jock. He's good. He knows what he's doin'."

"Ma officer aboard *Alabama* taught me. Ah've helped sailors with bad coughs. Ah'll clear the filth from your lungs."

"All right. I'm about ready to try anything to get rid of this damned cough. Come to my quarters after supper and when you've signed the enlistment papers."

* * *

"Shirt off, please," Jock said.

Buster Parris expanded his chest, rubbed the corded muscles of his arms and turned to show a well-muscled back. Jim raised his eyebrows and gave an approving nod to Jock.

There was a bout of thick, hard coughing as Jim propped a seated Buster Parris on a blanket and a pillow placed on the small table in his tent. Jock formed a cup with the fingers and thumb of his right hand, covered the congested area with his cupped hand and placed his left hand on top of the right.

"Sergeant Parris, take deep, steady breaths."

The Sergeant inhaled and exhaled with the power of a small steam engine.

"Slow down. Deep but steady breathing, or you'll get dizzy."

Jock vibrated his hands on the congested area, loosening and shifting mucus to the upper lungs where Buster Parris could cough and spit out the filth. There was an immediate success.

"Jim, bring the bucket near."

A hacking volley of coughs, from deep in the Sergeant's lungs. A violent expectoration and a dull clang as a mouthful of thick phlegm hit the inside of the bucket.

Jock had Buster Parris shift to an upright sitting position, had him lean forward and repeated the treatment to clear the upper back of the lungs. Rapid coughing and hawking followed. Jim dabbed his sweating face dry with a soft cloth.

"Feelin' better already," Sergeant Parris said.

He put on his shirt.

Jim took out the bucket for cleaning, filled it with water and heated it over the small fire he'd lit outside the tent.

"Take off your boots and socks, Sergeant. Lie down on your bed."

"What the Hell is goin' on, MacNeil?"

Jim came back to the tent. "Jock is goin' to get right down and shift the last of the phlegm," he said.

"This is not a Confederate Navy cure-all," Jock said. "It's a folk cure from Barra, ma family's home island. Tinker woman told ma mother about the onion poultice."

With a lack of proper grace, Buster Parris removed his footgear, exposing dirty feet.

"There's hot water on the fire outside. Best you wash your feet, and have clean socks ready."

"Goddammit, you two boys are like a couple of old wimmin. Haven't got clean socks. Ah missed the issue. This is a military camp, not a fuckin' country store."

"You can have a spare pair of mine." Jim said.

He looked at Jim and jerked his head towards a chest by his bed.

"Fine. Bring me the top pair of long deerskin moccasins."

"Roll up yer breeks," Jock said. "Lie on yer stomach."

In preparation for the treatment, the boys had gone into a nearby copse to gather a handful of small wild onions. They rooted around until they found wild garlic, and dug up four bulbs. In a dab of lard in the small pan they used on the trail, they browned the onion and garlic, adding water, to make a thick, generous handful of mash.

Back in the tent, Jim spread an old but clean flour sack lifted from the cook tent, over the small table. Jock had poured off surplus liquid outside the tent. With the blunt side of Jim's knife, Jock edged out the hot mash onto one half of the flour sack, spreading it evenly, to about a

Only The Leaves Whispering

couple of inches thick. He folded the remaining half of sackcloth over the paste and tied the ends.

Holding it to eye level, Jock showed it to Jim and bent down to let to Buster Parris have a look.

"An Onion Poultice."

Buster Parris' upturned feet rested on his folded slicker, placed there to keep the bedding dry. His chin rested on folded hands. Jock pressed the hot poultice against the soles of his feet. His patient gave a sharp intake of breath.

"Jesus Christ, MacNeil, you torturin' me?"

"No, Sergeant, sir. We'll leave it there for twenty minutes. The poultice'll draw out the phlegm from your chest. Try to keep still. Tomorrow, you'll be a new man. That's a promise."

Later that evening, Jim's worries surfaced.

"What if the Sergeant doesn't get better? He'll laugh at us. Or worse, come down on us."

"Don't worry. The cupping's loosened the congestion. The poulticing will clear out the rest. The Sergeant will feel better."

* * *

Two days later, a changed Buster Parris opened the flap to the boys' tent.

"Ah'm feelin' really well, young Mr MacNeil. Thank you, and you too, Jim for gettin' me on my feet."

Jim, relieved, relaxed and grinned.

"Glad we could help," Jock said.

The rough Sergeant had removed his uniform trousers and now wore buckskins and high moccasins but was still apparently a member of the Cherokee Mounted Rifles.

"Jim, you're stayin' here today. Take care of your mounts. Anyway, you know all about what Ah'm goin' to show Jock." He turned to him. "No training here, Jock. The men know how to live on the trail, and they can track. Learned these things from huntin'. We are one of the civilised tribes, but we're Cherokee warriors, too."

Jim Ellis

The pair of them walked through the Camp to Buster Parris' quarters. The news worried Jock, and he held his tongue. Sergeant Parris entered his tent and emerged a couple of minutes later carrying two beautiful long rifles fitted with scopes on the left side of the weapon.

"These are Whitworth Rifles, made in Britain. Took them off Yankees. Here." He handed a rifle to Jock who weighed the gun and examined it. His right hand caressed the polished wood butt.

"Have a look through the scope. It's offset on the left side. It ain't loaded."

Jock trained the weapon at the edge of the camp. He adjusted the scope, bringing distant figures closer.

"What a rifle!" Jock said.

Buster Parris described the Whitworth in greater detail.

"In the right hands, this beauty can hit targets at two thousand yards. The barrel gives the .451 bullet a wicked twist and a spin, and that makes it a stable round at long range. Real craftsmen made these weapons."

"First time Ah've seen one. Ah've hit targets at four hundred yards with the Hawken Gun. But two thousand yards!"

"I heard you shoot well, and I need a sharpshooter in the squad. I can order you, but I prefer a volunteer. You want the job?"

"Yes, sir, Sergeant Parris. Thank you."

They shouldered the rifles and carried the forked stick rests back to Jock's tent. On the way, they detoured to the horse herd. Two chestnut mounts with white face marks waited for them, one saddled for Sergeant Parris.

The Sergeant fed sugar lumps to the horses and patted their long manes.

"Chickasaw breed. Fine little mounts. Spaniards bred 'em and let 'em loose back in the fifteen hundreds. Gallop real fast in broken country. A raider's horse. Perfect for The Rifles."

They walked the horses to Jock's tent.

"Saddle up, Jock. You won't need the Hawken Gun where we're goin'. But get the rest of your hardware ready. Bring the sabre and the

Only The Leaves Whispering

lariat. So we're out for a couple of days, maybe three or four. Livin' on jerky and water. Might run into Yankees or that Kansas Red Leg vermin. Give you practice with the Whitworth. Ah'll tell you about The Rifles and how we do things out here in Indian Territory."

Jock's heart lifted. His education as a Cherokee soldier had begun.

* * *

"No need to worry about Yankee patrols this far south. Too close to our lines," Buster Parris said. "But we'll keep a watchful eye."

Half an hour in the saddle and well away from the camp, they dismounted.

"We'll walk the ponies. Give them rest," Buster said. "There's water up ahead."

They hit a comfortable stride, and the mounts' breathing slowed.

"Got to keep them fresh. A horse will run so fast and so far, then fall down. We ain't getting to that."

"My father said that. He was a sergeant, a farrier in the British Army. Ten years service in the Scots Greys, a famous Scots cavalry regiment," said Jock. "Taught me smithing, and how to tell when a horse was sick. I might have joined the Greys had my father lived."

Buster caught the wistfulness in Jock's voice. He looked at the young man's sad face.

"Look, son, wherever he is, your father will be right proud that you belong to the Cherokee Mounted Rifles. Finest light cavalry in the Nations."

Jock's melancholy subsided at Buster Parris' kind, thoughtful words. "Thank you," he said.

They walked on for a few minutes. Then Buster opened up.

"You know about Lincoln and the slaves?"

"I had a friend aboard *Alabama*, Davey White. I was his first white friend. He was the body servant of a Delaware man taken prisoner from the sailing ship *Tokonagwa*. Captain Semmes freed him, and he signed on as Wardroom Steward. I mean, Davey White joined the Confederate Navy. Paid the same wages as white stewards. Davey is a

Jim Ellis

grand lad. He was for the South but warned me to stay away from the deep South. His people had a hard time down there."

"That's good that you and he were friends," Buster said.

"In port, Federal Agents tried to get him to desert, but he refused."

Buster returned to Lincoln and said that the President had freed the slaves when he issued the Emancipation Proclamation.

"I know Lincoln's the Yankee President," Jock said. "But freeing the slaves... what happened?"

"First pass? A good idea. I don't hold much with slavery myself." Buster explained that Maryland, Delaware, Kentucky, and Missouri remained with the Union but kept their slaves. Parts of Virginia were for the Union and had slaves. Lincoln made these parts the new state of West Virginia.

"That's hard to understand. Surely Lincoln would have said all slaves are free?"

"Lincoln's astute, but he don't give a horse's ass about slaves. He's playing pure politics. Plenty of men from these states fight for the Confederacy. For Lincoln, it's all about holding the Union together. He's a goddammed cynic."

"Christ, it looks that way."

"I listened to officers. Eavesdroppin', I was," Buster said. "Federal newspapers captured by a raiding party. Even the Yankees don't much like what he's doin'. The Chicago Times called the Proclamation a criminal wrong."

Buster rubbed his hands and shook his head. He cleared his throat and spat a gob well away. "I heard that one old judge from the Federal Supreme Court said Lincoln was broken, a damned fool. Blue Bellies ain't fighting to free slaves. Bastards want to bring the South to heel. Cherokee Nation abolished slavery not long after Lincoln. I hope and pray them that keeps slaves do the right thing and sets them free."

"I'm with you there."

That evening, they unsaddled and hobbled the ponies. Unasked, Jock rubbed down both mounts. Buster Parris circled their saddles and bedding with the lariats.

Only The Leaves Whispering

"Rattlers won't cross the rope."

"Jim told me about it."

"We'll sleep easy, but with one eye open for trouble."

After a supper of deer jerky and water, Jock and Sergeant Parris lay inside their bedrolls.

"I said I'd tell you about The Rifles. You're not tuckered out?"

"No. I'm fine."

The Indians belonged to a warrior tradition and knew how to live in the field: setting up camp, hunting, tracking. They rode and shot well.

"The men know to put latrines downstream of drinking water. Plenty of marksmen around, and brave, too. Warriors, great light cavalry. Experienced raiders, deadly snipers. The men don't like standing guard, detest garrison duty, and it's like drawing teeth getting them to mount defensive patrols. But there's no training for recruits. A mistake."

"I think so. Aboard *Alabama*, everyone was trained in the ways of the ship. Me being a sharpshooter, I can belong?"

"I'd say so. I've been at this caper since the start of the war. Colonel Stand Watie's a natural. He's not a regular soldier, but he knows what he's doing. Not every officer does. Trouble is, there are no war leaders done any fighting since 1825. They became good farmers, ranchers and men of business."

"I see. How did you learn to soldier, Sergeant?"

"Well, I got in some fighting in the Light Horse. They're like Texas Rangers. Responsible for the law. When I joined The Rifles, I made a point of finding out what a good army sergeant does. And the hard knocks."

Jock lay quiet for a whole minute, taking in what the Sergeant had said.

"I don't want to put you off, Jock, you comin' to The Rifles from far away and the Confederate Navy. But I want you to understand what it is like out here in The Nations. The war'll be won or lost back east. But we stop fighting, Yankees'll occupy our land. Federal soldiers moving back east and elsewhere. What we're doing matters. I intend bringing my boys out of this war alive, and you're one of them now.

"You're a good shot, son. You put five rounds, one after the other, into a ten-inch target at two hundred yards. But you've never killed anyone, or been a sharpshooter?"

"Saw wounded men when *Alabama* sunk *Hatteras*. I killed a big feral hog down at the O'Leary Ranch. But, no, never a sharpshooter."

"Before we turn in, let me tell you something about sharpshooters. You might change your mind about volunteering. Yankees catch a sharpshooter, most likely they'll kill him. We'd do the same."

Sergeant Parris explained that sharpshooting would be part of Jock's work. He'd also be out riding with patrols and with larger formations attacking the Yankees.

"I heard from the Lieutenant that you're tagged to help injured and wounded."

"Correct."

"You've got a lot on your plate, son. Sharpshooting needs a cool head. Patient, hunting prey, finding cover, set an ambush. Scare the Hell out of soldiers, who'll hold you a murderer."

Parris raised himself on his right elbow and stared at Jock's prostrate body. Through the darkness, Jock felt the penetrating force of the Sergeant's eyes.

"Army of Tennessee – heard the Irishman, General Cleburne formed a battalion of sharpshooters. Wear fancy badges an' all. Call themselves Mahone's Brigade. Think you'd like it up there?"

"That I don't know, Sergeant Parris. But I'll tell you this. I'm not going anywhere. I'm not leaving the Rifles."

It was the response Buster Parris wanted. He rolled over and fell asleep.

Jock lay awake, worrying.

* * *

Only The Leaves Whispering

Day two, they rode towards Kansas. Buster pointed out silver maple woods. Later, the horses cantered through buffalo grass, and then Canadian wild rye, and gamagrass.

"Might find some Bluebellies or Kansas Red Legs," Buster Parris said. "Give 'em a bloody nose if we can."

Buster and Jock rode on until noon before they looked for shelter from the oppressive heat. They hid among a small wood of shimmered oak and unsaddled and tethered the ponies near sweet grass and water nearby.

Jock and Buster stretched out, resting head and shoulders on their saddles. From time to time, one of them rose and scanned all points on the horizon with a telescope.

"Don't want riders surprising us," Buster said.

Buster Parris talked while they hid from the heat of the noonday sun.

It surprised Jock to hear that the five civilised tribes, the Choctaw, Chickasaw, Cherokee, Creek, and such smaller tribes as the Osage and Delaware, had transformed Indian Territory. They adopted the culture and technology of white America.

"My people are not savages," Buster Parris said.

"I never thought they were," Jock said.

Buster Parris grinned.

"Smarter than many settlers."

The Sergeant surprised Jock yet again when he explained that the Indians built plantations, farms and ranches, dug mines, graded turnpikes.

"Goddammit, son, but we made Oklahoma Territory the richest part of the US west of the Mississippi. The Federal Government moved us. The war broke out and the Confederate Government offered compensation. They gave us voting rights in the Confederate Assembly."

Buster tugged his nose. "Tell you something, son. Rebel states? Friends for now. Folks out of Georgia, Alabama, Tennessee, and Mississippi forced us west of the Mississippi. Texas and Arkansas? They chased us. It's difficult, but the alliance with the South is the best deal for the Nations."

Buster stayed quiet for a time. He looked at Jock and jerked his head. "We take people as we find them."

"I like that. Jock Tamson's Bairns."

"Who the Hell is Jock Tamson, and what's a bairn?"

"A Scots expression. A bairn's a child. We're all God's Children."

"That's good, son. We married Americans and blacks. Now we're mostly mixed-bloods. Like I told you, I've got plenty of Cherokee blood, but I'm proud of my white and African blood. And you're a white man enlisted in the Cherokee Rifles.

"Lots of Baptists and Methodists among us. We created public schools. Heard it said that they were the first public schools in the country. Most of my people can read and write English and Cherokee. My father printed newspapers in English and Cherokee."

Buster Parris reached into his saddlebag and withdrew a battered and well-read Bible. He waved the Good Book at Jock.

"This is a King James Bible, but translated into Cherokee. How about that?"

"I'm impressed," Jock said. "I have a King James, back at the camp. A neighbour who took me in after my father died gave it to me when I went coasting on the schooner *Jane Brown*."

"Did you read it?"

"My experiences with the Catholic Church sickened me. A swine of a nun locked me in a dark cupboard. Her priest thrashed me with a cane. A mad Irishman, a bad man. The pair of them in the service of the Devil. I'm finished with the Faith. Yes, I read the King James for a while at sea. But aboard the *Jane Brown*, none of the crew lived the way of the Good Book. I drifted away… gave up. What about you, Sergeant? What did you do before you joined the Rifles?"

"Light Horse for a while. That's what got me my Sergeant's stripes in the Rifles when I volunteered. My family farmed, and I helped my father in his print shop. I'm proud that we printed in English and Cherokee."

Only The Leaves Whispering

"You married?

"My wife's name is Ghigau, meaning beloved woman." He turned away from Jock for a moment. "A boy, Waya, that means Wolf. My daughter's name is Ayhoka, it means She Brought Happiness. They're down in Texas. Safe, I hope, with my parents and my sisters. Had to get them away from this damned war. Haven't seen them in more than a year."

"That is hard for everyone. I like the names of your wife and children."

* * *

They'd ridden several miles closer to Kansas. Buster Parris and Jock hid in a thicket of dogwood trees. They had ample views of the broken country in front of them. Buster had his ear to the ground.

"Riders are coming," he said.

"How can you know?" Jock said.

Buster laughed "You have to be an Indian to do this. Ten of them," he said, lowering the telescope. "Federal patrol. Lieutenant and a sergeant. Raiding or foraging." He handed the glass to Jock. "Here. Your first look at the enemy."

Jock brought the patrol closer. He gazed at well-mounted riders in a column of twos, officer and Sergeant out in front. The horses moved at a steady, distance-eating pace that could last an hour or more. Jock again magnified the Yankee Cavalry. He saw salt marks on upper body garments, worn blue coats and shirts. Black sweat marks circled the crowns of battered slouch hats.

"Be walking the horses soon. We'll watch 'em," Buster Parris said.

"Then what?" Jock said.

"Reckon on setting an ambush."

"But Sergeant, we're two, and they're ten."

"Right. Ten Blue Bellies and we're Mounted Rifles. Odds about right. You scared, son?"

"A little."

Jim Ellis

"Me too. Look, Jock, ain't natural ridin', shootin' and killin'. Scared is all right. Means you'll stay alive. It's heroes get themselves killed."

Buster Parris knew how Jock felt, having been through that vale of tears at the start of the war. Now he had a grip on himself and would help Jock overcome his fear of combat. He'd meant to have Jock kill his first Federal with his sharpshooting. Jock had shown his skill when practising with the Whitworth Rifle on the first day in the field. Well, there'd be sharpshooting before the day was out, and an ambush, too.

Buster Parris knew the country and a plan was taking shape in his head. He doubted the patrol would expect an attack this far from Confederate lines.

"Few miles up the road, a bunch of elm trees off the trail. We're heading there. We'll get behind them and well off from their left flank. The ponies will get us there before the Yankees pass. Here's what we'll do."

* * *

The horses breathed slow. They'd recovered from the rush to outflank and overtake the Federal patrol. The sweat that was lathered on their coats shrunk to streaky white stains. Jock and Buster Parris hid among the elms. The loaded Whitworth rifles and the forked rest sticks leant against a small elm.

"They'll be passin' in twenty or thirty minutes," Buster said.

A pale-faced Jock looked at the Sergeant and nodded. Buster Parris had said they could ambush from far away and hit a couple of troopers bunched in the patrol. At long distance, even with the Whitworth, it was challenging to select and be sure of killing the target.

"Say we shoot at the Sergeant and the Lieutenant, and we miss one or both. Damned quick they'll come after us. A counter-attack, and we'll be runnin'. They'll pass close. We get one shot each with the Whitworth. You get the Lieutenant, and I'll get the Sergeant. No one to give orders after we kill them."

"I can do it. I won't miss the target."

"I know you can, Jock."

Only The Leaves Whispering

Fifteen minutes had passed in anxious silence. Buster Parris untied a cloth parcel about three feet long from the back of his saddle. He opened it.

"This here's an old Harper's Ferry blunderbuss. My father brought it with him from back east. His father got hold of it about 1812. A good charge of powder in there. Funnel muzzle'll spread a load of lead balls and nails when it's fired. Do a lot of damage. Confuse them Yankees. We ride at them about ten feet apart. Up close, after I hit them with the blunderbuss, fire the sawed-off shotguns, one barrel at a time. Get closer and finish them with our pistols. Use the Navy Colt and keep the .36 Colt to last. Use it if you have to. I'll hold one of my Navy Colts in reserve."

He patted the large Bowie knife attached to his belt.

"This is for dirty work. Have your sabre ready."

The Yankees came up, and Jock and Parris laid the barrels of their Whitworths on the forked rest sticks, magnifying the targets. Jock hit the Lieutenant close to the heart. Buster put a round in the Sergeant's head. The Yankees pitched from the saddles, the mounts galloping on. The patrol shuddered to a halt and shocked riders milled about. Jock and Buster secured the Whitworths and rest sticks to their saddles.

The Sergeant and Jock burst out of the thicket and rode straight at the cluster of confused Yankee horsemen. Jock's Rebel Yells and Parris' war whoops terrified the cavalrymen. Seeing their fear of him excited Jock, and he was not afraid. He wanted his father's ghost to be proud of him. At fifteen feet, they stopped. Buster fired the blunderbuss and cut down four Yankees and their mounts. He slung the blunderbuss from the saddle pommel and reached for the sawed-off shotgun snug in its saddle holster. Jock drew his sawed-off shotgun. They fired. One volley killed two troopers, and the second wounded a black gelding. The animal collapsed, pinning its rider to the ground.

Buster Parris and Jock rode up and down the Yankee patrol, knocking men aside and trampling over dead horses and riders. Three mounted troopers: one fired a pistol at Buster and missed. Jock and Buster each fired three shots from the Navy Colts, killing the Yankees.

Buster Parris rode to what had been the front of the patrol. Jock stayed back, looking at the mess of dead men and horses.

The trooper pinned down by his wounded mount had freed himself. He staggered a few steps on an injured leg and aimed a Cavalry pistol at Buster Parris. Jock spurred his mount forward, gun in left hand, steering the animal with his knees. He withdrew the sabre from its sheath. Jock raised the sword and brought it down on the man's arm, severing it at the elbow, and shot him in the head.

"Thanks, Jock. You should've shot him first."

Sergeant Parris dismounted.

"Cover me, Jock."

He holstered the Navy Colt and withdrew the .36 Colt from its shoulder holster. Eyes sharp, pistol cocked and ready, Jock surveyed the dead Yankees. Nothing moved.

Buster Parris turned over corpses with his moccasin toe. He looked in saddle bags; shot the wounded black gelding in the head; picked up a revolving Colt Shotgun.

"Reckon they're 6th Kansas Volunteer Cavalry. Probably out of Fort Scott. They're all dead. See if we can pack the McLelland saddles. We'll take the shotgun, carbines and sidearms. Check saddlebags for clothing and anything else we can salvage. Look at their boots. We're always short of footgear. Everything else they're wearing stinks. Let it rot with the corpses."

"'We're not burying them?"

It troubled Jock to leave the enemy dead to rot in the field. Even though he was no longer a believer, it felt un-Christian, not Catholic; a sacrilege. "The sacred, the dead," Jock said.

"Yankees? Maybe. Best we get away from here. You never know when another Yankee patrol might pass. They'd kill us. Nature'll take care of the remains."

"Nature?"

"Sure. Wolves, coyotes, buzzzards'll eat 'em all up. By tomorrow morning there'll be nothin' here but a heap of bones."

Only The Leaves Whispering

Buster pointed to the sky. Jock looked and saw buzzards gathering, riding the warm air currents.

"Smart birds. They know when the table's set."

Five horses that had survived, having run off in panic when the fighting began, began drifting back to the carnage.

"Let's get hold of the mounts," Sergeant Parris said. "We'll load the saddlebags and join the horses for the run back to our lines."

They reloaded the Whitworth rifles, shotguns and Colt revolvers. "That's thirty rounds ready, plus the Harper's Ferry Blunderbuss," Jock said.

Buster Parris took his time with the blunderbuss. "He's an old feller. I take care of him." He primed the weapon with powder and loaded it with lead balls and nails. They looked at the destruction. Sergeant Parris turned to Jock.

"Nasty work but we had to do it. You did well, son. Out here, keep your nose in the wind and your eyes along the skyline. With luck, you'll travel far."

They linked the five horses by reins and bridles, running the animals in a compact phalanx. Jock led and Buster rode behind the cantering animals, as rearguard. His eyes ached from sweeping the distance with the telescope for pursuers, Yankee cavalry patrols, or a guerrilla band out of Kansas.

At dusk, Buster called for Jock to slow down, and they walked the horses in the darkness. At first light, they remounted and urged the animals to an easy canter until they reached Confederate lines.

Chapter Five

Buster Parris signalled for Jock to slow the horses. They slipped into the camp. He meant to see to the needs of the men in his squad before any enterprising officer laid hands on the kit looted from the Yankee cavalry patrol. Buster knew who needed footgear and gave them the Yankee cavalry boots. It was the same with the clothing and blankets they had taken: he made sure that his bedraggled men got the looted uniforms.

Buster kept a carbine and gave the rest to the seven best shots in the squad. He passed the saddles on to his men who needed them. His squad was well mounted. He handed the captured mounts over to the wranglers looking after the horse herd.

Word soon spread about Buster and Jock's successful ambush of the Yankee Cavalry.

"Well done, sergeant – and you, too, young man," the platoon commander, a lieutenant, said. "You second-guessed me about distributing the kit."

"Thank you, sir." Buster nodded to Jock, who handed the officer the Colt revolving shotgun. "Thought you'd like that, sir," Jock said.

"That's a fine weapon. Thank you both kindly."

"We've got a dozen cavalry pistols. You want to have a look at them, sir?" Jock said.

"That's all right. Sergeant Parris knows what to do."

"Right, sir."

Only The Leaves Whispering

Buster picked up a bundle at his feet. He unfolded the thick cotton wrapping to reveal an 1860 Colt model Army Percussion Pistol. "We kept this one for you, sir. It's a forty-four gauge. Walnut grip, brass trigger guard, blue case hardened finish." He handed it to his commanding officer.

"Buster, that's a beauty."

Buster pointed to the half undone cotton wrap. "Ammunition too, sir." He reached down and searched among the folds of the cloth and brought out stock for the pistol. "Cut to fit, sir. Walnut stock matching the pistol grip, and brass finishings to go with the trigger guard. Shoot from the shoulder."

There was a solid click as the Lieutenant pushed the stock into the pistol. One-handed, he brought the Colt to his shoulder and aimed.

"Careful, sir. The Colt's loaded. I counted five rounds."

"Sorry, Sergeant, Jock. Don't want to hurt my good men."

The lieutenant went to his quarters.

They unsaddled the ponies.

"I'll get them back to the wranglers," Jock said.

"Thanks, son. We've kept him happy," Buster said. "He's keen, but he's young and ain't been long with the Rifles. He's like me, mixed blood, but I'd say he's mostly Cherokee. Get hold of Jim, give him one of the pistols. Get some grub and rest. I'm for my bedroll."

* * *

"You did well, Jock. I told you it'd be all right," Jim said. "You're now a mean old horse soldier. Have you ridin' soon with them Missouri Boys."

Jock handed Jim the Colt Cavalry pistol. "Tuck that in your belt."

Jim weighed the Colt and had a look along the sights. "Good, I like it. Thanks, Jock."

"I'm tired, Jim. Going to get some rest."

"No sleep for you, my friend. Surgeon Adair is looking for you. He asked for you to report to him when you got back."

"Oh, hell. After the ambush, we walked and rode all through the night. I'm dead beat."

"This is the Confederate Army. Raiding party on the way. Sent a rider ahead. Wounded men are coming in."

"I'll get over there then," he said, with a weary yawn.

"Jock MacNeil, sir." He came to attention and saluted. "Formerly Loblolly Boy, CSS *Alabama*. Now Cherokee Mounted Rifles."

Surgeon Adair came to attention and returned Jock's salute, his right hand touching the brim of his hat, the crown of which was decorated with a black feather plume. Glancing at the Surgeon, Jock took him in. The green sash of CSA Surgeon bound his waist. Just above middle height at five foot nine inches. Full beard. Knee-length coat, baggy trousers in need of pressing, scuffed boots wanting polish.

Adair removed his coat and put on a thick and none-too-clean thick cotton apron, and rolled up his sleeves.

"Wounded coming in, so we need to be ready. But first, Mr MacNeil, what's in that box by your feet?"

"I brought it from CSS *Alabama*. Assistant Surgeon Llewellyn gave it to me when I went ashore in Galveston." Jock paused and, with new pride in his voice, continued. "That was on the day my ship, I mean *Alabama*, sank USS *Hatteras*."

"I heard about that. Good job. Why ashore, son?"

Jock described nursing Midshipman Hollister back to fitness from pneumonia for sea duty. How he met Jim and the decision to enlist in The Rifles.

"So Doctor Merriweather gave you some medical training?"

"Yes, sir. But not just Doc Merriweather. Retired Surgeon Gavin of the Royal Navy trained me while I was convalescing from an injury back in Westburn. I looked after sick and injured sailors on the coasting schooner, *Jane Brown*. I was shown what to do aboard *Alabama* by Surgeon Llewellyn."

"Tell me, what can you do?"

Jock described his shipboard duties. "I can suture and dress wounds, poultice infected cuts and reduce bruises with poultices. I can bandage

Only The Leaves Whispering

a man up to help his cracked ribs heal. You can ask my friend, Cherokee Jim, about that. I know how to look after a man convalescing. I cleared Sergeant Buster Parris' lungs of phlegm and cured his cough. You can ask him. He'll tell you what I did."

"How did you treat him?"

"I cupped his lungs, shifting the phlegm from bottom to top, and got him hawking and spitting. Then I applied an onion poultice to the soles of his feet. That's an old Highlander's cure my mother used on me and my sister and brother. Two days and Sergeant Parris' cough was gone."

"Good job, son. Parris' cough had me neutered. Can you use the cautery?"

"I helped Surgeon Llewellyn a couple of times. I know what to do. I have a cauterising iron in the medical box."

"Ever seen a broken bone set?"

"Yes, sir. Helped Mr Llewellyn put splints on a broken arm, and another time on a broken leg."

"Ever set a broken limb?"

"No, sir, but I'd like to learn."

"Good. We'll get to that in due course."

Surgeon Adair decided to let this young soldier give his best shot. "Galloper that came in said two dead and five wounded. Two of the wounded got shot with Minnie balls, .58 calibre. One through the upper arm and the other in the thigh. Minnie's a heavy ball. Wrecks bones and tears flesh to bits, destroys what it hits. I estimate an arm and a leg amputation. Can you have a first look at the three wounded, see what you can do?"

"Yes, sir, I can do that."

"When I'm done, I'll come and see how you got on. You might need the cautery today."

Surgeon Adair's assistants would help with the amputations and administer chloroform or ether. Jock would be on his own. He sent for Jim.

Jim Ellis

The three wounded had minor injuries: suturing, poulticing an abrasion with the Black-Draught. And one soldier had a Minnie Ball lodged in his upper left pectoral, a spent round, the top third of the ball exposed. The poor man was in shock and pain.

"Ah'm Ah goin' to die, Doc?"

"No. Surgeon Adair is going to take care of you. He'll be here soon. And I'm not a doctor, I'm an assistant."

"You can get the Minnie ball out. You're the Doc."

"Keep calm, you're going to be alright."

Jock trembled with anxiety for an older Cherokee soldier with a deep slash across the top of his buttocks. Jock eased the man's pants down. "Christ, what a sore arse," he murmured. "Got to stop the bleeding. What happened?"

"Yankee got behind me. Cut me with an Arkansaw Toothpick. Blew his head off with the shotgun."

"Jim, can you get that brazier going?"

"Right, Jock." Jim worked the small bellows, shifting the cold heart of the fire to dull red.

Jock placed the tip of the cautery in the fire, waiting until it turned dull red. He put a leather bite in the soldier's mouth.

"Bite on this. It is going to hurt. I'll be quick."

Jock had indicated for Jim and two of the walking wounded to hold the man down.

He worked in short bursts, bit by bit, sealing the six-inch wound. The sweet smell of roasting human flesh made Jock feel sick. The bleeding stopped. Jock dressed the wound with salve and bandage.

Surgeon Adair appeared and inspected Jock's work on all the patients.

The wounded soldiers took to calling him 'Doctor Jock'. He protested, "All right, all right, but make it Doc MacNeil." That moniker stuck and amused Surgeon Adair.

"You know what you're about, Mr MacNeil. Good work. Help me move the man with the ball in his chest round to the operating tent.

Only The Leaves Whispering

Stand by. You'll learn something. Come with me tomorrow when I examine the patients."

* * *

Buster was on duty the day a band of Missouri guerrillas had come to the camp. They came in after pursuing and slaughtering Jayhawkers in a running fight when they crossed into the Nations.

He'd called Jock over.

"Have a look, son. Speak to them. Find out if they want something. A couple of young fellers with them. Got a feeling they might have ridden with Quantrell. It's a hard war up there. Ambushes, killin' anyone who gets in their way, burning farms, crops, killing animals. Families goin' down. Yankee irregulars, them Red Legs and Jayhawkers. Just as twisted, maybe even more. Like crooked timber."

Jock studied the band of fifteen riders. Good mounts; white sweat stains on their hides said that the horses had been ridden hard. Well-armed men, faces covered by the brims of their slouch hats, saddles and belted torsos bristling with hardware: carbines, sawed-off shotguns, Colt pistols and heavy sheathed bladed knives.

"How do, you all?" Jock said.

"How do, young feller?" an older man said.

Several men just stared at him through tired eyes. Two or three of the younger ones murmured, "How do?"

Jock broke fifteen seconds of silence. "Why're you wearing that kind of shirt?" he asked a young guerrilla about his own age.

"Want that pack of murd'rin' Jayhawkers, Red Legs, Union spies and thieves, to know who we are. Good Old Rebels. Missouri Bushwhackers."

He admired the many-coloured adornments of bright silk flowers and ribbons stitched to the front. "I like your shirts. Want to trade?"

The Missouri Boy withdrew a clean shirt from his saddlebag and held it up. "Maybe. What you got that's worth trading for this shirt?"

The Missouri Boys were trail-worn, dirty and bloodied. Jock figured they'd be looking to bathe. He'd noticed some of the men had dirty bandages covering wounds and injuries.

"Enough Confederate Army soap. There's a creek nearby where you can bathe. I'll take you there, and I'll treat all your wounds and injuries."

"How the Hell you're goin' to treat wounds? You're just a boy."

Jock held out his hand. "I'm about your age, going on fifteen. Jock MacNeil, from Scotland. Confederate States Navy, CSS *Alabama*. Loblolly Boy working for Assistant Surgeon Llewellyn. Now, I'm helping Surgeon Adair, Cherokee Mounted Rifles."

"Wait." The young Bushwhacker rode to the front of the column. "What you think, Frank?"

"He sounds like a good kid, Jesse. Scots – you can count on 'em."

"Jesse rode back to Jock. He reached out with his hand. "I'm Jesse James. The man at the front is my brother, Frank. We'll trade. We're obliged to you for looking at our hurt and wounded."

"Water the horses at the creek. There's sweetgrass there for feed. My friend Jim will take you."

Jock exchanged Confederate Army soap for a Missouri Bushwhacker's shirt. Then he treated the Bushwhackers' wounds and injuries. He painted arnica on bruised limbs. Sutured and dressed deeper cuts, poulticed infected wounds. Jock bound one man's injured ribs, sustained in a collision with a mounted Jayhawker.

"Ah killed the son of a bitch," he said to Jock.

Next morning, Jim brought a cauldron of coffee brewed from roasted acorns and a touch of chicory root to the Missouri Boys' bivouac. Jock went with him, carrying a dixie filled with flatbread and rancid fried bacon.

They had a cup of coffee with the Bushwhackers.

"Put something in your stomach," Jim said.

"Thank you kindly," Frank James said.

"Sure thing, and thank you for our care," Jesse said to Jock. "You boys ever come up to Missouri, look for us in Clay County, Little Dixie.

Only The Leaves Whispering

There's plenty of Good Old Rebels up there. Ride with us. Bit different from down here in the Nations. We're bleedin' Kansas, killin' them Red Legs and Jayhawkers, and have their widders wailin' *The Vacant Chair.*"

* * *

"See that wagon came in?" Buster said.

"Yes," Jock said, and Jim nodded.

"A roving photographer is in camp. Must have had permission from the Colonel."

The Regiment had paid the men. So the photographer was sure to pick up a few dollars.

"Round up the boys, and we'll get a picture of the squad," Buster said. "My treat."

Buster had a word with the photographer while the squad assembled.

"I'm what's called an itinerant photographer. The name is Jacob Duvalier, Creole. I ran a successful business out of New Orleans. I left when the Union forces invaded and occupied the city. Been travelling in Texas, Arkansas and the Nations. I'm making a living."

Buster noticed that Duvalier limped.

"I'm a Southern man. I tried to enlist in the Zouaves, but I was rejected." He patted his right leg. "Gammy leg kept me a civilian."

"You have a lot of kit in that wagon," Buster said.

"I do for sure." Jacob Duvalier explained the difficulties that went with wartime photography: transporting heavy equipment. "I use a Daguerreotype Camera. Takes wonderful pictures, but it's a dead weight and has to be mounted on a tripod. You need strong arms and shoulders to move it into position. Have to remember this damned leg."

Buster nodded.

"Then there's the chemicals – ethyl ether and acetic or sulfuric acid. Dangerous to handle. I have to make a chemical soup for the wet plate process. It's called a collodion."

Jacob Duvalier had lost Buster; he stood glassy-eyed and nodded an acknowledgement. "That's real interesting, Mr Duvalier. I'm counting on you taking some beautiful pictures of my squad."

"Depend upon it, Sergeant Parris."

The squad gathered, a compact line of twenty solemn men clad in a mixture of personal dress. A cap or belt badge, here and there a Confederate Army Kepi or slouch hat, a uniform jacket, said that they belonged to the South. Some men wore breechclouts, fringed leggings, and low-cut moccasins. A few soldiers had covered their trousers to above the knee with long deerskin moccasins. Here and there, a lucky soldier had tucked CSA trousers into looted Yankee cavalry boots.

The squad didn't smile and they didn't scowl, but stood rigid. To a man, they wanted it known that they were soldiers and warriors. Every soldier was weighed down with arms, a medley of destruction on display: two, three, even four Colts tucked into belts. Every man carried a two-foot Bowie knife, or Arkansas Toothpick, sheathed on his belt, or had the naked blade displayed in his hand. Soldiers cradled long rifles, carbines, or sawed-off shotguns. Buster Parris had joined in this martial display and Jock and Jim followed his example.

Once that picture was taken, Buster paid, and the photographer said he'd have pictures ready by the next morning.

"Let's have one of us, Jock," Jim said.

Jock had adopted some of the dress of Missouri Southern Cavaliers. He'd attached a feather plume to the hatband. He was proud of the loose, long-sleeved guerilla shirt of thick grey cotton adorned with bright silk flowers and many coloured ribbons stitched to the front. The guerrilla shirt covered a beautiful white shirt which reached down to his hips. The garment had an open V neck, two deep breast pockets, and two generous waist pockets. The collar and pockets were edged with an inch of black cloth. Jock cinched the shirt at the waist by his leather belt with the CSA buckle. He'd thrust two Colt pistols into the belt. A dash of colour came from his blue silk scarf, folded and tied sailor fashion. His red hair grew down his neck and beyond his ears.

Only The Leaves Whispering

"Not going to cut my hair until the South has won. Just like the Bushwhackers," he'd said to Jim, whose hair was already shoulder-length.

The boys refused to stand before the photographer's studio backdrops, insisting on a natural scene where they lived and fought: the company's tents and, further back, a stand of small oaks.

Buster watched. He'd taken a liking to these two young men. He admired the friendship between a full-blood Cherokee and a young Scot. Jock had come far by sea and land, and Jim had ridden from the Snowbird Mountains to the Nations to enlist. Buster had let himself get close to the young men; but not too intimate, for he had to command them in battle.

Their hats displayed CSA badges. Jim insisted on having a long feather stuck in the hatband.

"I want them all to know I'm an Indian, a Cherokee."

Buster watched the boys finish their preparations for the photograph. "You boys figuring on starting your own war out here?" Buster smiled.

They had removed their jackets and were armed to the teeth. Jock had added another two Navy Colts, making four pistols tucked into his black leather belt with the CSA buckle. His .36 Colt revolver was thrust snug in a tan shoulder holster on the left side. The fingers of his left hand held the barrel of the Hawken Gun, its butt touching the ground. The round edge of the Mameluke sabre rested on his left forearm, the ivory handle jutting beyond his elbow.

Jim had three Navy Colts tucked into his black leather belt with the CSA buckle. He cradled a sawed-off shotgun in his left arm. His right hand grasped the handle of a Bowie knife with a guard and a broad two-foot blade.

"For God's sake, smile," Buster said. "Keep them scowls, and you'll wreck the camera."

The boys cemented their frowns, matching the seriousness of the occasion. But they relaxed again when Duvalier finished.

Jim Ellis

"Going to rub down my horse and feed him. I went out and cut some sweet grass for him. Enough for your horse, too, Jim," Jock said.

"No feed for my horse, son?" Buster said.

"Course there is, Sergeant. I don't forget."

Jim hesitated, shuffling his cavalry boots.

"Gonna get a picture myself, for Miss Harriet," he said.

Buster went to his quarters and brought back the yellow sash of Confederate Cavalry. Jock brought his Naval Officer's round jacket and his black leather sword harness.

"Your britches will do, but brush and clean your boots. Impress the young lady," Buster said.

Jim cut a smart figure, long black hair touching his shoulders, hat on straight. He looked slim and martial in the round jacket. The yellow sash at his waist, the leather sword harness, and sabre sheath added an elegant touch. The point of the sabre rested on the earth. Jim rested both hands on the pommel.

"Young man, you're slouching," Duvalier said. "Your girl will think there's something wrong with you. Get your shoulders up and back and stand up straight."

Duvalier returned to the Daguerreotype and made some final settings. He got behind the camera and put his head under the black hood. A few seconds later, he came out from the cover.

"For God's sake, young man, smile, or you'll scare the hell out of your sweetheart."

Late the next morning, Duvalier brought the prints, and the squad were pleased. Buster looked over Jim's shoulder as the boys admired their portrait. He slapped them on the shoulders. "You boys are lookin' good. Jock, I'm glad you came in with Jim. You belong with us. You're a pair of proper Cherokee Horse Soldiers."

Jim went off by himself and sat against a tree. He stared at his portrait that he meant to present to Miss Harriet someday. But in addition to the full-length portrait, he'd asked the photographer to take a head and shoulders; a picture that, was she inclined, Miss Harriet could insert in a locket. Jim wished there was some way to buy a silver locket,

103

Only The Leaves Whispering

but out here, where the Regiment camped, there was no chance of finding a suitable shop. He waved Jock across.

"You coming over, Sergeant?" Jock said. "I think it'll be a fine picture."

"You'll be right about that, Jock. I'll wait here. Don't want to embarrass Jim."

* * *

Several days after the photographer had left, Buster got hold of Jock.

"Noon, Jock, come to my quarters. Something I want to show you. I'll get some wittles and coffee from the sutler."

"Sutler, Sergeant?"

"He's a camp follower. Sells food and kit to the soldiers. There's more than a few rogues among them. But this one is more or less honest."

The boys sat on saddles waiting for Buster. He threw coffee dregs into the dust. Jock drained his cup.

Buster unfolded brown paper wrapping and laid out a beautiful, long-sleeved buckskin shirt.

"When we go out on a raid or attack enemies, many of the Cherokee wear the warrior's shirt. I wear one under my regular shirt, for protection. We're the civilised tribe, but we're still Cherokee braves. My mother made my shirt when I joined the Rifles.

"You been out with me and on patrol with the squad as well as doing good work with Surgeon Adair. Been quiet, garrison life these past few weeks, but I figure we'll be going out in strength soon. I like your get-up. You look good. But it could get you killed for a Missouri Bushwhacker. Get taken prisoner with that shirt on, you'd be shot or hung right away."

Buster's forefinger moved across the deerskin shirt, resting on a symbol as he explained its meaning. "We use red for the spirit of power, success, and triumph. Sometimes weapons are coloured black to destroy the enemy's soul. The arrow gives us strong defence and protection. The wolf gives strength, endurance, intelligence and makes the family strong. The Bear makes us strong and able to face danger. The coyote warns us against taking the wrong path. The eagle works for success on the hard path."

"Jim has some of those signs tattooed on his arms. I didn't like to ask him about them."

"I've seen that arm work. Anyway, a young brave from another squad got killed last week. Horse shot from under him. Only seventeen or eighteen. Was in the Rifles for less than three months. His kit was sold, and the money went to his family."

"That's the custom in the Navy."

"He was about your age and build, so I bought his shirt for you. It's hardly worn. A gift. Wear it when we're out. You need the protection that comes from the spirit of the Cherokee."

"Thank you, Sergeant, for thinking about me."

"Mind if I ask you something, Jock?" Buster said.

"Ask away."

"Well, son, I see changes in you."

A worried Jock broke in. "Is something wrong, Sergeant?"

"No, No. Nothing's wrong. What I see is good. You're doin' good work and sound like you're from the Nations, and I figure you understand some Cherokee."

"Jim has been helping me with the Cherokee tongue."

"Scots tongue has taken a back seat. You've got the Cherokee sound now when you speak English. I think you're becoming a Southern man."

Buster wanted to know how Jock felt about his role in the Rifles.

"You been with us a while, Jock. Travelled far to get here. Life's no bed of roses in the Nations. How you feelin' deep down, son?"

Jock fell silent as his life since joining the schooner *Jane Brown* passed in front of his eyes.

"Well, Sergeant, I'm happy," he said eventually. "I'm not in Scotland and a prisoner in a Catholic orphanage, a slave of Irish nuns and priests. Sailing on *Jane Brown* opened the door to the Confederate Navy and my ship CSS *Alabama*."

Only The Leaves Whispering

"You liked the Navy?"

"Yes, I liked it a lot. For me, *Alabama* will always be special. She was a clean ship."

Buster smiled. "Yes, I see what you mean. Gets dirty here at times and in the field." He worried that Jock felt he'd taken the second prize by enlisting in the Rifles.

"You wish you were still in the Navy?"

"Was my duty to leave *Alabama* and look after Midshipman Hollister. Jim kept me on the right path, getting me up to the Nations and joining the Rifles. I'm serving The Cause, and I'm supporting the Cherokee. I didn't expect that, and I like it."

"You're doing good, Jock. You're one of us."

Buster was glad that, with the addition of the warrior shirt, Jock would look the complete Cherokee Confederate soldier. Jim had been in the Rifles for a long time. He could see that Jock identified with the Cherokee, and he belonged to the Regiment and the South.

* * *

Two days later, Buster spoke to Jock and Jim. "Colonel wants an order for fodder delivered to Pete O'Leary," Buster said. "Lieutenant brought it."

Lieutenant Colonel Stand Watie and Pete O' Leary were acquainted. Pete had supplied fodder and grain to the Rifles.

The Colonel had Pete O'Leary's letter concerning the boys' residence with him and working for the war effort.

"One rider to deliver the order," Buster said. "Want to volunteer?" He glanced at Jim.

"Go on, Jim," Jock whispered.

"I'll go."

"Too late to leave today. Be ready to leave at first light," Buster said.

Jock worked on Jim's horse, checking shoes, driving a nail here and there, taking up the slack. He gave the animal a thorough rub-down. Jock covered the beast with a blanket to keep him warm in the night and tethered the animal close to their quarters.

Jim Ellis

Jim, adept at hunting and scouting, the perfect mounted rifleman, lacked domestic skill.

Jock placed his housewiff, brought from *Alabama*, at his feet. He sponged and brushed his naval round jacket and made sure the gold buttons were tight, then laid a square of muslin out on the floor of their tent.

"Want you looking the part when you meet Miss Harriet."

Jock folded the round jacket and laid it in the centre of the muslin.

"Give me your best pants."

Jock examined Jim's dark grey worsted trousers and found a small tear.

"Damn it. There's a hole in the seat, too. I thought those were your best pair!"

"Can you fix them?"

Jock got out his darning needle and a near-matching ball of wool and got to work. After ten minutes' close and careful work, he'd repaired them with the needle, darning yarn and thread. He held the trousers up for Jim's inspection.

"How's that?"

Jim ran his fingers over the darn, a patch as tight as from a weaver's loom.

"Thanks, Jock, that's a wonderful job."

Jim handed the trousers back to Jock, who folded them and laid them on top of the round jacket. He added clean small clothes and socks, and a small brush.

"Put in your wash bag. Travel in your field kit. One night you'll sleep out. Bathe in a creek next morning and change for arrival at Pete O'Leary's ranch. Tell everyone I send good wishes."

Jim rolled his new kit in a neat roll inside a blanket and his slicker.

* * *

In the quiet mid-morning, Jim walked his horse along the avenue lined with Prairie Fire crab apple trees. He listened to the soothing thud of the horse's hooves on the sandy path. Jim doffed his hat to the field

Only The Leaves Whispering

hands he passed. They waved, for they recognised him from his earlier visit with the young Scot.

A boy scouting the woods hurried back to the house. He took a shortcut to announce to his mother that Jim had been spotted on his horse.

"You tell Mister Pete, the soldier called Jim is comin' in and make sure Miss Harriet knows her young man is here," she called from the kitchen.

Jim cantered towards the main door of the O'Leary house. He wasn't expecting to be greeted by the O'Learys, and the Sullivans lined up at the foot of the portico stairs.

Jim dismounted and tied his mount to the hitching post. He straightened his hat, held Jock's sheathed sabre in his left hand and turned to salute Pete O'Leary.

"Good morning, Mr Pete. I have a letter for you from Colonel Watie."

Jim unfastened the round jacket, withdrew an envelope and handed it to Pete O'Leary.

"Thank you, Jim. We'll get to that soon. Right now, everyone wants to meet you again."

'How do's,' handshakes and embraces, kisses on the cheek from Miss Estella and Miss Sally. Solemn handshakes from the children. Miss Harriet stood at the end of the line, her head turned left to gaze at Jim. Excited and eager, shifting from the left to the right foot, her brow perspired as she polished the mist from her spectacles for a look at Jim before he came up to her. Miss Harriet had never seen a smarter, better-looking soldier.

Jim removed his hat and held her hand. "How do, Miss Harriet?" He raised her hand to his lips.

"Oh, fiddlesticks, Mr Cherokee Jim. I'm just so glad to see you again." Miss Harriet put her arms around Jim's neck and kissed him.

* * *

Pete was pleased that he could help the Confederate war effort by filling Jim's order for fodder and supplying Stand Watie's command.

The company dined well that evening at Pete and Miss Estella's table, on an excellent honey glazed ham, greens and mashed potatoes. And everyone took pleasure in the quiet but obvious delight that Miss Harriet and Jim had in each other's company.

"Ah think that our daughter is in love with Mr Cherokee Jim," Miss Sally said to Willie as they moved to the parlour. "Oh, Willie, she's just sixteen."

Willie nodded. "Well, my love, you were about that age when we went away together."

He squeezed Sally's hand. She smiled. "So I was."

"Ah do believe the feeling is reciprocated," Willie said. "Jim cares for Harriet. He looks at her most affectionately. Jim's a fine young man."

The younger children sat quietly while Pete served glasses of port to the ladies. He handed Miss Harriet a glass, half full. "Your pa said you can have this, seeing that Jim has come."

Willie filled three small crystal glasses with a measure of Pete's whiskey for Pete, Jim and himself.

Their happiness was tinged with sadness for the Confederate fortunes. By the autumn of 1863, the war had not gone well for the South.

"Damned Yankees captured Vicksburg and Port Hudson back in July," Pete said, after tossing off two glass of liquor. "Federals control the Mississippi."

Miss Sally and Miss Estella looked at each other and returned to sipping port.

"Much information comes down to The Rifles?" Willie asked.

"Heard about Gettysburg, and General Lee's Army withdrawing from the North."

"Southern Boys under Lee and Jackson did well at Chancellorsville in May," Pete said. "Chickamauga too, a couple of weeks ago, under Bragg and Longstreet. Wonder what's coming next?"

By October, depressing word would come down from Tennessee of the Union victory in the Chattanooga Campaign.

The conversation moved on to Jim's situation in The Rifles.

Only The Leaves Whispering

"Colonel attacked a Union wagon train with supplies for Fort Gibson, at Cabin Creek at the beginning of July, but we didn't stop them. Supplies getting through meant stronger Federals. We got a bloody nose at Honey Springs in mid-July."

"You was there, Jim?" Willie asked.

"No, sir. I was out with raiding parties. We rode from south of the Canadian River and attacked Indian Territory to the north, into Kansas and Missouri."

"Tying down Blue Bellies?"

"Yes, sir, Mr Pete."

"Jim," Miss Sally said, "how is your young Scots friend?"

"Ma'am, thank you for asking. He is well, and the soldiers like him. Surgeon Adair showed him how to set broken bones. He wanted Jock transferred to his staff."

Jim explained that Jock had been out on raids, and in camp was kept busy treating the minor wounds and injuries of soldiers who'd been fighting or knocked about. But he did not want to transfer.

"Told Sergeant Parris he'd desert and go north to join the Missouri Bushwhackers if they forced him to transfer."

"Perhaps he'd have been happier in the Confederate Navy," Miss Estella said.

"That might be the truth, ma'am. But it was his duty to leave *Alabama* and come ashore to nurse the sick Midshipman back to health. There was no road back to his ship or any other blue water Confederate ship. Jock is doing good work, and he's happy belonging to The Rifles."

"Any word of *Alabama*?" Pete asked.

"No sir, Mr Pete. It's quiet where we are."

"We had word from Texas about *Alabama*. The ship is a credit to the South. She's everywhere and nowhere. Damned Yankee Navy is chasing a phantom ship. Texas officer said *Alabama* had been seen in Jamaica, then destroying Yankee ships mid-Atlantic, berthed in Cape Town. Last this Texan heard, Captain Semmes had taken the ship into the Indian Ocean."

Jim Ellis

"I'll be sure to tell Jock."

The ladies retired, Miss Sally and Miss Estella to put their children to bed. Miss Harriet lingered a few minutes.

"I'll see you tomorrow. Pa might let us go for a drive in the buckboard." Harriet turned to her father.

"That'll be all right, Harriet. But not far from the house."

"Thank you, Pa."

She turned to Jim, who stood up. He took her extended hand and she kissed him on the cheek. "Goodnight, Jim."

A flustered and red-faced Jim sat again. "I should really start back tomorrow for the Regiment."

"The Hell you will," Pete said.

"Right enough," Willie said. "You stay another day, Jim. Make Harriet happy. Confederate Army can stand your leave."

* * *

After breakfast, Pete and Willie took Jim around the property. "Bring your Colt pistol," Pete said. "Strangers have been sighted a few miles away. Confederate or Yankee deserters, it don't matter. Killers all the same."

Willie carried a seven-shot Spencer carbine. Pete had a Colt pistol in his belt and cradled a sawed-off shotgun in his right arm. They stopped at the hog pen, and Willie called Emily the pet hog over.

"They're so clean and fresh," Jim said.

"Emily's a sweet girl, and she's smarter than any old hound dog," Pete said.

"Emily came closer, hearing her name again. She rolled on her back and grunted.

"Go on, son," Willie said. "Stroke her belly. She loves it when Harriet pets her. Reckon Emily knows you're sweet on Harriet."

A blushing Jim leant over the low fence and petted Emily until his complexion paled and he cooled down.

"We'll walk," Pete said. "Keep a sharp watch."

Only The Leaves Whispering

Pete and Willie showed Jim the fields that grew the fodder for the Regiment's horses. The acres turned over to cotton cultivation looked well.

"Aim to get that crop on a blockade runner out of Galveston," Pete said. "Send her to England. With the money for the cotton, I'll buy ether, chloroform, morphine too, plus bandages and any other medical supplies I can get my agent to lay hands on. Confederate Army needs medicines and supplies."

"Pete intends covering the cost. No profit on this cargo," Willie said. "Maybe a few luxury goods come back on the ship. Sell up north, Pete?"

"Correct, Willie."

Cattle and horses grazed in the mild autumn weather. The tour of the ranch was uneventful, and they returned to the main buildings around noon and ate jerked venison and crisp flatbread.

* * *

Jim and Harriet sat in the cushioned seat of the old but well-maintained buckboard, a chestnut mare harnessed to the vehicle. Behind the bench was a covered picnic basket with finger food and lemonade.

"Pa, who are those strange men?"

Four mounted black men cantered towards the ranch. The leader rode ahead. A small-brimmed bowler hat was perched on his head and around his neck was a long, knotted, red neckerchief. His coarse black woollen trousers were tucked into high, fringed moccasins which were tied at the knee. A long blue calico shirt with ruffled front was cinched at the waist by a brown leather belt that rested below the hips. Two Colt pistols were tucked into his belt next to two black leather cartridge boxes. A sheathed knife was attached to the belt on the right side, while a fringed buckskin bow case and a quiver of arrows were tied to the rear of the saddle. He controlled his horse with his knees, right hand holding the reins, a seven-shot Spencer Carbine butt resting on his thigh, held upright in his left hand.

Jim Ellis

The leader looked to be in his early fifties. He had a sombre face with black, deep-set eyes. A thin moustache lined his top lip and a bunch of straggling hairs at his chin might have been a beard.

His men wore wool turbans, neckerchiefs and long shirts of many colours: blues, greens and red. The Maroons rode easily. They were well-armed with Enfield rifles, knives, cartridge boxes and Colt pistols. Black-skinned men well in their forties, clean-shaven, dark eyes, impassive faces.

"Why, Harriet, they're friends of Mr Pete. Seminoles settled in the Nations."

Jim had met Seminole warriors serving the Confederacy as soldiers and had heard their stories. "They're warriors, sometimes known as Maroons from Florida. Followers of Billy Powell, better known as Osceola. The Yankees took Osceola under a flag of truce and kept him prisoner. He died from malaria about 1838. The Maroons hate Yankees."

"Maroons come to the Nations in 1843 after the Second Seminole War," Pete said. "They help me from time to time."

Just before Jim arrived, Pete had called on his Seminole friends to patrol the property for several days when rumours spread of strangers in the vicinity. Probably Confederate and Yankee deserters – or worse, Federal Irregulars, Jayhawkers and Redlegs.

Willie stayed by the buckboard. Pete rode out to meet the Seminoles. After ten minutes, he returned with the Maroon leader.

"This is my friend, Palmer Brown," Pete said. He kept it to himself that his friend had a tribal name that was used in the band. "Tomorrow when you leave, Jim, they'll ride with you."

"With respect Mr Pete, I don't need an escort."

Pete held up his hand. "Don't argue, Jim. You're riding with an escort. There might be trouble," Pete said. "Fact is, there's been trouble about a mile out."

Pete asked Willie and Jim to stand by the residences. Harriet twisted her fingers and swallowed tears. Pete rode off with the four Maroons.

Only The Leaves Whispering

"Ambushed them here," Palmer Brown said. "Didn't hardly use guns. Kept it quiet. Killed them with arrows." Five corpses, each with two arrows sunk in their flesh, lay in stiff, awkward crouches. Five horses with McClelland saddles were tethered nearby. The mounts had been loaded with looted Colt pistols, two Spencer seven-shot carbines, three Enfield rifles and useful goods.

"Burn them," Pete said.

"Sixth man got away," Palmer Brown said. "Shot him in the back with a rifle ball. Probably die on the trail… bleed to death. Sorry about that, Mr Pete."

"Palmer, send your best tracker after him. Finish him off."

The tracker set off at once. Pete was worried by what he saw.

This was no dishevelled band of deserters from either of the two warring armies. These men were well-mounted and well-armed raiders. The Yankee riders wore a mixture of Federal blue jackets, a kepi or cavalry slouch hat, and homespun trousers held up by Union Army leather belts. Each man had scuffed but whole Yankee cavalry boots.

Pete turned to Willie and Palmer Brown. "Figure this was a reconnaissance party for a raid."

"Reckon that's it, Pete," Willie said.

"Yes, sir, Mr Pete," Palmer Brown said.

Within the hour, the tracker was back. "I found him. He was dead already. Left him for the coyotes. Tracks near him. I'd say two riders but long gone."

Harriet and Jim spent a quiet afternoon sitting outside the Sullivan house. They ate some of the food and had a sip of the lemonade.

"I've no appetite, Jim."

"Me neither."

Harriet took the picnic food and drink to the pantry, hoping that it might be eaten the next day.

* * *

Jim Ellis

A quiet evening meal in the O'Leary house. Pork chops, greens and fried potatoes.

"Eat heartily," Pete said. "Reckon the Yankees are gone. But Palmer Brown's men are on watch through the night. A few more will arrive tomorrow morning before Jim leaves us."

The meal over, Jim and Harriet left the table and stood by Willie and Miss Sally.

"Ma'am, sir, might we speak in private for a moment?"

Willie and Sally, wise in the guileless ways of young love, had anticipated an approach.

"Speak, son. We're like a family here."

Miss Estella and Pete sat quietly, but exchanged a smile. Pete squeezed Estella's hand. Harriet looked at Jim as she twisted her handkerchief back and forth.

"Well, sir, Miss Harriet and I have an understanding. I gave her my new photograph to make my pledge for her hand when the war ends. I wanted to give more, but where Stand Watie goes is desolate. We ask for your blessing, Miss Sally, ma'am, and you, sir."

Willie linked his hands under his chin and pursed his lips. Miss Sally looked at her husband. Willie took his time, figuring that it was good for the young people to wait.

But the silence was too much for Harriet. She dropped her handkerchief and didn't pick it up.

"Well, now, Harriet and Jim, this is a grave thing you ask..."

"Please, Pa, don't say no."

Jim handed Harriet his neckerchief.

"Well, girl, stop fretting and let your Pa finish. Your mama and I are pleased to give you and Jim our blessing. It's a fine thing, and I'm sure Miss Estella and Mr Pete agree."

Miss Estella smiled and Pete, approving, slapped the table several times. He went to the sideboard and fetched the whiskey decanter. "Good news, indeed. It calls for a toast."

* * *

Only The Leaves Whispering

It was a subdued leave-taking next day. Jim shook hands with Pete O'Leary. "Thank you, Mr Pete, for your kindness and hospitality."

Jim carried Pete's written agreement to provide fodder for the Regiment.

Pete compressed his lips. "Look after yourself, Jim. Try and come and see us again. Want to see you back here when this damned war is over, and bring Jock with you. We like that young Scot."

Jim turned to Willie and clasped his outstretched hand. Willie's left hand gripped Jim's shoulder. "You listen to Pete, son. Don't go getting yourself killed or wounded up there."

Miss Sally and Miss Estella came forward. Miss Estella kissed Jim on the cheek, followed by Miss Sally.

"Go on, Sally, you tell Jim," Miss Estella said.

Miss Sally dabbed her eyes. 'Don't you worry, Jim, we'll take good care of Harriet and keep her safe. She'll be waiting for you."

"Thank you kindly, Miss Sally, Miss Estella."

Miss Sally kissed Jim on the cheek.

A brave smile creased Harriet's face, her eyes bright. Jim saw the tears welling behind her spectacles.

"You'll wait for me?" Jim asked.

Harriet nodded, unable to speak.

"I do love you, Miss Harriet, and I'll come back to you."

The tears spilt from under Harriet's glasses and fell on Jim's Confederate grey round jacket.

"And I love you, Mr Cherokee Jim."

They kissed.

Jim mounted beside his Maroon escort. He wheeled his horse and tugged on the bit, raising the animal on its hind legs; a brief protesting neighing shattered the silence. Jim removed his slouch hat with the CSA badge and swept it down in farewell. The breeze lifted Jim's long black hair from his shoulders.

Palmer Brown grinned. "You ready, Mr Jim?"

Jim, mouth dry, voice breaking, answered, "That I am, Mr Palmer Brown." He forced the slouch hat down on his head.

Jim Ellis

Palmer Brown turned to the women and touched the brim of his bowler hat. "Ladies."

He raised a hand to Pete and Willie as he led the warriors and Jim in a canter down the avenue lined with Prairie Fire crab apple trees. Sandy soil spurted from the hoofs of the horses.

Chapter Six

The Maroons escorted Jim to within sight of the Rifles camp. They'd had an uneventful ride from the O'Leary ranch.

"Thank you, Mr Palmer Brown," Jim said.

Palmer Brown gave a nod of acknowledgement. The four Maroons turned their mounts south, gave Jim a wave and rode off. He reported to the Colonel.

Jim sat in Buster Parris' quarters. They waited for Jock to come over after finishing his duties with Surgeon Adair.

"All is well, then, Jim?" Buster Parris asked.

Jim grinned. "Real well. Colonel is happy getting Mr Pete's agreement to supply fodder."

"Saw you ride to the edge of the camp. Four riders with you. They waved and then left. Trouble, son?"

"Maroons. Mr Pete wanted me escorted. Pleased Miss Harriet."

"One man name of Palmer Brown?"

"The leader."

"A great warrior. Fought with Osceola. Has no time for Blue Bellies."

Jock arrived at Buster's tent. He removed a dirty, blood-soiled, thick cotton apron.

"You're glum, son," Buster said.

Jock nodded. He spoke in clipped, rapid sentences, the result of his depression after treating a foul wound. "Young soldier, right forearm arm removed below the elbow. Gangrene. Surgeon Adair's saving his life. I gave him chloroform. He was out. No pain. After the surgeon finished, I released pus, poulticed and dressed infected wounds. I bound sprains. Handed out tonic – sassafras and iron root, a dab of meat. Walking about and talking to wounded men. God knows, but I cheer them up. It's not why I came here." He pulled a face as he shook hands with Jim.

"Glad you're back," Jim said. "You're doing good work here."

"That's what Surgeon Adair tells me, most days."

"Why the Maroons?" Buster asked.

Jim remembered the tension and anxiety felt by everyone at the ranch when they heard the news. "Six scouts for a Yankee raiding party. Maroons caught up with the raiders near the O'Leary ranch. One raider galloped off, but Palmer shot him in the back with a rifle ball. A tracker found the raider dead. Signs of two more Yankees who escaped."

Jock looked at Jim. "You see them?"

"No, I stayed with Willie and Miss Harriet. We was set for a picnic but stayed by the house. Mr Pete and Willie were worried that strangers, Federal raiders or irregulars, were in the area. Pete had his friend Palmer Brown and three of his men to patrol the ranch. Come dusk, ten to twelve Maroons came to guard the ranch."

"I have to work," Buster Parris said. "Goin' to have a word with the wranglers. Let you two catch up. Come to the squad, say in an hour." He turned to Jock. "Take it easy, son. Be careful what you wish for. My nose tells me fightin' is comin' our way."

* * *

The friends sat for a few minutes, letting the tension ease. Jim's thoughts turned to happier events.

"Miss Harriet and me, we have an understanding. I gave her my new picture. That made her happy."

"What's an understanding?' Jock asked.

Only The Leaves Whispering

"Well, she's waiting for me, and when the war is over, I'm goin' back to her. Miss Sally and Willie gave their blessing. Mr Pete and Miss Celestina was right happy, too."

"You mean to marry Miss Harriet?"

"What's wrong with that?"

"Nothing wrong – no, sir! You're my friend, and I've high regard for Miss Harriet."

"She gave me a small, framed portrait. It's packed with my kit. I'll show you later."

"They all said to bring you back to the ranch. There's a place for you. They're right fond of you, Jock."

Jim had found love with Harriet and happiness among the O'Learys and the Sullivans. He shared his euphoria with Jock. "I've been fighting since I got out here at the start of the war. Never expected to find good things in The Nations while I soldiered with The Rifles."

Jock raised his head. "Everything is good. I'm happy for you and Miss Harriet."

"I never thought about the end of the war. I want the South to win, then get back to the O'Leary ranch and Miss Harriet."

Jim, effervescent with the flush of first love, could not stop talking. "Don't you wish you had a girl, Jock?"

"You're ahead of me in years, Jim. Reckon I'm too young."

* * *

Jim's happiness made Jock cheerful. He, too, had memories that warmed his heart. "Bagged a young rabbit yesterday. How about you get the fire going, and I'll skin, gut and clean it for the spit?"

The boys held the spitting sticks securing the roasted tender young buck and wolfed it down. They threw the bones into the dying embers. Jock wiped his mouth with the back of his hand.

"We had fine times in Westburn before my mother died. When she passed, my father went to pieces. He drowned himself."

"That's bad. A soldier, a strong man, going down," Jim said. "Your mother's death struck him low."

"At first, I couldn't figure it out. I grieved, and I raged at my father for leaving us. My brother and sister were terrified and cried. Then I had an inkling of my father's sorrow. He couldn't go on without my mother's love." Jock flushed, talking about matters of the heart.

"I see," Jim said.

Jock moved to the safe ground away from melancholy and sad memories. He described the happy times to Jim.

"On Sundays, after Mass, the family would walk through the rich west end of Westburn. The toffs drew us frosty looks, but my father stared them down. They could see he was healthy and not afraid. He told us stories about his years as Sergeant-Farrier in the Scots Greys. My mother told us about growing up on the island of Barra."

Jim smiled but did not interrupt Jock's reminiscing.

"We stayed in a tenement in the Old Vennel. It was a grim slum, the weans barefoot in the worst weather, but the good people there made up for it. The Irish and Highlanders come to Westburn for a better life. The wifies wrapped in their tartan and plaid shawls were the backbones of the Vennel. The Irish loved a laugh. The Highlanders were dour, but underneath they were good folk. Catholics and Presbyterians tried to get along."

Jock paused and a stern look shadowed his face.

"We buried my mother right, but my father lies in a pauper's grave. No marker to say he'd been in this life." Jock wiped his eyes. "Me, my young brother and sister finished up alone. Made foundlings by sickness and death… headed for a Catholic orphanage. A good neighbour, a Presbyterian, a blacksmith, took me in as his apprentice. But he couldn't help my brother and sister. He had his own children to think about."

"What happened to your brother and sister?" Jim asked.

"The Irish nuns and priests got a hold of them – sent them away from Westburn. I never saw them again. In school, one swine of a priest beat me with a cane. I've had enough of Irish priests. I swore I'd never go near one of those damned orphanages."

Only The Leaves Whispering

Jock wrung his hands. The pain of guilt he felt about abandoning his brother and sister cut him to the quick. "What the Hell could I do? I was just thirteen. I saved my skin."

"You did right, Jock," said Jim.

"But the Southern Cause got hold of me. Southerners and Highlanders, people that fought and suffered. And I found out from you how the Cherokee struggled. I went to sea to get away from Westburn and damned Irish nuns and priests. The Highland struggle is over, but not the Cause, nor the struggles of the Cherokee. I'm here until we win this war. I'm not going to desert to Missouri Bushwhackers, and I'm never going back to Westburn."

"The sea… It was a hard life, you said."

"Tough life, alright. At sea, I stood up for myself. I learned to cook and care for injured sailors aboard *Jane Brown*. I saw off a filthy drunken cook and an evil, drunken steward. The crew of *Jane Brown* liked and respected me. When she docked in Liverpool, I took my chances and passed Surgeon Llewellyn's tests. I enlisted in the Confederate Navy."

Jock's eyes shone with tears as he bunched his right hand, slamming it into his left palm. "Jesus, Loblolly Boy aboard *Alabama*, and Captain Semmes, a proper Southern officer. There was never a better ship. I belonged to her."

"What about the Rifles?"

"I'm with the Cause and close up. There's no doubt about it. But there's more doctoring than I'd like."

"You're doing well here, working for Surgeon Adair. And you can fight. You're the best shot in the squad. One of the best in the Regiment."

Jim's compliments cheered Jock up. He grinned. "When I went out on patrol with Buster, I worried that I'd run. When we started shooting, I went mad. Worse, I went berserk, but inside I was cold. Buster Parris and me, we massacred that Yankee patrol."

"You belong to the Rifles, like you belonged to *Alabama*. You're one of us, Jock."

Jim Ellis

* * *

Two days later at the Rifles camp, Buster approached. "Going out on a raid," he said. "Band of Pins causing trouble. You boys need one of the Whitworth Rifles. Jock, bring the Hawken Gun. Make sure you have your shotguns and sidearms."

Buster handed Jock a pair of spectacles. "These are Sharpshooter's Glasses. The centre of the lens is clear, to get a bead on your target. The rest of the lens is opaque. Gets you focussed on the kill."

Jock tried on the spectacles. Looking around, he whistled. "I see what you mean." He cased the glasses and placed the container in his shirt's deep pocket.

"Pins, Jim? Tell me about them?"

"They are Cherokee on the Federal side. Full bloods, most of them. Wild Indians. Make a lot of trouble. Not Redlegs, but bad enough. They're Cherokee, Creek and Seminole. They wear cross pins on their coats, turbans on their heads and want to live the old longhouse culture. They hate white Southern culture. Pins walk the 'Red Path' and go after bloody revenge. Some of them switched sides and went over to the Union in 1862. We don't get along. There's bad blood between us and the Pins. It's hard fighting when we go up against them."

"The Pins think the men of the Rifles are not proper Cherokee?" Jock asked.

"They don't care for Southern ways. Reckon they don't like Cherokees and whites marrying. You know I'm full blood, and my family is Cherokee. We kept to the old ways. Hid out in the Snowbird Mountains when the tribe moved west to the Nations. I'm for the South, but I was not for serving in Thomson's Legion in the Army of Northern Virginia. I prefer the Rifles."

"Me too. I like the life," Jock said. "More scope out here than you'd likely find in Northern Virginia or Tennessee."

Buster had the squad mounted and lined up for inspection before the Company left camp for the raid on the Pins. He'd badgered the Company Commander to have Jock bring medical equipment. "Treat

Only The Leaves Whispering

wounds and injuries in the field. No point in leaving it until the Company gets back," he'd said to the Major.

Buster stopped his horse opposite the young Scot. "Jock, that medical box all set?"

Surgeon Adair had augmented the medical chest Jock had carried from *Alabama*. He'd added a bottle of bootleg whiskey. "A man might need a drink before you look after him." Bandages and lint; arnica, iodine. Quinine for the treatment of respiratory ailments; peppermint as an antiseptic and numbing agent; a bottle containing opium and camphor to ease the pain.

"Ready and correct, Sergeant."

* * *

Dawn. The sun rose, lighting the prairie and the Pins' camp. The officers and braves had gathered around an abandoned ranch and outbuildings.

Before sunrise, Jock and Jim hid in a hollow about four hundred yards from the Pin camp. Jim kept watch, armed with a seven-shot Henry rifle. Jock watched the raiders with a powerful Dollard and Atcheson telescope.

"Be about fifty Pins. I counted six wounded. Reckon they'll be in camp for a couple of days. Officers are in the old ranch house, the braves scattered throughout the outbuildings. Horses corralled. Four mounted pickets patrolling the perimeter."

"Well-armed?"

"I counted four Enfield rifles. The Braves have bows and quivers of arrows. Most men are carrying muskets and muzzle-loading pistols. About as well-armed as the Rifles. Reckon the officers are better armed. I saw one wearing a Colt pistol."

"Better get out of here. Report back," Jim said. The boys cradled their rifles and lay down. They slithered and crawled, hidden by prairie grass, out of the hollowed ground. Jim went first, followed by Jock, rolling over a small ridge five hundred yards distant. They slung their rifles and hit a distance-eating lope back to the Company.

Buster and the Lieutenant brought the boys to the Company Commander.

"We outnumber them, two to one," Jim said.

"Good," the Major said. He glanced to the east. "We'll attack tomorrow. Out of the sun. About fifty yards from the Pins, our centre will hold the charge, with a third of the Company to each flank. Attacking the Pins on three sides, drive them back on the ranch. Nowhere to run."

The Major deployed the Company Sharpshooters on the flanks of the Pin camp. "The best shot fires and the other man reloads. You'll have a couple of minutes to shoot once the line charges. Want you putting three, four rounds a minute into the Pins. Make every round count. Cease fire when our line divides at fifty yards."

Jim and Jock hid on the right flank armed with a Whitworth Rifle and the Hawken gun. On the left flank, two sharpshooters had a Whitworth and an Enfield Rifle.

The camp came to life as Pins lit cooking fires for breakfast. The unsuspecting Pins went about morning ablutions. The Rifles spurred their mounts, moving out of the shadow at a brisk trot, riding under their battle flag. The sharpshooters commenced firing on the flanks of the Pins. Jock wore the Sharpshooter's Glasses. He fired first with the Whitworth and passed it back to Jim for reloading, receiving the Hawken Gun for the next shot. He'd get a Pin in the sights, set the trigger and fire, smashing heads, torsos and limbs. It was a cold, methodical slaughter.

Jock and Jim heard their comrades moving out. The drum roll of hooves on the hard prairie changed to a thundering beat as the Rifles' line galloped. The charging Confederate horse, the Rebel Yells and war-whoops of the Rifles reached Jock and Jim.

"I hope the boys are scaring them Pins," Jim said. "They're sure as Hell scaring me."

Jock shook his head in admiration for his comrades.

The line of horsemen divided at about fifty yards, the centre continuing straight on. The left and right of the line swept out and turned in to envelop the Pin flanks. The boys stopped shooting.

Only The Leaves Whispering

Pin officers improvised a line of resistance. The Cherokee horse charged and shot down Pins with shotgun blasts. With no time to reload, they cut and killed enemies with long-bladed Bowie knives and pistol shots. Jock and Jim watched for Pins trying to escape.

Three Pins stopped killing Cherokee Rifles with knives and tomahawks and broke off. The Pins vaulted the corral rails, leapt on saddled mounts and forced their mounts to jump the fences.

Attacking Pin horsemen, coming in fast on nimble ponies; leaden arms and legs weighed Jock down. He couldn't move, reduced to a helpless child convinced a wild Indian would kill him. Fear drove Jock upright, and he almost dropped his weapons, preparing to run and save his skin.

Jim caught Jock's shoulder and held him in a crouch. He understood how his friend felt. In the early days of the war, he'd lived through and overcome the horror of cowardice. "Jock, you're all right. The Pins, they're coming for us. If we don't kill them, they'll cut us to pieces."

Jim had shaken Jock out of his funk and handed him the Hawken Gun. "Shoot!"

Jock aimed, fired, and missed the leading Pin horseman. Jim's breath whistled in Jock's ear as he snatched the Hawken Gun and handed him the Whitworth Rifle. Jock's fear of combat vanished. He gazed through the Sharpshooter's Glasses. The Pin closed in, growing large in the rifle's sight. Buckskin-clad legs astride the pony, moccasins brushing the ground. Bony knees dug into the horse's ribs. The animal surged ahead. The Pin clenched the reins in his teeth and set an arrow in his bow. Jock glimpsed the face streaked with white lines of war paint below a blue Federal kepi. He sighted the Whitworth, fired and smashed a hole through the blue Union Army shirt near the Pin's heart. The Pin shot out of the saddle and cartwheeled in a blur of buckskin and Union Blue. The pony cantered off a few yards and stopped.

Buster had drummed into Jock that the best defence was an attack. Jock checked his weapons and touched the Colt pistol holstered at his shoulder. He gripped the sawed-off shotgun in his right hand. He felt the weight of pistol ammunition attached to his belt. A bandolier of shotgun shells crossed his torso from left to right. The Whitworth Rifle and the Hawken Gun were laid safe, side by side on the ground.

"Come on, let's go. Watch for the arrows," Jim said.

Pin war cries carried over the drumming pony hooves. The boys rose, boosting their courage with war whoops and Rebel yells. They moved towards the enemy in a swerving zigzag. An arrow flew by Jock's head, startling him. Jim fell, an arrow gouging his left shoulder. He got up and shuffled a few steps, then held his ground. The Pin slung his bow and came up fast, a stone club in his right hand. Jim fired both barrels of his sawed-off shotgun, missed the warrior but killed the pony. As it collapsed, the warrior vaulted off and hit the ground running. He unsheathed a long-bladed knife with his left hand, meaning to club and knife Jim to death.

Jock had fared better. He'd fired one barrel and shot his adversary out of the saddle, but not killed him; the man, his left arm riddled with buckshot, lay doggo and waited for Jock. The Pin rose and thrust at Jock with a short lance. "Fucking white man-boy!" he screamed.

Jock ducked and swerved, avoiding the thrust at his belly. The lance knocked off his hat and made a bloody cut on his scalp. Close up, a terrified Jock fired the shotgun, leaving a gory hole in the Pin's belly. He bled to death in minutes.

Jim was down. He held his left arm up in a futile gesture to protect his head. The Pin struck Jim on the forearm with the stone club, and he screamed. Jock felt sticky blood seeping into his hair. He slung his shotgun, and, by the time he reached Jim, he had pulled the Colt pistol from the shoulder holster. Jock put two rounds into the Pin's head. It was over.

* * *

The boys made a sorry pair as, laden with arms, wounds hurting, they staggered towards the Company. The Rifles had looted the Pin camp for horses, weapons and supplies. They left the Pin dead where they fell.

Only The Leaves Whispering

"Good work, boys," the Major said, then he looked at them more closely. "Why, you're wounded!" He sent for the Lieutenant. "Get Sergeant Parris to see to them."

Blood from the head wound covered Jock's face. "You're hurt bad," Buster Parris said.

"Not so bad. Head wound. Bleeds a lot. Need to look at Jim. He's hurt. Shoulder wound from an arrow and I reckon a broken left arm. Try to get a bandage around my head, stop the bleeding."

Jock cut a comical figure. A bandage, knotted under his chin, secured a padded dressing to stem the blood-flow from his head wound. He wore his slouch hat. Doc Merriweather had given him the hat but now it was ruined by the Pin lance-thrust that had cut the brim and made a hole in the crown.

Jock cleaned Jim's shoulder wound, applying arnica and a thick dressing. "It'll scar. Surgeon Adair will look at it when we get back."

"What about my arm? Can you set it? It hurts like Hell."

"Going to check for our wounded. Then I'll come back." He looked at his friend's pale and sweating face. "It's best that Surgeon Adair fixes your shoulder. I've dressed it. You're my first broken arm, though. I've seen it done aboard *Alabama*. I helped the Assistant Surgeon. He explained it to me. I made notes in my little book. I can do it. You'll be all right, Jim."

The friends clasped hands. "Thanks, Jock."

Buster escorted Jock around the fighting ground. The scale of the carnage appalled the young Scot. He'd seen dead Yankee soldiers after the ambush that he and Buster had sprung on the cavalry patrol. Here, the field was strewn with corpses in the grotesque moulds of a violent end. Faces with jaws shot away. Dead eyes, gaping mouths and a parade of bad teeth; lolling, discoloured tongues. Broken arms and legs twisted out of shape. One headless body. Soon, the field of honour would reek with the stench of the dead. Jock looked up. Buzzards floated in the hot air currents.

"Shall I help wounded Pins, Sergeant?

"Like Hell, you will, son."

"But Sergeant Parris, it's right to help the wounded. My officer on *Alabama* told me."

Buster Parris' eyes bulged out of a face pale with fury. "You fuckin' listen to me, you insolent Scotch fucker. Out here ain't the fuckin' genteel Confederate Navy. This is the Nations. This Civil War is dog eat fuckin' dog. Fuckin' Pins never look after our wounded. Was you lyin' out there sufferin', fuckin' Pins'd carve you up and lift your scalp. This is a real civil fuckin' war, son. Send the Sons of Bitches to meet their ancestors."

They'd finished the inspection and recovered the Rifles' wounded. Jock swallowed hard and thanked God that there were no Pin survivors.

The Rifles had suffered ten per cent casualties. Six dead and four soldiers with arrows or rifle balls embedded in torsos and limbs. The removal of arrows and bullets, an amputation, lay beyond Jock's skill. He'd make the wounded men comfortable for the journey back to the main camp.

Jim had broken his left forearm in the fight with the Pin. It was a clean break. Jock studied his notebook before attempting the set. He handed Jim a small glass of laudanum. "I'm ready. The setting will hurt. Drink this to help the pain."

Buster had improvised splints from a couple of floorboards left in the ranch's main room. He removed britches and shirts from two dead Pins, cutting bindings and pads to prevent chafing. From a dead Pin officer, he removed a broad, blue-chequered silk neckerchief to make a sling.

Buster stood by and helped Jock lay Jim on a blanket. Jock gave Jim a thick piece of leather to bite on. Setting the broken forearm was straightforward. Buster held Jim's shoulders and a burly soldier pinned his legs.

"Jim, I'm going to set your arm now."

Jim nodded.

"Hold him steady."

Only The Leaves Whispering

Jim's arm lay by his side, fingers turned up toward the front of the arm, muscles relaxed. With the least force, Jock pulled the lower bone fragment away from the upper. It was a clean break. In one swift movement, he put the bone into the natural position.

The leather bite moved, but Jim did not and made no sound.

"Keep still, my friend. We're almost done."

Jock splinted Jim's arm, put pads in place and bound it. It was a good set, and his arm would not shorten as the bone repaired.

Buster wiped the sweat from Jim's face with his own cotton scarf.

"Sit him up, and I'll make a sling with the silk neckerchief," Jock said. He turned to Jim. "Surgeon Adair will check what I've done. I'll see you get proper splints and bindings when we get back. You'll have the splints on for six weeks. I'll adjust the bindings every week."

The Rifles had fought hand to hand. Many of the men had cuts from long-bladed knives and bruises from clubs and musket butts. Jock meant to look after them: bandaging, dressing injuries, and suturing wounds.

The column of twos rode south under the battle flag of the Cherokee Braves. The sun cast long shadows over weary soldiers slumped in their saddles. Buster Parris had supervised the construction of travois to carry the wounded at the rear of the column. There were two men riding point. Wranglers ran the captured Pin horses. Further back, two men kept a lookout for Federal pursuit. Jock rode beside Jim, who'd mounted awkwardly with his broken arm, and he kept watch on the wounded.

* * *

The Company was a week into the rest period. The men were refitting as much as the Rifles' meagre supplies allowed.

"You ain't been working with the surgeon," Jim said.

"Surgeon Adair said I've seen enough fighting and dead and wounded men for a while. Reckon Buster took care of it and spoke to the Lieutenant. He was rough with me out there with the Pins. Still, he's a good man."

Jim Ellis

"Buster was right about the Pins. He was getting you ready, Jock. Hard fighting coming, I feel it. He's the best Sergeant in the Company," Jim said. "The best in the Rifles."

Jock laid his hand on Jim's shoulder. "You're dead right, Jim." Jock rubbed his hands. "I've been worrying. Can't sleep, get up at night and go to the latrine. One day I'll piss and shit in my drawers. Can't get it out of my head that I'll not be fit when we go out again."

"Before we go out, take part with me in the Cherokee way for battle. You'll be ready, Jock. I know tactics."

Another week passed, and the boys felt well again. At dusk, Jock and Jim walked the camp perimeter. They carried Colt pistols and ammunition pouches attached to their belts. Jock carried his sabre on the left side. Enemies might appear; if attacked, they'd fight.

"Riders coming in," Jim said.

Jock listened for many horses above the camp bustle. "How the Hell do you know that, Jim? It's all quiet."

"Buster told you, Indians know these things." They walked on. After a few minutes, Jock stopped and listened to the distant rumble of many horses coming. "I hear them."

Jim shaded his eyes and looked south. "I can see them. They're coming in."

Jock got his telescope on the riders. "That's Mr Pete and Willie leading a column of twos. Palmer Brown's behind them. He's holding a flag." Jock refocussed the telescope in the poor light, capturing the fluttering Gideon. "They're riding under a black flag. Something's wrong, Jim."

Chapter Seven

Pete O'Leary's column had been in the Rifles camp for about an hour. Pete conferred with Colonel Watie. Wille organised space where the men could bivouac. Palmer Brown worked with the wranglers on the care of the horses.

Jock and Jim moved back and forth outside their quarters, anxious to find out what had happened. They saw Buster approaching from the direction of the Colonel's quarters.

"You boys had better come with me."

"What's wrong, Sergeant? Tell us," Jim said.

Buster grabbed Jim by the shoulder. "Follow me, son – an' you an' all, Jock."

The boys waited outside the Colonel's quarters while Pete spoke to Stand Watie. Willie paused on his way in, removed his slouch hat and issued a curt, "How do, boys?" He didn't wait for a reply.

"What the Hell is wrong with him?" Jim asked.

"Right, something must've happened," Jock said.

Stand Watie rose. "We'll complete arrangements in the morning." He waved the boys into his quarters. The Colonel placed four glasses on the table. "Pete, drink up some of that whiskey you brought me." He turned to the boys. "You young fellows will need a drink. Jim, you and Jock take a seat."

Bad news was coming. The Colonel sensed the change in mood and left the tent to walk around the camp with his adjutant.

"Ah see you boys lookin' at me."

The boys flushed and turned away from Pete.

"It's all right, boys. Six months or more since you was at the ranch, Jim. Longer for you, Jock. Bad times came. Hair turned white overnight. Worse, can't eat... been livin' on jerky and whiskey. My complexion is like mud, cheekbones like knife edges. Lost twelve, maybe fifteen pounds last time I checked."

The change in Pete's appearance astonished Jock. Pete's clothing hung on his skeletal frame, his body reduced to skin and bone. A grey coat covered his hips, beneath it a heavy blue shirt with a black scarf tied at the neck. A black leather belt held two holstered Colt pistols, and two Colt Dragoon pistols tucked in. The belt carried ammunition pouches and a sheathed Arkansas Toothpick. His black wool trousers were tucked into knee-high boots.

Willie looked up, haggard and heavy-eyed. "I look like I'm comin' apart. My hair peppered grey like it was old birdshit. Too much whiskey. Pete and me aged ten years since the bad days."

His worn buckskin jacket covered a heavy grey wool shirt with a red sash tied at the neck. Black wool trousers were tucked into stout black mule-eared boots. Thrust into his belt, two Colt Dragoon pistols and a Bowie knife. A sawed-off shotgun hung from his right shoulder. Two bandoliers crossed his torso; one held shotgun shells and the other, rounds for the Colts.

"The last of the Sullivan-O'Leary mash." Willie filled the glasses. Pete downed his whiskey in one gulp. Willie followed him.

The boys eyed each other, puzzled. They finished their whiskeys in two swallows. Pete uncorked the bottle and refilled their glasses. "Sip it. Keep you right."

"Pardon me asking, Mr Pete," Jim said. "You and Willie comin' up here to the Nations with about a hundred armed men... Talking about bad times and bad days... What the Hell is goin' on?"

Pete O'Leary and Willie Sullivan exchanged a look. Pete started.

"Happened a couple of months ago. Ranch sacked. Destroyed by Federal irregulars. Reckon a bunch of fuckin' cutthroat Kansas Redlegs

Only The Leaves Whispering

and Jayhawkers did it. A few militiamen. We found discarded Union Army kit."

"They killed a lot of our people," Willie said. "Wiped out the Maroons guarding the ranch."

"Murdered families nearby and burned-out properties," Pete said. "Maroon families suffered, too. Palmer Brown brought some men to help."

Willie downed another whiskey. "These Union bastards talk about freedom and fuckin' Lincoln and emancipation. No slaves or bonded servants where we're from. White folks, and black folks, Mexicans and Indians, all gettin' along just fine. Show them murderin' Northerners how to live." Willie drew his right sleeve across his eyes.

"We're goin' up there an' put things right," Pete said. He filled the boys' glasses to the brim. "Go on, young fellers. Drink up. Brace yourselves."

"What about Miss Sally and Miss Celestina?" Jock asked.

"Dead. Raped and murdered," Pete said.

Willie looked up. "Jim, I'm sorry, but all our children, Pete's and my children, are dead."

"Miss Harriet?"

"Violated and cut to pieces with knives. Must've been four or five Yankees got at her."

Jim turned corpse-pale. "Easy, Jim," Jock, said. He was worried that Jim would be sick, and caught his arm, keeping his friend from pitching out of the chair on to the groundsheet.

"Bad, was it?" Jock asked.

"Cruel and savage," Pete said.

The raiders hit the ranch while Pete and Willie were inspecting the borders of the property. When they heard rifle and pistol shots, they rushed to the accommodations.

"A fuckin' orgy of destruction, rape and murder," Pete said.

"Big party of raiders. More than fifty," Willie said. "Must've had scouts checking the place for a couple of days before they attacked. They moved through the land wrecking farms, killing and burning."

Jim Ellis

"Two ranch hands with us. One a Cree and the other a Yaqui from Mexico," Pete said. "We caught up with their rear."

"The Yaqui killed one straggler. Shot him in the head, and the Cree got one with an arrow; killed him outright," Willie said. "Pete wounded another straggler with the Henry repeater."

Jim had been silent, pale and shaken. Now, he asked, "What'd you with him?" hoping this Yankee barbarian had met a bloody end.

"We got it out of him that they came from Jim Lane's riders out of Kansas," Pete said.

Willie chimed in: "Clark Tough led them. Federals from Missouri joined for the raid."

"We said we'd keep him alive." Pete looked at Willie.

"He was worth nothing. Yankee vermin. I cut out his vital parts, stuffed his member in his mouth. He bled to death. Left him for the coyotes. Ah'll tell you this, boys, to hell with justice. There'll be no rest until we get our revenge."

Pete whistled a tune then hummed the melody. A tight grin creased Willie's face, a mask of hate.

Buster Parris stared at the back wall of the tent.

Pete O'Leary's harsh, mirthless laughter shattered the silence. He sang in a reedy, tuneless voice:

> "*We shall meet, but we shall miss him,*
> *There will be one vacant chair;*
> *We shall linger to caress him,*
> *When we breathe our ev'ning pray'r.*
> *When one year ago we gathered,*
> *Joy was in his mild blue eye.*
> *Now the golden cord is severed,*
> *And our hopes in ruin lie.*"

He stopped singing and continued to speak. "The bastard Red Leg got what he deserved, an eye for an eye from Sullivan and O'Leary. When we're done killin' Red Legs, and Jayhawkers, Federal vermin,

Only The Leaves Whispering

there'll be a choir of widows and lovers singin' their fuckin' hearts out for empty chairs and dead men."

Jock heard his own breath. He listened to the heavy breathing of the four comrades, and he recalled Jesse James talking about *The Vacant Chair*.

"You boys take some time to think about what we've told you," Pete said, breaking the silence.

"Come on, boys," Buster said as he led them out of the tent.

"What's going on, Mr Pete singing and all?" Jock asked.

"I heard about it," Buster said. "Song's called *The Vacant Chair*. From up North. Yankee infantry officer, William Grout, only eighteen. Killed at Ball's Bluff. Southern families sing the song. The Major and the Captain… I've never seen men so near broken by grief. Reckon I'd feel the same if Yankees had murdered my family. The song, it's all about loss. North and South."

He turned to go. "Goodnight, boys. Get some rest. Much to do before we go out."

Jock led Jim away from the tent. He placed his hand on Jim's shoulder, and felt tremors through the shirt as Jim fought against sobbing. "It's all right, Jim. I can only imagine how you're feeling."

"I feel like giving up, Jock. What kind of men would rape and murder a young, innocent girl like Miss Harriet?"

"Bad men."

"They defiled her. I'm grieving and sick at heart. I'm going to pray that Harriet has passed to the other side. I'm attached to the old Cherokee ways. I believe in the Three Divine Beings, and Harriet should be with them forever in perpetual light. But the rage is starting in me. When I'm done mourning, I'll avenge Miss Harriet. We loved each other. Damned Yankees will pay for killing her."

"I'll pray for her, too." It came to Jock that for Harriet Sullivan and Jim, he should recite the *De Profundis*. The words came to him: *Out of the depths I have cried to Thee, O Lord…*

Jock wakened in the small hours, startled by a soft wailing. In the half-light, he saw Jim, wrapped in his bedroll. His dear friend wept for Miss Harriet, his lost love.

Next morning, Jim's mourning continued. He fasted and prayed, then changed into his oldest clothing. Jim prepared to go to a quiet bank of the creek at the edge of the Rifles camp. Buster had told Jock to stay with Jim.

"I know Harriet's buried at the ranch," Jim said, "but I don't think I'll ever go to her grave. It would drive me mad with grief."

"Will I stay, or do you prefer to be by yourself?"

"Come with me to the creek."

The boys walked to the creek. "My people bathe the dead," Jim said. "I prayed that someone washed and purified my Harriet with water and willow root. If only I could've closed her eyes."

They came to a quiet spot by the creek. Jim removed a small cloth parcel from a sack he carried. He spread ashes on his head and sat a while on the bank. "I'm going to purify myself. Pray for me, and for Harriet, Jock." Jim entered the water, and faced east, then west as he immersed himself seven times in the waters of the creek. He prayed, "May Harriet dwell in the place of light and happiness."

Once out of the water, Jim shivered as he dried off and put on fresh clothing. "I'll burn my old clothes when we get back to the camp."

* * *

Colonel Stand Watie welcomed Pete's volunteers into the Rifles. He appointed Pete a Major in the Confederate Army. "I've sent a dispatch to General William Steele. Official letter of appointment will come back in due course," he said to Pete. They agreed to name Pete's outfit O'Leary's Rangers, riding under the battle flag of the Cherokee Braves. Pete had two requests.

"Sir, back a generation or two, my family came from Ireland. Can we have a gold harp stitched to the battle flag? I want them Federals to know when it's O'Leary's Rangers."

Stand Watie agreed. "You had another request, Major?"

Only The Leaves Whispering

"Yessir." Pete explained about Jim's understanding with Willie's daughter, Harriet. "Jim's grieving, Colonel. Reckon he'd like to be with the Rangers when we head north. And there's that young Scotchman, Jock MacNeil. He and Jim, they're good friends."

"You want both of them?"

"Yessir. Jock's doctorin' be a boon for the Rangers' fighting men. And I know he's an excellent shot."

"Jock MacNeil is one of the best sharpshooters. I'll agree to your requests, but I can't give you much in the way of surgical supplies and medicines. Everything is so damned scarce out here. Don't have enough for the Rifles." The Colonel paused. "Tell you what, Major. We have two Whitworth rifles. I'm going to give you one of my best Sergeants, Buster Parris. Speak to him and see that you take a Whitworth with you. Annoy the Red Legs at long distance."

"Depend on it, Colonel. I thank you kindly. I brought medical supplies with the mule train. I took them off the French in a raid into Mexico."

Pete had not come empty-handed and had brought well-mounted, clothed and armed men.

"With your permission, Colonel, I'd like to keep the Rangers here for a few days and give them some training. I want them to move and fight like soldiers. They'll not be shy when we go up against the Federals. I'm not taking a mob to the war."

"The Sergeant will help you with training and organising. Buster Parris knows what he is about."

* * *

"I'm enough of a soldier from my time as a Captain in the Union Army to want to lead a disciplined outfit," Pete said. "Not interested in parades. I want the Rangers to be a fighting outfit."

Willie, Jock and Jim kept quiet.

A cough sounded outside the entrance to Pete's tent. "Come on in, Sergeant."

Buster Parris entered and saluted Pete, who gestured to a camp chair. Buster nodded to Willie and turned to the boys. "I heard what happened down at Major O'Leary's ranch. I'm right sorry. But we're goin' north. Make them Redlegs regret they ever come down here. Y'all got to keep goin' ahead."

Pete had made Palmer Brown acting Sergeant in charge of the Maroons and responsible for scouting. Willie Sullivan was second-in-command in the rank of acting Captain. Buster was appointed Sergeant Major, working for Major Pete O'Leary; Jock, sharpshooter and medical orderly, Jim sharpshooter with Jock, reporting to Buster.

Every Ranger was armed with a Bowie knife or Arkansas Toothpick. Pete wanted his men to have modern weapons and not antique rifles and pistols. Pete had made sure he had a handful of small squads ready: expert bowmen from among the Maroon and Creek. Men who could launch five arrows before the first arrow hit an enemy. A good number of the men had sawed-off shotguns, and he had twelve men armed with Henry repeating rifles.

"Major, the Rangers are about as well equipped as the Rifles," Buster said.

"You're right, Sergeant. We'll take more and better guns, and ammunition, from the Yankees."

Pete and Willie inspected the Rangers, checking horses, saddles, harnesses. Buster tested weapons and drilled them in basic manoeuvres. Jock, assisted by Jim, examined the men for minor injuries, aches and pains. At Pete's urging, Jock mentioned personal cleanliness and staying well.

* * *

On the eve of their departure for Kansas, Jock and Jim sat by their quarters drinking acorn coffee saved from supper.

"Captain Semmes is a proper Southern Officer. Never killed anyone when he captured a ship," Jock said.

Only The Leaves Whispering

"Confederate Navy at sea is a gentleman's war," Jim said. "Different war out here in the Nations. Mr Pete and Willie don't respond, Yankees'll figure them weak and come back and kill again. Worse, they'll reckon Southern men are cowards. Them Federals'll think they can get away with burnin' and murderin'."

"But that's revenge. I worry what'll happen," Jock said, feeling a surge of his latent Catholic conscience.

"Sure, it is. But we'll hurt the Yankee sons of bitches so damned bad, they'll be real careful about comin' down here again.

"You know some of the war we're fightin', Jock, through going out with Buster and battling the Pins. Can't all be new to you."

Jock let that observation sink in. Riding with Buster; setting a murderous ambush and killing a Federal cavalry patrol. They had left no survivors. The horror, and yes, the excitement of war: the dog-eat-dog battle with the Pins; Rifles slaughtering wounded Pins.

"I understand. But we fought soldiers and warriors that were not killing civilians and murdering women and children."

Jim shook his head. "They were guerrillas that attacked O'Leary's. Farmers and the like by day, Devil Riders by night, come out to kill and burn. Hard to say who they are. But Mr Pete has names. We'll find them. Don't reckon Mr Pete's a killer of wives and children."

He waited, but Jock kept his mouth shut. Jim spread his hands. "It's hard, I'll grant you that. Try lookin' this way at what happened. These swine out of Kansas and Missouri destroyed a safe, happy place. No slaves. It's drivin' Mr Pete and Willie, and the men who joined with them. It's drivin' me, Jock."

"I understand."

Jim was still grieving for Miss Harriet. He could see why a Yankee raid on the land, the livestock, the crops, hurt the Confederate war effort. But killing innocents should have had no part in it. "Evil men," Jim said. "We're goin' up there to punish the killers. I want to find the men who killed Harriet. We'll knock a hole in the Federal war effort."

"You're right, Jim. A good dose of their own medicine for these Federals. Pay them back. But I'm not killing women and children."

Jim Ellis

"As long as they don't fight."

Jock was among the youngest men of the Rifles. He was battle-hardened, but idealism still clung to him. He liked the Missouri Boys he'd helped when they came to the Rifles camp. Called them Missouri Cavaliers. Good southern men. "The Missouri Cavaliers. Better than Redlegs and Jayhawkers," he said to Jim.

"Word came down to the Nations. Southern men for sure," Jim said. "But they fight the same kind of war as the Federals. We cross the Kansas border, we'll be ridin' with Mr Pete and Willie. We run into Quantrill's Raiders or them that rides with Bloody Bill Anderson, don't get carried away. Remember we're all Cherokee Mounted Rifles, Confederate Army."

"I can't forget I'm a Confederate soldier and I belong to the Cherokee Braves," Jock said. "It's the main reason why I rode with you from Galveston."

"You're one of us. Let's take a walk, Jock. I want to show you something."

Buster stepped out from the shadows of the tent. "Evening, boys. I was passing and you were talkin' loud. Quiet talk and silence, Jim, are strengths of the Cherokee warrior."

* * *

Buster walked with the boys to a quiet clearing among cottonwoods at the western edge of the camp where they were unlikely to be disturbed. They sat by the creek.

"It doesn't answer, you fretting before we go out. Jim, you're a time served horse soldier, and you, Jock, you know what you're about. So stop worrying."

"But O'Leary's Rangers are a mixed bunch," Jock said.

"That's a fact, Sergeant," Jim said.

"Sure enough," said Buster, "but I've been training them in cavalry manoeuvers. You've seen the Seminoles and Creeks. Natural horsemen. Maroons are fine warriors and fighters. The black riders sure

Only The Leaves Whispering

learn fast. And the Americans who settled with us are all frontiers-men. All these boys can ride and shoot all right. Major O'Leary ain't forgotten what he learned in the Union Army in the Mexican war. He's the right man for the commanding officer. Captain Sullivan doesn't say much, but he has a grip all right. Kind of man I like to have by my side in a fight."

"You think so, Sergeant?" Jim asked.

"Goin' into Kansas and Missouri plays to our strengths. We merge with the terrain. We're the best at raidin', ambushin', and surprise attacks. The Red Legs and Jayhawkers will be expectin' something. Don't think they'll have figured out what's in store for them. They've stained Southern and tribal honour. We'll be fixin' that."

Jock rubbed his hands, and the tension that had built up in his chest eased off. "I'm ready to ride with the Rangers."

Buster could see that he'd had a good effect on the boys' confidence. He wanted to do more.

"We'll fast. It's good preparation," Buster said. "Bring that Bush-whacker's shirt, Jock."

"What about our buckskin war shirts?" Jim asked.

"Them too."

"We'll ride out in war paint. Jim knows how. I'll show you what to do, Jock, at first light. Major Pete doesn't mind. We'll use black for strength and to show we've fought well in battle. Red, too, for war, for blood and strength, for our power and victory in battle. A touch of blue that the Great Spirit may send us wisdom. Let us think about tomorrow and the days ahead."

Buster knew he'd have to fight hard when the Rangers were out. He hoped his courage would hold.

Jim searched for strength and bravery to kill the enemies who'd sullied Miss Harriet's honour and murdered her.

Jock felt strong and ready for the warrior's path.

"I'm going to pray to the wolf," Buster said.

Buster's voice rose, and he chanted. The boys swayed in time with the rhythms of the sacred words.

Jim Ellis

"Spirit Of the Wolf
You who wanders the wildlands,
You who stalks in silent shadows,
You who runs and leaps
Between the moss-covered trees.
Lend me your primal strength.
And the wisdom of your glowing eyes.
Teach me to relentlessly track my desires.
And to stand in defence of those I love.
Show me the hidden paths and the moonlit fields.
Fierce spirit,
Walk with me in my solitude,
Howl with me in my joy
And
Guard me as I move through this world."

* * *

O'Leary's Rangers: Creek, Maroon and Seminole warriors, Mexicans, free Blacks, and Americans. Expert fighters to raid and ambush.

Major Pete O'Leary and Captain Willie Sullivan, carrying the black flag, led a column of twos. The shabby Rangers, bearing ancient arms, were riding north towards the Canadian River. Pete was taking his command to invade Kansas and Missouri and wreak destruction.

Colonel Watie assembled his Staff to salute the Rangers passing in review. They acknowledged the battle flag of the Rifles dipped in salute.

At the rear, Jock and Jim rode with Buster and the mule train. Jock was glad that many of the braves in the column wore war paint, though it differed from the patterns used by the Cherokee.

He turned to Buster and asked, "Seminoles and Creeks, they look different. Why?"

"They follow their own old ways," Buster said.

Only The Leaves Whispering

"Tell me, Sergeant."

"Three main colours, Jock. Black means a man's prepared for war. Yellow is the colour of death. It means the warrior has lived his life, and he'll fight to the finish. Never wear too much yellow. Red is for blood and war. Warriors dab green under the eyes to make night vision stronger. Up close, you might see a few warriors have painted hands."

"They look fierce."

"They do. The Rangers are ready for what needs doing up north."

"What's that?" Jock asked, when he heard the brassy trumpet notes blend with the rhythmic creak of saddle leather and jingling harnesses.

"It's a couple of Mexicans playin'. They was in the Mexican Army. Soldiered with Santa Ana a while back. *De Guella's* the name of the tune. Reckon now it's our slow march. Goes with the black flag Captain Sullivan's carryin'. Santa Anna's trumpeters played it at the *Alamo*." Buster cleared his throat and spat. "Means we're not askin' for quarter or givin' it."

* * *

The column crossed the border into Kansas, heading east towards Osceola just across the Missouri state line. Major Pete would try to contact Bushwhackers. On the way to Osceola, they meant to raid, kill and plunder. After Osceola, the command would head back to Kansas, attacking on the way south.

"The Federals don't know we're here," Pete said to Willie Sullivan and the non-commissioned officers. "So we move and strike hard at Jayhawkers when and where they least expect it.

"I'm not forgetting that the Missourians attacked us," Pete said. "We'll attack them at the right time. Get help from them Bushwhackers."

"Beggin' your pardon, Major, but Jock MacNeil knows some of the Missouri Boys. He met Frank James and his younger brother, Jesse. Patched up them riders after a raid. Met them myself. Told us we could find them in Clay County. Be happy to ride with us, I reckon."

"Thank you, Sergeant. I'll remember that."

144

Jim Ellis

The Rangers had bivvied in among trees. They meant to destroy the property a mile distant, which belonged to the Jayhawker, Clement Rayburn. He'd led the raid on O'Leary's ranch.

"Jock, you've got the aid station ready?" Buster asked.

"No, Sergeant. I joined the Rifles to fight."

"You've done plenty. You've nothing to prove. Listen, son. Major Pete prefers his men to be willing. So he asked me to ask you to get ready to treat our wounded. Bound to be wounded after a big fight."

Ten seconds of silence. Buster rose and stood over Jock.

"This is O'Leary's Rangers, Confederate Army. We're soldiers, and we obey orders. Major Pete asked you, and Ah'm givin' you a fuckin' order. Git that aid station ready."

"Yessir, Sergeant."

A chastened Jock sulked as he finished his supper. He rose and did what he knew he should've done from the start: Jock attended to his duty.

That evening, Buster sat with the boys, eating a supper of cold fatty bacon, beans and hard, stale biscuits. They drank water. No fires that night so close to the enemy.

"Could sure do with hot food," Jim complained. He shivered.

"Yeah, right, Jim and you'll have Jayhawkers kickin' your ass in five minutes. Finish your supper."

The trio munched their way through the last of an unappetising repast. They washed away the taste of congealed bacon fat with swallows of cold creek water.

"Jock, you've got the aid station ready?" Buster asked.

"All set, Sergeant."

Buster spooned the last of the bacon and beans. He got up. "I'll be back soon."

After supper, Buster escorted Major Pete and Captain Willie through the bivvy. They stopped to speak to the small groups of men.

"Commanding Officer, and Captain Sullivan here. 'Tenshun," Buster said.

145

Only The Leaves Whispering

The boys rose and came to attention. "At ease, boys," Major Pete said. "Show me around, Jock. You come too, Jim."

Jock had laid his medical kit out on a white cloth which covered a makeshift table made of planks, sheltered under a canvas lean-to. The most durable mule had carried the legs and top. Major Pete picked up the bottle of cheap whiskey.

"Liquor, Jock? For drinking?"

"Not for drinking, sir. I'd some training back in Westburn with a retired Royal Navy surgeon, James Gunn. He said that applying spirits kept wounds free of infection."

"That's a new one."

"Well, sir, James Gunn didn't know why it worked but he knew that it helped save the lives of injured and wounded sailors."

Major Pete looked at the case of surgical instruments. His eyes lingered on the saws, probes, scalpels, regarded with horror by wounded and injured soldiers. He turned his gaze to the splints, ligatures, bandages, lint and jars of the black salve. The Major picked up the bottle of ether.

"A Godsend. Ether will save our wounded from misery."

The quiet talk of Captain Willie and Buster broke the silence. "Let's take a seat." Pete jerked his head towards a fallen tree. "Go on, boys, sit down."

The boys sat, elbows resting on knees and waited.

"I know you're disappointed because you want to fight them Jayhawkers. And that's how an O'Leary Ranger should feel. We'll fight with care, and we'll kill them Yankees. But some Rangers will get killed or wounded on this raid; that's war. You, Jock and you, Jim, can help the wounded live to fight again, or get them recovered and home. I lose you two, and it means more good men'll die. You understand now?"

"We understand, sir," Jock said. "But I'm not a doctor. If a wounded man has a ball lodged near vital organs, or broken arms and legs needing amputation, I can't do that, sir. If I tried, most likely I'd kill the patient."

146

Jim Ellis

"The men like you, son. They know about your work with Surgeon Adair. They have faith in your healing hands. You have all that medical kit. A good Ranger adapts and improvises; he overcomes. It's not for nothing that they call you Doc MacNeil. You have my confidence. I know you'll do your best, Jock, and you too, Jim."

* * *

"Two Maroons scouted the place at first light," Buster said. "Two guards is ridin' the edge of the property. Two on foot patrolling close to the main house and outbuildings. Reckon on some hands around the place, right now, sleepin' in the bunkhouse. Can't be sure how many. But we'll get 'em when we attack. Oh, I near forgot. Dogs. A couple of Border Collies."

"Smart dogs," Jock said to Buster, who turned to him and said, "Major Pete is sending men in the old Indian way."

"How's that?" Jock asked.

"You'll see tomorrow morning."

The chilled hour before dawn. Sun rays on the horizon, giving some light. The mist hung on in the hollows of low ground and the corners of fields. Buster and the boys watched the four Creeks preparing to leave for the opening phase of the attack. They were armed with bows, quivers full of arrows, knives, and Colt pistols and ammunition. The warriors had tied back their long black hair with a bandana. Stripes of red war paint bisected their faces from the bridge of the nose to their lower ear lobes. War shirts, long buckskin leggings and moccasins completed their dress.

"They look good," Jock said.

"They are good. Real fighting Creek – warriors for the South," Jim said.

The warriors vanished into the shallow ground. Experts in fieldcraft, they melded with the contours of the land, making a silent, hidden approach.

Pete had Buster ready the men in columns of two. They waited for the signal – a flaming arrow overhead, meaning the guards were dead.

Only The Leaves Whispering

* * *

The Creek hidden near the dwellings killed the two collies with arrows. Two Creeks hid by the edge of the property. They launched four bolts. A faint hissing cut the air as the missiles flew at the guards. The mounted guards tumbled dead out of the saddle, killed by arrows sunk deep in their chest cavity. A warrior moved over open ground, grabbed the reins of the horses and hid the animals in a thicket.

The other two Creeks had got closer to the ranch and shot two arrows into the hearts and necks of the guards on foot.

A Creek lit a prepared arrow and launched it in a fiery arc.

Pete saw the arrow reach its full height and ordered the Rangers to move out. Horses cantered forward. The jingle and creaking of working harnesses and saddles added sinister notes to the morning bird song. They halted at the locked gate of the Jayhawker place.

Pete waved Buster over. "Open it, Sergeant."

"Yes, sir."

Buster brought out his Harper's Ferry Blunderbuss. He'd loaded it with heavy buckshot, small stones, metal fragments and splinters of metal.

"Been in the family since 1812. Double-charged, sir. Knock a wall down."

A nod of approval from Major Pete. Buster fired and blew the gate into kindling wood.

Jock heard the crash of the blunderbuss. "That's Buster at his work."

He looked with the telescope at two older Maroons guarding the temporary aid station. Jim and a guard, a former farmer, had gone down with two mules behind the main column. Their job was to ferry the wounded back to Jock for treatment.

The trumpeters played *De Guella* as half the column surged through the gate. They divided into two bands of twenty-five men and proceeded to set fire to the outbuildings. Men dashed from blazing wooden structures and fired at the Rangers, who shot them down.

A white flag waved from the edge of the main door of the house. A man crept out. He gazed, horrified by the sound of the trumpets, the sight of the black flag and the battle flag of the Cherokee Braves.

"Let our families go," he said.

"You're Clement Raeburn?" Pete asked. The man nodded. Pete doffed his slouch hat. "Major Peter O'Leary, commanding O'Leary's Rangers, Confederate States Army. You have to answer for all that killin' at the O'Leary Ranch." Pete shot Clement Raeburn in the heart.

Rangers burst into the house, killing, looting and burning. Comrades watched doors and windows and killed Raeburn family and followers who were trying to escape.

The attack was almost finished. Pete and Willie waited while Buster rounded up the men for departure. Buster came towards them, half dragging and half carrying a bedraggled, terrified black girl.

"Look at what Buster found, Pete," Willie said.

"Found her hiding in the hay when we set fire to the barn," Buster said.

The girl appealed to Pete, having guessed that he was in charge. "Ah ain't done nuthin', suh. All that hollerin' and shootin'… why suh, Ah'm scared to death."

"Are you a slave?"

"No, suh. Ah'm a bonded girl. Least that's what ma master told me. Said Ah'm owed to him forever."

"You have a name, girl?"

"Ah'm Abigail, suh."

"And your last name?"

"Don't have one, suh. Everyone calls me Abby."

"Wages?"

"Board and keep, suh. Never had a dollar to ma name."

Pete beckoned to Willie, and they steered their mounts out of Abigail's earshot. "Wait there, young lady. Sergeant, please join us."

"What are we going to do with her?" Pete said. "Can't leave her here. This is wild country: Bushwhackers, Redlegs, Federal troops, Confederate raiders. She'd be raped and dead in a week."

Only The Leaves Whispering

"I reckon she's an orphan," Willie said. "Been sold into bondage by her family, who were too poor to care for her. This girl is no better than a slave."

Pete turned to Buster. "What do you think, Sergeant?"

"Sir, she's genuine. A good girl who's had no life. Treated by this Jayhawkin' lot as a dogsbody. Like Captain Willie said, no better than a slave."

There was a silence, that seemed to last forever. Buster looked at Pete and Willie. "Sir, I reckon we could use her help at the aid station. She'll get along with the boys. I'll protect her. Point of fact, sir, I'll deal with any man who bothers the young lady. And you remember there are black Cherokees in the tribe."

Willie smiled. "You're a good man, Buster, as well as a first-rate Sergeant Major."

"Captain Willie is right," Pete said. "She'll come with us."

Pete beckoned to Abigail. "Your master, his family and all the men and their families he had here are dead. We killed them. They had to answer for the murder of our families and the destruction of our homes in Oklahoma. Do you understand what I am saying?"

"Yes, suh."

"You can come with us, and we'll take you to the Nations. Then we'll see. You don't have to come, but we –" Pete gestured to Willie and Buster – "think you should come. But you should know, we're O'Leary's Rangers, attached to the Cherokee Mounted Rifles, Confederate States Army."

Abigail smiled. "Reckon, suh, Ah'm safer with the Rebels than with this Jayhawkin' family. Ah'm pleased you makin' me such a kind offer, suh."

"We'll sign you on as a supernumerary, and pay you the same wages as a private in the Confederate Army. You'll assist two of my men to look after our wounded."

"Thank you, suh."

Buster sent a Ranger off to find a bedroll, a good horse, saddle and harness for Abigail. He looked at the girl's dirty bare feet. Reckon Jock can help her get those tired, worn feet in shape, Buster thought.

"Abigail, have you personal things? What about clothes and shoes, riding boots?

"Ah have not, suh."

"Well, let's get you some kit before we finish burning down the house."

Jim and the guard brought in the casualties. Jock examined them. One dead Ranger, a Creek, would be taken care of by fellow tribesmen. Five wounded. One man had the third finger of his left hand shot off. Jock would cauterise the wrecked digit. Bruised limbs, he'd treat with arnica, and bind injured ribs. One man had a back peppered with buckshot that would have to be dug out with a surgical blade and probe, the wounds dressed with the black salve.

At last, Jock finished treating the wounded. Jim poured whiskey on Jock's hands, and he dried them off with a clean cloth before tackling the buckshot wounds.

"Look at that," Jim said. "Buster's brought a black girl."

"This is Miss Abigail. She's under my protection," Buster said. "You boys show her what to do. Help her, and she'll help you.

"Miss Abigail, meet Cherokee Jim. He's from back east and this here is Jock MacNeil, the Ranger from Scotland."

"How do, Miss Abigail," Jock said.

"Yes, Miss Abigail, how do," Jim said.

The boys saw a very dirty barefoot waif. Abigail, eyes lowered, made a small curtsy.

She had nothing to say to these youths. The Cherokee was bristling with Colt pistols and an Arkansas Toothpick. Cherokee Jim stared at her from beneath his slouch hat. Abigail glanced at the feather sticking out of the hatband. She saw the fringes of a buckskin war shirt protruding above his Missouri shirt. This man was a wild Injun, and she was afraid of him.

Only The Leaves Whispering

Abigail had never heard of Scotland. This Jock seemed to be a doctor or a nurse. She did not care for his long red hair that hung to his shoulders, or the Missouri shirt worn over a buckskin war shirt. Would this white man be like her master, who beat her and invaded her bed?

* * *

Buster took Abigail aside. He'd noticed her guarded approach to the boys when she met them.

"Don't worry. You'll get on fine with the boys."

"Yes, suh."

But Abigail's fear remained, though she said nothing about it. Buster had brought her back with the column to the temporary lines. She was afraid of the Rebel soldiers: white frontiersmen, Mexicans, a mix of tribesmen and black Cherokees, clad in a shabby patchwork of Confederate uniforms and personal clothing. She did not understand why the white commanding officer worked with a black officer.

Jim took the horse and the bundle of clothing and kit brought for Abigail. He arranged a bedroll and made adjustments to the saddle and harness.

Jock dealt with the injured. Abigail paid attention when he had a Creek remove his war shirt and laid him belly-down on the table. With scalpel and probe, Jock dug out the buckshot embedded in the warrior's back and dressed the wounds with black salve. Jock's skills, his gentle hands as he worked at the wounds, impressed Abigail.

"Mr Doc. Ah ask you a question?"

Jock looked up. "Go ahead."

"Ma back, suh, please look? It's hurt bad."

"Alright, Abigail. Jim, will you pick clothes for the trail for Miss Abigail?"

Jim left to search through the bundle of gear Buster had taken from the Jayhawker house.

Jock reached for a basin, washcloth, towel, and a small cake of Confederate Army soap. He handed them to the girl. "Wash over there, by the small pool No one will trouble you, but you need to be quick."

Jim Ellis

In five minutes, Abigail returned, covered by a shift. Her damp hair was pulled back to reveal high cheekbones and firm lips.

"She's so pretty," Jock murmured. Too bad Abigail had not belonged to a loving family like the Sullivans and lived alongside the O'Learys.

Jock had her lie on her belly on the table. He covered her bottom with a cotton towel, and lifted the shift. Abigail's back was crisscrossed with angry, inflamed red welts. Broken skin and raw flesh in three places; the open wounds leaked pus.

"Jesus Christ, Abigal! Who did that to you?"

"The master, suh."

"Why? What did he do to you?"

"Come to ma bed, suh. Ah asked him to please leave me alone. Beat me wid a belt. Hit me wid the buckle. But, suh, Ah covered ma face. Said he goin' to hump me."

A few tears escaped her eyes.

"I'm sorry, Abigail. Lie still, and I'll dress your back."

Jock applied arnica to the bruises. He washed away surface pus with a damp cloth. "I'm going to bathe your cuts with whiskey. It'll sting, but it'll clean up the wounds."

Abigail quivered through Jock's hands when the whiskey entered the wounds. "Oh, suh, that's strong moonshine."

Jock grinned. "Texas whiskey. Rotgut. I wouldn't drink it. This ointment will help soothe your wounds." He applied the black salve to the raw flesh. "What about your chest and belly?"

"Ribs hurt, suh."

"Turn on to your back and raise your shift."

Jock was relieved when Abigail raised her shift, exposing her ribs but keeping her breasts covered.

"You don't have small clothes?"

"Small clothes are for white folks, suh."

"There's no small clothes here. One of our raiding parties can pick up small clothes for you. We'll see about getting you more personal things back at camp."

Only The Leaves Whispering

Jock handed Abigail the cotton towel. "Keep yourself covered with your shift and lay the towel over your private parts."

Jock painted arnica on her bruised ribs. "Is your back stiff?"

"Yes, suh."

"I'll help you sit up." Jock put both hands under Abigail's shoulders and raised her. It was close to the start of an embrace. Abigail went rigid and turned her head away. "Ah'm Ah goin' to be all right, suh?"

"Damn and blast, miss!" an angry Jock yelled. "Of course you're going to be all right! What the Hell do you think I am? I'm not some Kansas ruffian. I'm a Confederate soldier, and I learned my trade in the Confederate Navy."

Abigail stifled a sob. "Ah'm real sorry, suh. You good to me. But white man picks me up, bad things happen."

He sat Abigail up and bound the bruised ribs. Jock realised his gruffness had frightened Abigail. "I've put pads with black salve in the bandages to protect your back wounds,' he said gently.

"Didn't mean to yell, Abigail. Sorry, I spoke rough. You're safe here. You're under the protection of Seargeant Buster Parris, O'Leary's Rangers, Confederate States Army."

"Thank you, suh."

"You're all right now?"

"I am, suh."

Jim returned carrying riding boots, socks, pants, shirt, jacket and a slouch hat. "Here you are, Miss Abigail. You'll want the hat for the sun. Your horse is ready."

"You can get dressed, Abigail," Jock said. "The column is moving soon. Don't ride barefoot."

"Reckon the boots'll hurt, suh."

"Sit down. Hold your right foot up, then your left foot."

Abigail's broken and battered feet suggested a life of overwork and neglect, knocked about by rough Jayhawkers. Jock had grown up beside mothers working hard for their families. Abigail had missed family life.

Jim Ellis

The MacNeils had lived beside impoverished, barefoot Irish and Highland children. But Jock and his younger brother and sister had never gone without footgear.

Jock chatted while he attended to Abigail. "I've worked with doctors looking after sailors and soldiers. You're my first young lady."

"Well, suh, thank you. You the first young white man called me a young lady. Them Jayhawkers called me the coloured help, or 'that Nigger girl'."

"Can't say I like that, Abigail."

Jock worked on Abigail's feet. He clipped, pared and shaped her toenails.

He showed Abigail a round of pumice stone. "Hard skin needs to come away. The rubbing won't hurt."

He finished by putting black salve on Abigail's split heels.

"Next time you can do it."

"Thank you, suh. You have good hands, an' you've been real nice to me."

"Jim, can you get a pair of moccasins from one of the smaller men?"

Jim left and came back in a few minutes. He handed a pair of moccasins to Abigal.

"Deerskin moccasins," Jock said. "Wear them. Your feet will heal. Then you can wear the boots. Hold on a minute."

Jock cut a length of clean white cotton. He trimmed the ends to a ribbon-like V cut.

"Tie your hair back with a bow."

Abigail smiled. "Thank you, Mr Doc. Help me tie a pretty bow, suh?"

Abigail, a fine young woman, had flattered Jock. That this pretty black girl had favoured him delighted the young Scot. Abigail's smile erased the shameful memory of his sordid deflowering. He'd lain with a wretched tart who had worked the ship when Alabama took crew on board anchored at Anglesey.

"Sure, I'll do that." Jock knotted the bow and spread the wings. "There, it's done. Nice shape, too. The neat way I tied my sailor's scarf when I was in the Confederate Navy."

Only The Leaves Whispering

"Mr Doc, you was on a ship?"

"Yes, Loblolly Boy, helping the Assistant Surgeon aboard the Confederate States Ship, *Alabama*."

Buster appeared, carrying two metal containers. "Major Pete decided on hot food before we move out. Cooks have done well. There's hot beans and back fat bacon. Biscuits and coffee, too. Jock, take Miss Abigail down to the cooks, draw her eating irons and bring the biscuits."

They sat on bedrolls in a loose circle. Buster served Abigail first. He spooned out beans and bacon and placed two biscuits on each tin plate. Jim ladled coffee into tin mugs. Abigail moved away to eat by herself.

"What are you doing, girl?" Buster asked.

"Coloureds don't eat with white folks, suh."

Buster moved along his bedroll and patted the waterproof slicker covering. "You come right back and sit here, Abigail. Like I told you, I'm Cherokee with white and African blood. Jim's a full blood Cherokee. The only white man here is Jock, an' he's goin' to be right upset if you don't eat with us."

Abigail, eyes downcast, sat beside Buster and ate her food.

Jim grinned. "Miss Abigail, you're now a Rebel soldier."

"You're one of us," Jock said.

* * *

The Rangers cut deep into Kansas, killing and destroying the property of Jayhawkers. Much of the damage to communities consisted of the assassinations of known Jayhawkers. Major Pete would send a small party to a farm to kill the man of the house. They shot women and children if they fought.

Jock and Jim were used for impersonal long-distance killings with the Whitworth Rifle and the Hawken Gun.

Rangers out raiding helped themselves to superior Yankee Colt pistols, a few Henry repeating rifles and ammunition, discarding their old ordinance. Where they could, they took fresh horses.

Major Pete said to Willie and Buster, "The Federals must be getting pursuit organised. Time to think about heading south for the Nations."

"What about the Missourians who attacked us?" Willie asked.

"We should hit them before we head for home," Buster said.

Pete let the decision rest for a day, but events brought matters to a head. A shift in tactics that might permit the Rangers to wreak more significant damage on the Federals.

Chapter Eight

In the morning, a sentry approached Willie. "About twenty riders comin' in, Captain. Lookin' like Missouri Boys. Bushwhackers, sir."

Jock and Jim had just finished dosing a Ranger suffering from acute constipation.

"Head for the bushes," Jim said. "Here." He handed the soldier a few scraps of packing paper.

The boys doubled over in silent laughter. "If you run out," Jock yelled after the soldier, who was doubled over, fumbling with his belt, "get a handful of grass and leaves. All hell going to come loose when the Blue Mass does its work!"

The mercury and chalk mixture of the Blue Mass was dreaded by soldiers. A dose left a man emptied and embarrassed by the eruptions in his bowels.

"Shame on you, Mr Doc and Mr Jim," Abigail said. "You takin' after that poor, sick man."

The sound of the approaching riders reached the boys and Abigail. Hooves drumming on packed earth, creaking saddle leather, ringing bridles, Southern voices.

"That's Bushwhackers comin' in," Jim said.

Abigail, ever curious, moved towards the riders. Jock went after her and laid a restraining hand on her shoulder. He walked her back to where they'd laid out the medical kit.

"Watch with us, Abigail. They're fearsome hard men. They ain't O'Leary's Rangers. I'm sorry we spoke rough."

"Thank you, suh, for sayin' that."

The Bushwhackers were suitably attired. The Missouri Boys were no posse of ruffians. A couple of men wore scraps of Confederate Grey, a kepi, trousers with a yellow stripe. But the general tone of appearance said threatening field elegance.

"Smart lookin' fellers," Abigail said.

Every man wore the pullover guerrilla shirt in several colours, open down the front. The shawl-collar front, cuffs and pockets was decorated with elaborate ribbon work and needlework.

"They've had help from their women," Abigail observed, casting an admiring look at their shirts. "Four real big pockets."

"Called guerrilla shirts," Jim said. "Bushwhackers carry iron and ammunition in them pockets. Small pistols, too, I reckon. Look at their belts."

There was a sharp intake of breath from Abigail when she saw that the riders had two, or even three Colt revolvers tucked into their belts. A big, imposing man at the front had tucked four Colts in his belt.

"What you think, Jim? Bet them revolvers are .36 Navy Colts."

"Yes, Jock. A right good handgun when fighting in the saddle."

"Ah see big knives some of them is carryin'," Abigail said.

Jock grinned, pleased by Abigail's keen eyes and shrewd appraisal. "Bowie knives and Arkansas Toothpicks. Up close, you'll see some of them packing small axes, like a tomahawk. Them that think they're officers are carrying sabres."

Abigail smiled at Jock.

The Bushwhackers wore wide-brimmed, buff to dark brown and black, slouch hats. A few men displayed CSA badges on the crown.

"Can't see their eyes under them hats. Ah like to see people's eyes," Abigail said. "Oh, them hairy faces make them look mean."

Abigail turned to Jock "Why they wear their hair so long, Mr Doc?"

"Many Missouri Boys vowed not to cut their hair until the South won this war."

Only The Leaves Whispering

* * *

The lead rider dismounted. "David Porter, Major. Outta Missouri. We heard about you from our bushwhackin' friends over in Clay County. Them James an' Younger Boys. Good Southern men. They're engaged fightin' the Yankees. So we come down. Assist you in destroying the Federals. There's about two hundred and fifty Yankee cavalry out lookin' for you. 16th Volunteer Regiment, Kansas Cavalry. About forty miles north of here. Reckon they aim to destroy your Rangers. They've been around since April '63. Had their share of fightin'."

"Appreciate the offer, sir. We sure can use your firepower. You boys like coffee and vittles?"

"That'd be fine, Major."

Coffee was swallowed, biscuits and back fat bacon devoured in five minutes.

"Get the Federals to follow us into the Badlands," John Anderson, the second in command of the Bushwhackers, said.

Pete and Willie referred to the map to examine the Bushwhacker's suggestion. Badlands ran from Nebraska Territory south into Northern Oklahoma.

"I like it. A big area. Thirty to a hundred miles wide," Major Pete said.

"Lead the Yankees into the Little Jerusalem Badlands. Get them thinking we're heading home," Captain Willie said. "Could be perfect for an ambush. A good place to turn south for the Nations." He turned to David Porter. "You know the area, sir. What do you think?"

"Who is this fuckin' Nigger talkin' like he was a Confederate Officer?"

Pete had prepared for prejudice when the sentry brought word that the Bushwhackers were coming in. He ordered Buster to organise a body of armed Rangers. He wanted to avoid a fight for the sake of The Cause. Pete lifted his right hand. Twenty-five Rangers led by Sergeant Buster surrounded the twenty Bushwhackers. Men cocking rifles and revolvers broke the silence.

Jim Ellis

"Listen to me. This gentleman is Captain Willie Sullivan, Confederate States Army, second in command. We got Indians, Blacks, and we got Whites. All O'Leary's Rangers. Southern men. There's no fuckin' Niggers. Your thinking is what I don't like about the South. Captain Sullivan is my particular friend. He's no man's Nigger."

Major Pete let his words sink in. Sweat trickled down his lower back and into the cleft of his arse. "Get the fuck out of here, unless you're fixin' to meet your Maker."

His right hand rested on the butt of a Colt pistol, one of two tucked in his belt.

"We fight this war without the likes of you," Captain Willie said. "Leave, 'fore accidents happen."

"Didn't figure on meetin' uppity Niggers and Injuns, fuckin' Red Niggers thinkin' they're Southern men, did we, boys?"

Grunts of approval rippled through the Bushwhackers as they reached for weapons.

Major Pete gave the signal to spill Bushwhacker blood.

Jock, Abigail and Jim watched, horrified, as the killing unfolded. "Oh, ma God!" Abigail shrieked. "They shootin' an' killin' each other."

Rounds hissed overhead.

"Get down." Jock pulled Abigail to the ground. Jim crashed down beside them. "Don't want to be killed by stray bullets."

Buster directed fire into the Bushwhackers, who fought huddled together, only to fall, shattered and broken by rifle fire, blasts from sawed-off shotguns and Colt pistols. Silence. A black cloud of powder smoke hung over the killing ground, then drifted away in the south wind.

"A few wounded Bushwhackers, sir," Buster said. "Four or five."

"Kill them, Sergeant. Strip all them of anything useful. Take all the weapons."

The Rifles collected personal kit, and a mix of firearms – Henry repeating rifles, single-shot Henry carbines, a good weapon for any mounted soldier.

"Burial party, sir?"

Only The Leaves Whispering

"Carrion. Leave them for the animals, the coyotes and the buzzards."

A sigh of relief swept through the Rangers gathering around Major Pete and Captain Willie.

* * *

"What do you think, Willie? We got to deal with that Yankee column. Damned Bushwhackers killed four and wounded five. And we lost men fighting Jayhawkers. We're at seventy fighting Rangers. Might get that to seventy-five if the boys can fix the wounded."

"Jock and Jim will do it," Buster said. "Abigail's a real treasure. She'll help, too. That girl learned quick."

"You mean to fight them, and we're down to seventy-five Rangers? Them Federals are two hundred and fifty. Fresh horses and well-set troops out of Leavenworth."

"Don't mean to fight them, Willie, just kill them."

"Yes! Hit and run. We don't stand and fight. Ambushes and skirmishing. No pattern. Keep them on edge," Willie said. "Hurt them, so they keep coming after us. We got to stay ahead of them."

"We can't take them on in the field," Major Pete said. "They outnumber us more than two to one. The Maroons can scout places for ambushing and skirmishing. Let's get Parris Brown and Buster. They're our senior Sergeants, and they've been around the territory a while now."

Pete gathered his thoughts. "Get them Federals following us by harassing the Hell out of them," Pete said. "We're Rangers, and we're guerrilla fighters, we can outsmart them. We start with the initiative and keep it. If them Union Boys bring us to action or get ahead of us, catching us on the ground they've picked to fight us, it'll be hard for us. Reckon we'd lose. Can't have that." He meant for O'Leary's Rangers to hurt these Kansas Cavalrymen. Teach them a lesson they wouldn't forget.

"You're right," Willie said.

Parris Brown and Buster nodded in agreement.

162

Jim Ellis

They pored over the map, etching to memory the terrain and possible lines of march. The Rangers had come into Kansas near the Red Hills, then turned east and raided. Each of them knew that after the destruction of the Missouri Bushwhackers, there could be no crossing into Missouri.

"Them Yankees'll be on fresh mounts," Buster said. "Let's make them run – tire them out. Get them edgy and angry. Might not be thinking' straight 'fore we're finished."

"Our horses are in good shape," Willie said. "We captured a bunch of fresh animals in the raids. And we're better armed now than when we started from the Nations."

Palmer Brown said nothing while he read the map and thought about a strategy. "We can lead them Yankees astray, sir," Palmer Brown said. "I've been through the Badlands. Let's get them running after us to Little Jerusalem. Perfect for the last ambush."

"How far?" Pete asked.

"Say a couple of day's riding. I can scout the route. Suggest places for an ambush. Two of us for the job. How about Cherokee Jim coming with me in case one of us gets hurt? Jim and me can guide us to the points of ambush." Palmer Brown laughed as he rubbed his hands. "When we're finished with them Yankees, Little Jerusalem is a good place to turn south and go home."

The Rangers needed a handler for a couple of mules carrying ammunition. The wagon with medical supplies, ordinance, and food went on ahead with a small escort. They waited at a rendezvous for the column once the fighting was over.

Major Pete wanted all fit men in the fight.

Abigail had overheard Major Pete, Captain Willie and Buster discuss it. She moved closer, overcoming her reserve. She touched Buster on the arm.

"Yes, Abigail. What is it? I'm busy right now."

"Beg pardon, suh. Ah heard you talkin' about mules with Major Pete and Captain Willie. Ah can do it. Ah can take care of mules, ride with the skirmishers, hand out ammunition. Ah'm good with mules. Used

163

Only The Leaves Whispering

to look after animals for them Jayhawkers. An' Ah can ride. Them old teamsters drives the wagon, Ah believe, suh, they too old to handle a pair of mules from horseback and on the trail."

"You never said anything about mules, girl," Major Pete said.

"Never asked me, suh."

Captain Willie came over all protective, thinking about the family he'd lost. "You're just a young girl. Abigail, you remind me of my daughter, Harriet. We don't want you hurt, or worse, killed. Can't have you too close to danger. But thank you all the same."

Abigail, crestfallen, turned away. "Wait, Abigail," Buster said. "Tell Captain Willie and Major Pete why you want to help."

"First time in ma life, Ah've been treated right. Rangers been good to me. Now it's ma turn to help you."

"I'm for it," Buster said." Abigail's under my protection. There'll be Rangers nearby and coming in. Abigail volunteering gives us one more fighting Ranger."

So Abigail had charge of the mules and rode with the skirmishers and ambushers.

* * *

The Rangers navigated to Little Jerusalem, Parris Brown guiding the column through prairie grass and on to terrain marked by strange and outlandish chalk formations. He pointed to a cluster of chalk columns of varying heights. "The tall one is real pretty, a willowy woman. Nature at her work. But the columns are fragile. They erode and collapse."

Major Pete grunted and turned to Parris. "Any game hereabouts?"

"Pronghorn, Major. When we're through with the Federals, we could have a quick hunt?"

"Right. Fresh meat be good, once we're done. Leave it with you, Sergeant Brown."

"Major."

They rode at the front of the column: Major Pete, Captain Willie, Buster and Parris Brown. Parris turned to Captain Willie. "Real pretty, the Chalk Lillies. Spiky leaves and white petals."

"I hadn't noticed, but glad you pointed them out, Sergeant."

"We get to the cliffs, might be lucky and hear cliff swallows sing. It's a sweet bird song."

Palmer Brown was not deterred by the lack of response from his companions.

"Well, Major Pete, I have a suggestion," Palmer Brown said. "Snakes, sir. I've been thinking about snakes. There's the nasty Prairie Rattler. They den together, wrigglin' an' horrible."

"I hate snakes," Captain Willie said.

"Don't love 'em," Major Pete said. "Let's hear Sergeant Brown."

"Called Canebrake Rattler hereabouts," Sergeant Brown said. "A little feller, but you can find them at three feet, even four feet long. Once, I killed one of six feet. Dark brown, yellow or grey. They have a chevron or cross-band pattern. Black ones and fat snakes that like their grub. The bite is painful, and can be fatal."

Palmer Brown laughed. "Someone gets bit, that young Scot, Jock, that takes care of sick and wounded – well, God damn it, he can suck out the poison!"

Buster, Sergeant Major of O'Leary's Rangers, glared at Palmer Brown. He rode ahead a few yards and turned his mount to face the column. Major Pete held up his right hand, and the column halted.

"What the hell are you doin', Sergeant?"

"Him, sir," Buster said and pointed a long finger at Palmer Brown. "You're fuckin' about, Palmer. Jock is suckin' out nuthin'. You're the snake man; you take fuckin' care of it." Buster laid his right hand on the butt of a Colt pistol tucked in his belt. He drew the weapon half out of his belt.

"Right, you two, calm down. Act like fuckin' sergeants," Major Pete said. "Share your thinking, Sergeant Brown. But I'm telling you now. Any risk of snake bites to the men, then we have nothing to do with goddamned rattlesnakes."

"We got fifteen good bowmen with us. Tip arrows with snake venom. The Creeks, Maroons, Seminoles can have three to five arrows

Only The Leaves Whispering

in flight. Showers of poisoned arrows rainin' down on the Yankees. Ain't goin' to like that."

"I like it," Captain Willie said.

"Grief for them Yankees," Palmer Brown said. "The last thing they'll be thinkin' about is Indian bowmen shootin' arrows. I'll get the snakes up in Little Jerusalem. Catch a bundle to milk. I can do that too. If Mr MacNeil can give me a beaker, I'll take care of everything."

"Jock don't love snakes, but I reckon he'll be all right helpin' with the beaker and workin' with you," Buster said. "I'll speak to him."

"Good," Major Pete said. "Now, you two, shake hands."

"Last thing, sir," Parris Brown said. "Make the snake attack from a high place, but not too high. I'll have my Maroons throw sacks full of rattlers right in among them Yankees… cause panic after we've shot them up."

* * *

Palmer Brown approached Jock. "Sergeant Major Buster speak to you?"

"He did, Sergeant. I have the beaker, one with a tight-fitting cap."

They found snakes lurking under stones, or hidden in clumps of vegetation. They discovered reptiles on flat rocks taking the sun. A deft movement with the curved stick and Parris had an elapid secured by the neck. Their rattles did not disturb Palmer Brown. He grabbed the rattler behind its head and let it hang to thrash about. He turned to Jock.

"Hand me the beaker and make sure the gunny sack is open wide. Don't want an angry snake getting loose and biting you or me."

Palmer Brown forced the serpent's mouth open on the edge of the beaker. The snake struck, and the venom trickled down into the vessel.

"See, Jock, the two fangs are hollow. When it strikes, the poison flows into the victim through the two holes the fangs make when it bites. We're milkin' the venom into the beaker. Takes a while for the venom to gather again in the sac inside its mouth. He'll be ready to poison Yankees when they come up. Hold the sack open. Close it once he's well inside."

Parris kept a hold on the snake's neck and thrust the reptile into the open gunny sack.

Buster caught more snakes, and they milked them. Jock stopped counting after Parris caught the tenth rattler. He packed another ten snakes into the sack.

"I'll catch a few more. Make it twenty snakes in one sack and fifteen in the other sack."

"That'll do it," Parris said. "Thirty-five snakes in there." He prodded the gunny sacks and the gathering of serpents writhed and rattled.

Jock shuddered. He'd secured the neck of the bags with a tightly knotted thin rope. He handed the gunny sack to Parris.

"You take them."

* * *

Major Pete had deployed the Rangers. Jim and four men had moved the supply wagons far in front of Little Jerusalem to protect vital supplies of food and ammunition. Fifteen marksmen were in a position to attack the Federal right flank. Fifteen bowmen waited to launch their arrows on the left flank. Fifteen mounted skirmishers, undetected, were in the rear of the Yankee column. On the canyon rim, Major Pete and Captain Willie waited with twenty-five Rangers.

A couple of miles from Little Jerusalem, the Rangers launched the first attack. Six riders swept across the rear of the Federal column, and nine riders galloped down the left flank of the last third of the column. War whoops and Rebel Yells mingled with gunfire and drumming hooves, as Rangers killed and wounded Yankees. Riders hanging from the saddle were hidden by their horse, firing round its front then turning away, riding out of range. One Yankee shot back with a Sharps Carbine, killing a brave. Some crazy braves, yelling their war cries, rode close enough to use the bow. Arrows killed Federals. Jock, well

Only The Leaves Whispering

hidden among rocks, worked with the Hawken Gun, killing a lieutenant and two sergeants. He joined the skirmishers, shadowing the Yankees from the rear but out of range of rifle fire.

Major Pete and Captain Willie watched the skirmishing through binoculars and telescope.

"Reckon we have them on edge," Major Pete said.

"Looks like it," Captain Willie said. "Our boys in the Federal rear are keeping up the pressure. Want the Yankees angry and out for blood. Keep coming after us."

Major Pete sent the Mexican trumpeters forward, visible to the Command of the Federals but out of rifle range. They played *De Guella*.

"No quarter asked or given," Major Pete said.

"They'll come up now," Captain Willie said.

* * *

The 16th Kansas Cavalry advanced to Little Jerusalem, keeping watch for more attacks in their rear from Ranger skirmishers. The Rebel forces hidden here and there along the canyon waited. The Yankees entered a canyon which ended in a narrow, funnel-like egress. The confines of the canyon walls obliged the Yankees to keep the tight column of twos. Hidden on the left side of the trail, the bowmen lay among the dead ground. On the right side, fifteen Ranger marksmen sheltered behind rocks. At the head of the canyon, Major Pete and Captain Willie waited with twenty-five marksmen. They kept back from the canyon rim.

Major Pete lowered his binoculars. "Yankees should be in sight anytime now. That dust rising is from their horses. Must be trotting at a good clip."

Captain Willie lowered the telescope. "They'll move faster once the boys down there get busy."

The sound of many hooves striking the hard ground and the distant ring of harness and creaking saddles travelled up the canyon. The middle of the column passed the hidden bowmen and marksmen. Parris Brown gestured for the bowmen to rise. The men raised their bows, ready to launch poisoned arrows in a high curve, to drop on the Yankees. Before a minute passed, a shower of sixty arrows hit the middle of the column. Riders fell, panicked, killed, the wounded, set to suffer or die from snake venom. The bowmen launched another flight of poisoned arrows, cased their bows, secured quivers and mounted.

Major Pete and Willie heard volleys from the Sharps carbines and a few Henry repeating rifles of Rangers hidden on the other side of the trail. Archers now using firearms, and marksmen, broke off the action to join the skirmishers some hundred and fifty yards behind the rear of the Yankee column. They dashed forward, fired rifles and carbines into the heaving mass of confused cavalrymen, then moved back, out of Yankee carbine range, to reload, advance and fire again. The rear of the Yankee column pushed the body of cavalrymen, moving them towards the head of the canyon. Major Pete and Captain Willie waited with the marksman for the mass of blue-clad riders. Buster had sent Abigail and the mules, their work done, away from the skirmishers in a move well out from the Yankee left flank. A Ranger rode with her until she reached Major Pete and Captain Willie.

The body of Cavalry came up. From the rim of the canyon, twenty-five Rangers discharged five volleys from Henry repeating rifles, and single-shot Sharps carbines. The cavalry staggered under the weight of the Rebel fusillade. Two young Maroons sent by Parris Brown held tight the gunny sacks full of dangerous serpents. On Captain Willie's nod, they dashed to the rim of the canyon, opened the gunny sacks and emptied the compacted mass of famished, aggressive ophidians on the hapless Yankees.

The Ranger force pressing the rear of the Yankees broke off the action. Parris Brown and Buster led the men to the rendezvous with the Ranger's wagons.

Pete and Willie waited, reins held loosely as the men passed, forming a column of twos for the ride to the rendezvous with the supply wagons.

"Reckon them Yankees won't follow, Pete."

Only The Leaves Whispering

"Reckon not. But we'll have a rear guard, just in case. Fighting wasn't too hard. There's more empty chairs in Kansas tonight. We bled them Federals. We're about even for now. Let's get the men back."

* * *

O'Leary's Rangers' raid was over. They were back in camp recovering and refitting. Abigail's life had been short of kindness and affection; and bereft of decency. At first, she did not know what to expect, riding with these rough Confederate soldiers., but the Rebels treated her better than the Federal Jayhawkers. Sergeant Buster and the two young men showed her how to help the sick and wounded. They looked after her and treated her as an equal. She considered Jim distant; quiet, remote, keeping to himself. But Abigail recognised that he was mourning Miss Harriet, the girl he had loved.

She was glad that she'd come through to the safety of the Rifles main camp.

In the weeks and days of the raid, she saw that Jock liked her and she liked him. At times, she was sure that what they felt for each other went well beyond liking. But Jock was white, and Abigail was black. And plenty of cruel people – black and white – up north and down south, would be ready to make their lives miserable. Anyway, they were just two young people.

Buster told Abigail to be ready to leave for Texas and safety, where Buster's family waited out the war. A wagon train would leave in two days. Buster had arranged a place for Abigail. But she could take the pistol, the horse and the kit Buster had given her.

"I sent a letter," Buster said. "My wife and children are expecting you. Stay with them. I'll come when this goddamned war is over. Then see about starting again in our home in the Nations." He smiled. "Before the war, I worked as a printer and rancher with my father."

Buster found it awkward, dealing with emotion and feeling. He tugged his nose and stared south towards Texas. "No family, girl?"

"No, suh. Can't remember my daddy or mama."

Jim Ellis

He shuffled the toe of his boot in the sand and dust. "Everything works out, Abigail, and if you want to, stay with us as part of my family. What do you think?"

"Oh, Sergeant Buster, Ah don't know what to say." She wiped away tears. The Jayhawker family had treated Abigail as a worthless dogsbody. Buster's kindness overwhelmed her, rooted her to the spot.

Buster went to Abigail and, overcoming his own shyness, he hugged her, an avuncular embrace. "You'll be all right, Abigail. You'll stay with us."

"Yes, suh, Ah'll stay."

Everyone in the Rifles who had been out campaigning was dirty and trail-worn. Jock had gotten used to seeing Abigail clad in men's clothes. A slouch hat, wool shirt, pants and riding boots. Garments too big for her petite figure. She packed a small Colt pistol in a holster at her side. And she was grubby. Yet no matter how Abigail looked, Jock's affection for her grew stronger. He didn't say how he felt, but he prayed that this wonderful girl would know and somehow understand. He dreaded Abigail leaving for Texas; he didn't want her to go.

Jock rode to the nearby settlement of squalid shacks and rough eating places. He visited the knocking shop and asked the Madam for help.

"You got money, young feller? Real money? Not goddammed Confederate paper?"

"Yankee dollars."

"We can do business."

He bought two white petticoats, adding a worn, pale blue dress with a full skirt. The Madam showed him a slim white dress and hung it for Jock to examine. "Pretty on a young girl. Catches them right here." She cupped her breasts with her right hand and pushed upwards. The woman grinned, exposing worn, stained teeth. Jock remembered how pretty and fetching Miss Harriet had looked in her Empire line dress.

"I'll take it."

Overcoming his shyness, Jock asked for decent stockings and small clothes.

Only The Leaves Whispering

He went to the bathhouse, where he organised and paid for a hot bath for Abigail.

He paid the woman at the laundry to wash, dry and iron the garments. Back at the camp, Jock fashioned a broad sash for Abigail's waist from a clean cotton sheet.

Later, Jock called at the laundry for the garments. He rode back to camp and went to see Abigail. He handed her the folded bundle of clothing.

"Fixed a hot bath for you at the settlement. I'll take you there. When you've bathed, you can change."

He blushed when Abigail held up the stockings and small clothes.

"You kind to me, Mr Doc, Mr Jock MacNeil. You treat me right. Ah feel like a lady. Thank you, suh."

Abigail abandoned the unwritten rules. She came close to Jock and kissed him on the cheek. "Ah'm so grateful. First real dress, underwear, stockings Ah ever had."

"No shoes for you out here. Your boots and moccasins will have to do."

"Ah don't mind."

Once she was bathed and dressed, Jock brought Abigail back. She turned and walked up and down.

"Abigail, you're looking good."

"Looking good, suh?"

"You're beautiful. The slim dress becomes you. Fits right, but the skirt drags the ground. I can make a hem right quick. I'll pin it up and hem it while you stand still."

"Mr Doc, you a wonder. Where you learn all this?"

"I was a sailor on the schooner, *Jane Brown*. We took cargoes between Scotland, England and Ireland. Picked it up aboard her. Then I joined the Confederate Navy, my ship, CSS *Alabama*. I learned more about tailoring from the blue water hands. Sailors can do everything."

Abigal laughed. "Mr Doc. Only one Mr Doc."

* * *

The evening before Abigail left, Jock made a small fire outside her sleeping quarters. Earlier, he'd prepared a rabbit for roasting, and scrounged the makings of biscuits, and shelled out precious Yankee dollars for a quarter pound of real coffee.

They sat on bedrolls by the fire, and he cooked the rabbit on a spit and made biscuits in a skillet.

"Jim went out this morning with the bow and got this rabbit for us."

Abigail smiled. "You spoil me, Mr Doc, treatin' me, dressin' me and cookin' for me, too. Thank you, Mr Jock. Where you learn to cook?"

"I taught myself on *Jane Brown*. The cook was a drunken sot. Came near to poisoning the crew. Captain got rid of him and promoted me to the ship's cook. I learned real quick."

"An' you just a child."

"Not for long. I had to be a man."

They ate in silence. Knowing that Abigail was leaving next morning weighed on Jock. Abigail was the one who broke the silence.

"You fixin' to stay with the Rifles?"

"Yes. I signed the paper. But Major Pete ordered Jim and me to work with wounded soldiers."

"I've seen it. You and Jim doin' good work, Mr Doc."

"Surgeon Adair said that, too. But Jim and me, we spoke up. Reminded Major Pete we signed the paper to fight. We decided that if we couldn't be healers and fighters, we might go over the hill, and desert."

"You keepin' men alive. You gotta stay here, Mr Jock MacNeil."

"Major Pete fixed things after we mauled that Yankee cavalry back there in the Little Jerusalem. We're fighting and healing. We did some good sharpshooting with the Hawken Gun. Jim and me, we're Good Old Rebels. We're with the Regiment until the South's won."

Abigail had heard enough as a girl bonded to Jayhawkers, and seen enough Yankees when out raiding with the Rangers, to doubt that the Confederates could win. She'd never seen braver men than the Rangers. They'd treated her like a real person. But how could these scarce peerless fighters defeat the sheer weight of the Yankee juggernaut?

Only The Leaves Whispering

"An' after the war?"

"Can't see that far ahead. Reckon Jim and me'll stick together. He's my good friend. One thing, Abigail, I'm not going back to Scotland. What about you?"

"Ah'm goin' to belong to a family. Somethin' Ah used to dream about. Goin' to be a Black Cherokee."

"I'm glad for you. Buster is a good man. If I get a furlough, I could come down to Texas and see you. But I might be here in the Nations when the war is over, and Buster brings you all home."

Jock drained his coffee cup, leaving dregs in the bottom.

Abigail reached towards Jock. "Please give me the cup, Mr Doc."

She swilled the dregs around, searching for patterns where the coffee grains settled.

"What are you doing?"

"Lookin' ahead. Gipsy woman come round the Jayhawker place. Told me Ah had the gift. Said ma grandmother or ma mother must've been a Hoodoo Woman. Your heart is opening, suh."

Abigail gazed into the cup. An impassive look shrouded her bright eyes and warm smile. "Ah'm sure goin' to miss you."

"I'll miss you too, Abigail."

"Oh, Mr Doc, Mr Jock MacNeil. We just a couple of youngsters. Black and white in these days can't be together. Plenty white and coloured folks make troubles for us."

"I could stay in the Nations with the Cherokee. Wait for you coming home."

"Ah know that. Ah want it, but it ain't for us. It can't be." In the firelight, Abigail saw Jock's eyes filling. Embarrassed, he turned away from her and rubbed his shirt sleeve across his eyes.

"Oh, Mr Doc, you special. You an' Mr Jim, great things for you is comin', Ah can see. Not every man goin' to like what you an' Mr Jim goin' do. But you do good. Ah know the truth." Abigail gazed again into the coffee grains. "Nice pretty girl. She find you. Can't see to say more. But she make you happy, Mr Doc. You wait for her."

Jim Ellis

At last, Jock MacNeil overcame his paralysing shyness. He stood in front of Abigail. "Give me your hands." She took his outstretched hands and Jock raised Abigail to her feet. "I'm so glad I met you, Abigail." He held her close.

"Oh, Mr Doc, ma Mr Doc."

Abigail kissed Jock. He held her a while longer and then kissed her in return.

Parting, they turned to look back at each other.

* * *

The Federals planned to send provisions, arms and clothing by boat to Fort Gibson in the east of Indian Territory. They controlled the Arkansas River after winning at Cabin Creek on 17th July 1863.

Texan Confederate units withdrew from Indian Territory. Indian soldiers of the Five Civilised Tribes defended the Nations against Union Army attacks.

Buster sent for the boys.

"Lieutenant's come from Company Commander. Need you two for sharpshooting. Colonel Watie's goin' to ambush a Federal supply steamboat."

"A boat, out here?" Jock said.

"She's the *JR Williams*. A sternwheeler. Wood-fired boiler for steam-drivin' her stern-mounted paddle wheel."

"Back at sea again," Jim laughed.

"Doubt that," Jock said.

"It's no laughing matter, boys," Buster insisted. "This is an important job callin' for fine work. Them Blue Bellies are afraid of us. We attack their wagon trains comin' from Fort Scott, Kansas. But goin' on the water ain't goin' to save them. Colonel says you'll have the two Whitworth Rifles."

"Me loading and Jock shooting?"

"That's how you'll do it," Buster said. "Take them Sharpshooter's Glasses, Jock."

Only The Leaves Whispering

"Too bad the Rangers are not here," Jock said. "Major Pete and Captain Willie have them out raiding."

"The Rangers'll be doing good wherever they are," Jim said.

* * *

Fifteenth June 1864. Colonel Stand Watie led four hundred men to Pleasant Bluff. They gathered at a bend in the Arkansas River below the mouth of the Canadian River.

Jock stood, the barrel of the Whitworth Rifle resting on the V of the firing stick. He brought the bridge house of the boat into the scope sight and fired.

"Reckon I wounded the Captain," Jock said, as he handed the Whitworth to Jim for loading.

Jock made a quick count of twenty-odd Union soldiers guarding the boat. With his second shot, Jock wounded the Lieutenant commanding the detachment of soldiers.

"Damnit it to Hell. I meant to kill the pair of them."

"You done good, son," Buster said. "Bein' hit by a .451 rifled ball, they'll be feelin' low."

Colonel Watie gave the command and his artillery opened fire, crippling the *J R Williams*. The gunners hit the smokestack, pilothouse and boiler. Riflemen shot at the Federals. Union troops shot back through the fog of escaping steam. Jock looked again for the Captain. He intended to kill him, but did not find him, or any suitable target.

The Captain grounded the vessel on the river bank opposite the Confederates. He and the Sergeant launched the yawl and sailed it towards the Confederates. The Union men abandoned the *J R Williams*, retreating to a nearby Union Army camp to report the ambush.

"Come on, boys," Buster said.

They joined the press of Confederate troops boarding the abandoned steamboat. The soldiers manhandled a couple of small boats and towed the steamer to a sandbar on the south side of the river. Junior officers and NCOs organised unloading before relieving Federal forces came up. The Rifles took four hundred Sharps rifles and six hundred new revolvers.

Then they plundered the vessel, piling bacon and flour on to a sand bar. They meant to deliver the food to their starving families.

The ill-clad soldiers of the Rifles plundered the cargo of men's dress clothing. They looted top hats, jackets with tails, fancy trousers and spats, adding them to their uniforms.

"We could be in trouble," Buster said." So many men heading for home with grub for hungry wives and children. Look at them sportin' dress clothes. Yankees come up, we could lose the artillery."

The Lieutenant appeared. "Federal troops are in sight. Time we moved out."

Buster scanned beyond the east bank of the river with his telescope. "About two hundred men in the column. Looks like the Indian Home Guard."

Federals came up and fired on the Rifles. The river rose, covered the sand bar and carried away part of the cargo. The loss of flour and bacon to the flood vexed the boys.

As the withdrawal gathered momentum, Colonel Watie ordered a party of men to set fire to the *JR Williams,* destroying the vessel.

* * *

Buster knew the taking of the steamboat would cheer up Confederates in the Nations. Gloomy Southerners clung to any good news about the war.

"Reckon that was the first and the last naval action out here in the Nations. A useful haul of guns. Worry the Yankees with them. All that food and fancy dress, too," Buster said that evening, after supper. "I figure the Colonel might get promoted, Brigadier General. Doesn't mean we'll win the war, though."

A few men wandered the camp wearing outlandish, ill-fitting dress clothes taken from the *J R Williams.* They would leave soon with food and clothing for their families. The majority of the command had already gone home.

Only The Leaves Whispering

"They'll come back in a few days, "Buster said. "Can't say I blame them."

Jock and Jim declined to take part in the looting of dress clothes. They preferred their worn medley of bushwhacker and Confederate garments. The boys hooted with laughter at the sight Cherokee Braves capering in top hats, and tailcoats over buckskin leggings and moccasins. Helpless mirth gripped them when they saw soldiers with spats on the wrong feet, worn over cavalry boots.

"Don't look like Southern Blades with them pistols and knives tucked into Yankee coats and belts," Jock said. He wiped his eyes.

"Jock, wipe that grin off your face. You an' all, Jim, or I'll do it for you. Better if the goddamned Confederate Government sent enough of the right supplies." Buster gestured to the few remaining Braves. "That's all most of them have to keep out the cold and damp."

"Sorry, Sergeant," Jock said.

"Didn't mean no harm," Jim added.

"All right, all right," Buster said, waving his right arm. Anxious to repair fences with the boys, he reflected on the state of the Confederacy in the first six months of 1864.

"We're holding on, but can't afford to be too optimistic."

"You mean capturing the *JR Williams* was not a real win," Jock said.

"What we're doin' is critical, tying down Federal troops. Farragut took New Orleans back in 1862. It's no picnic down there. Major General Benjamin Butler, he's a hard man. Earned the moniker Spoons Butler because his men looted silverware.

Buster and the boys fell silent for several seconds.

"What else has he done?"

"The bastard is mistreating women. Any who insult or show contempt of Union officers and men will be treated like a whore plying her trade."

"Jesus Christ," Jock said.

"Hate sayin' this, but we lose this war, it'll be a bleak living. Sherman's attacking Georgia with three armies, Grant took Vicksburg last

Jim Ellis

year and he's bound to be movin' against Lee in Virginia. I'm a Good Old Rebel still, but it looks terrible."

* * *

A few days after the Rifles had returned from wrecking the *J R Williams*, a merchant came to the Rifles camp. He'd brought two wagons filled with medical supplies, more bacon and flour, fifty Enfield rifles, and ammunition.

"We have bandages, surgical dressings, chloroform and ether," Surgeon Adair said.

"That's good for us, sir," Jock said. "I saw the Mexican escort and the cattle. First time I've seen vaqueros."

"Yes. I spoke to the Texan owning the herd. He brought the cattle from Mexico. Joined with his friend, bringing the wagons from Galveston for protection from outlaws."

The merchant and the cattleman supported the South but wanted to be paid in Yankee dollars. Stand Watie had Yankee currency which he'd taken in raids. He made a bargain with both men.

Buster approached Jock. "The merchant out of Galveston has word of your old ship, *Alabama*. Let's go and see him."

The merchant sat on a comfortable canvas camp chair. He sipped whisky from a crystal glass. He wore quality clothes: a heavy, worn, but elegantly cut three-piece grey tweed suit, the trousers tucked into black polished riding boots. Jock noted the bright, silvery spurs on the heels. His jacket hung open, revealing the handle of a Colt pistol tucked in a shoulder holster. A black, curly-brimmed derby hat tilted over his right brow. With his left hand, the merchant eased his starched white collar and tugged loose his grey silk tie.

"My goods came off a blockade runner from England. I took a risk and paid for my stuff in advance."

"What about *Alabama*? I served on her as Loblolly Boy. My Sergeant said you had word of her."

"You're a Scotchman, young feller?"

"Yes, sir. From Westburn."

Only The Leaves Whispering

"William Watson, a countryman of yours, captained the *Pelican*, a fast screw steamer. Sailed her from London to Havana. Then brought her into Galveston, right under the nose of the Yankee blockade. There were some Westburn men on board the ship."

"Right glad to hear that, sir. But what of *Alabama* and my old shipmates?"

The merchant reached for a pewter flask standing on a small folding table and had his Creole manservant bring two more crystal glasses. He unscrewed the cap from the container and poured two shots of whisky, handing a glass to Buster and Jock.

"Battle of Cherbourg, some called it. Best you have a snort – liquor from Scotland. It was the Captain of the blockade runner told me. He was loading the cargo in London when word came in about *Alabama*."

Jock had seen crystal glasses aboard *Alabama* but had never drunk from one. He held it close and sipped the whisky. He liked the smooth finish when the glass touched his lips.

"Lovely glass, sir."

"Stewart Crystal, from Scotland."

Jock listened to the news about his former ship. On 11th June 1864, *Alabama* had docked in Cherbourg after twenty-two months at sea. The Confederate ship needed a complete overhaul to function as a man-of-war. The French permitted *Alabama* to restock and make small repairs.

Outside Cherbourg, the USS *Kearsarge* had arrived on 14th June and blockaded *Alabama*. *Kearsarge*, a screw sloop of war, had pursued *Alabama* for two years.

"*Alabama* was a tired ship after twenty-two months at sea, and never a visit to a Confederate port. Captain Semmes was not shy. He offered battle to Captain Winslow of *Kearsarge* and came out to face the Yankee on 19th June," continued the merchant.

The ships fought for an hour. Each Captain had tried to cross the other's bow and deliver a raking fire down its length. *Alabama* maintained rapid fire. *Kearsarge's* armoured cladding protected the hull.

Her guns had poured missiles into *Alabama*, holing her below the waterline. The Confederate ship began to sink.

"Captain Semmes struck the Confederate colours, but the Yankee kept firing. A sailor aboard *Alabama* waved a white flag, surrendering, and *Kearsarge's* guns stopped firing."

Captain Semmes had sent his remaining dinghy across to *Kearsarge* requesting assistance. More than forty Confederate had sailors died.

"The Assistant Surgeon, David Herbert Lewellyn, was my commanding officer. Did he survive?" asked Jock.

"No, son. This good man drowned when the ship went down. There was word about him. A brave officer. Captain Watson said he'd read the surgeon's obituary in an English county newspaper. Seems he declined an offer to get into one of the boats. He wanted the wounded to be saved first."

Jock swallowed the last of his whisky. The merchant reached for the pewter flask. "Have another drink, son. You need it."

Jock asked about Davey White.

"He was a friend of mine, an officer's steward. A slave freed by Captain Semmes."

"No, I can't recall that name. I guess he went down with *Alabama*."

"The word is all bad. It's terrible." Jock drank more whisky.

"There's some light. A British yacht, the *Deerhound*, rescued thirty Confederates and fourteen officers. Three French pilot boats were on hand. They got away. Captain Semmes did not surrender his sword to the Yankee."

"I'm glad the Captain escaped," Jock said to the merchant. "Thanks for taking the time to tell me and thanks for the whisky."

Jock, depressed, wandered through the camp. He found it hard to accept that the Yankee Navy had caught up with his beloved *Alabama* and sunk her. He was saddened by the death of shipmates. But his mood swung to the edge of despair knowing that David Herbert Lewellyn and Davey White had died. Jock knew that the loss of *Alabama* meant the Cause had taken another wrong turn.

Only The Leaves Whispering

* * *

13th September 1864, Camp Pike, Choctaw Nation. The Rifles remained in the field, waiting. The news of the war depressed the soldiers: Lee under siege in St Petersburg. On the 5th August, the Federal fleet, commanded by Admiral Farragut, sealed the port of Mobile, Sherman taking Atlanta on 2nd September. The Yankees were celebrating Sherman's victory with a national holiday on 5th September. The word from the Western Theatre said the army was in poor shape. Throughout the Confederacy, food was scarce.

By 17th September, the Rifles grew fed up with waiting and were ready for action. When he had the opportunity, Buster dined with Jock and Jim at supper. He soaked up the last cornmeal and fatback bacon on his tin plate with a wedge of biscuit. A satisfying burp escaped the Sergeant as he patted a full stomach. Buster drained his mug of acorn coffee and tipped the grains on to the ground.

"Grub is good as far as it goes, but I could do with some home comforts, or even a spell of tepee livin'. Buffalo tongue, broiled venison. A real treat, Jock, would be one of your roasted rabbits."

"Hereabouts," Jim said, "good-sized rabbits are hard to find."

"Shoot me a rabbit, Jim," Jock said. "I'll cook it right. And scrounge the makings of biscuits. Real coffee, that would be good, too."

"Anyway," Buster said. "Good to hear Colonel Stand Watie is now Brigadier General Stand Watie! He got word after we fixed the *J R Williams*. The men are happy that their Colonel commands not only the First Indian Brigade, but also two regiments of Mounted Rifles and three battalions of Cherokee, Seminole and Osage infantry.

"We're keeping south of the Canadian River," Buster added. "We're well placed to cross the river into Union territory and hit the Yankees."

Jock gathered the knives and spoons, tin plates and mugs.

"I'll clean up. Be back soon."

The Rifles waited on the word to attack. Meanwhile, Brigadier General Richard Montgomery Gano met Brigadier General Stand Watie for the forthcoming expedition.

Gano commanded several Texan Confederate units. He'd agreed to join with Stand Watie as co-leader of the Campaign. General Watie had developed the plan to attack the Yankee supply train.

"We have to win this fight," Buster said. "It's the second battle of Cabin Creek. We lost the first one back in 1863. You was there, Jim?"

"I was. First and second of July. We got licked trying to ambush a Federal supply train. Yankees shelled us for half an hour. Didn't like it much. We fought coloured troops. Ist Coloured Kansas Infantry. Have to say it, they fought well. We was in trenches and them Federals drove us off the field."

"General Watie's a good man. He's a fine officer; a gifted natural soldier. Ain't going to be any repeat," Buster said. "Some of our boys and Texans got off to a good start yesterday. Maybe you heard?"

"There was talk of a fight," Jock said.

"Fifteen miles northwest of Fort Gibson at Flat Rock, near Flat Rock Creek and the Grand River. A detachment of 2nd Kansas Cavalry and some fellers from the 1st Kansas Colored Infantry. They was making hay. Our boys surrounded them. Stalled a breakout. A handful of Federals got away. Captured the hay-making machine, and several hundred tons of hay. Took out a hundred Yankee casualties, including prisoners. Hardy, awkward men, them Texans."

Word had leaked through the ranks that the Texans hated Indians; including allies. They resented Stand Watie's promotion to General in the Confederate Army.

"One fuckin' Texan, a Colonel De Morse, 29th Texas Cavalry, refused to serve under the General," Buster said. "He's forgetting the Cherokee are the finest Confederate light cavalry. We've kept them goddamned Blue Bellies out of south Indian Territory and good parts of north Texas."

"Bloody Texan brass neck," Jock said.

"The South wins or loses this war," Jim said. "You couldn't trust them Texans to consider Indian interests."

"Not just Texans," Buster said. "Be other Southerners thinkin' the same way. Yankees, too. Indians got to look after themselves."

Only The Leaves Whispering

* * *

The Confederates attacked at one o'clock in the morning on 19th September. All fit men were directed to fight.

"Boys, you're in this one all right. We'll be attacking. We're after a big Yankee wagon train. No sharpshooting," Buster said. "Reckon Surgeon Adair has the help he needs."

"I'm fine with that," Jock said.

"Me too," Jim said."

"General put The Cause first," Buster said. "Said Morse had more seniority, so he should command. The General's a better man than any goddamned Texan."

The Confederate force advanced. Gano's Brigade of twelve hundred men comprised Texas cavalry and artillery. Stand Watie commanded the Indian Brigade of eight hundred men. The Texans covered the left flank and the Indian Brigade the right flank.

Union gunners opened fire, and the Confederate artillery replied.

Gano led the attack on the Union flank, driving the Federals back, scattering them among the trees along the Creek. Confederate shells fell close to panic-stricken mules of the wagon train. Here and there, a few active animals dragged wagons into the Cabin Creek. Some terrified animals fell into the waters of the Creek. Wattie's men gave the Rebel Yell. They discharged revolvers and rifles at escaping teamsters, riding mules they'd cut loose, across Cabin Creek Ford to safe ground.

Jock and Jim rode with Buster's platoon straight for the wagon train. The Kansas infantry retreated towards the river.

An infantryman shot Jock's hat off his head, leaving a bloody graze across his scalp. The excitement of battle flooded Jock with adrenalin and he rode on, knocking the young soldier down. He pulled the horse round, unsheathed his sabre and cut down the black infantryman preparing to swing his Enfield Rifle in a futile attempt to club Jock to death.

By nine o'clock in the morning, the Rebels had routed the Federals. They captured one hundred and thirty wagons and seven hundred and forty mules valued at one million dollars.

After the battle, the boys rode with Buster's platoon back to camp. He brought his horse up beside them.

"We did well this morning. I'll be surprised if the General doesn't get some recognition from the Confederate Government in Richmond."

Jim and Jock, still young at heart and idealistic, knew that The Rifles and the Texas Cavalry had done well at the Second Battle of Cabin Creek. They felt and shared the soaring spirits of the men who'd won a victory.

"Think we helped Lee up in Petersburg?" Jim said.

"And what about the Good Old Rebels in Tennessee and Georgia?" Jock said.

"Like I said, boys, we're keeping Yankees down here. If we wasn't fighting, be a pile more of them Blue Bellies all over them good Rebel soldiers."

They rode on, Jock and Jim feeling more than a little deflated by what Buster said.

"We're still Good Old Rebels, Sergeant," Jim said.

"We are, too," Jock said. "We're here for the South for as long as it takes."

Buster smiled. "Come on, you boys. Might be better grub when we get back."

* * *

The boys, wearing heavy jackets and scarves, hats pulled down to break the wind, sat warming their hands over the yellow flicker of weak flames. They finished their supper.

"More fresh biscuits and hot beans," Jim said. He looked over at Jock.

"You doin' that white man thing, Jock? Shaving?" he asked.

"Not exactly. I like the red hair on my face. It ain't quite a beard, but it makes me look older. I trim it with a razor, scissors and comb."

"You cut yourself?"

Only The Leaves Whispering

"No, God damn it! I can hone and strop the razor. Keeping it sharp is the way to avoid cuts. Why the Hell don't you shave? You're older than me."

"I'm an Injun. Don't have as much hair on my face as a white man. Take out the hairs on my face with tweezers."

Jock looked at the dying fire, then broke the silence. "How much longer?"

"Can't say. I've thought about what Buster said about the war. Have to say it looks bad for the South. The Yankees got men, guns, horses and kit. We kill them and beat them, and they keep comin'."

Word came about the troubled state Army of Northern Virginia, and Confederate forces to the west.

"How you feellin' about it all, Jock?"

"I'm sorry the South is hangin' on and not winning. But, no regrets, Jim. I loved my time in the Navy. Servin' on *Alabama* was an honour."

"And what about Indian Territory, and your time in the Rifles?"

"Glad I came up with you from Galveston and enlisted. I worried that I'd be afraid. Got over that. Proud to have served in the Cherokee Mounted Rifles."

"You done good, Jock. You saved lives and limbs. And you're the best sharpshooter in the Rifles."

Both boys quietly thought about the time they had spent helping Doc Merriweather. And the month living on the O'Leary Ranch, meeting the O'Learys and the Sullivans. The happy time.

"Miss Harriet was the best thing in my life. I miss her every day," Jim said, looking at his boots to hide the emotion working on him. Cherokee Braves shed no tears.

"Did we avenge Miss Harriet?"

"Well, we caused mayhem and killed Yankees on the raid with O'Leary's Rangers."

"We did. Paid back them Blue Bellies."

"I reckon, but that was the war. I don't know if we killed the men who raped and murdered Miss Harriet." Grief choked Jim off. He swallowed hard and recovered. "But all that killin' won't bring her back."

Jim Ellis

"True. Pete and Willie are out raidin', burnin' and killin'. All they want is war. I'm glad we're back with the Rifles proper."

"Me, too, Jock. We're here fightin' for the Confederacy and the Cherokee until the General says we can leave."

"We'll do our duty, Jim."

"Ever hear anything about Abigail? Did she write? Sorry, I forgot. She can't write."

"Abigail was a bonded girl, she got no schooling from them Jayhawkers. Buster said she was getting along fine. I said I'd wait for her. She had the second sight, a Spey Wife."

"A Spey wife?"

"Abigail had the gift to see the future. Said we couldn't be together. I like her. She was kind and smart. Buster's family'll teach her to read and write. I cared for Abigail, and she cared for me. She worried that she's black and I'm white."

"I see what you mean. Might have been easier for Miss Harriet and me. A black girl and a Cherokee."

Jock felt a twinge of envy, but a surge of regret killed it. Miss Harriet was dead... murdered. Jim was without hope.

The feeble yellow flames turned their thoughts to what might have been.

Jim had longed to marry his beloved Harriet. The war destroyed his yearning.

For the first time with Abigail, Jock had known young love, but hatred of Southerners and Northerners stymied their desire to be together. Abigail, smart and lovely, knew the hard road facing them if they were together. At that moment, Jock realised she had gone in order to protect him. Abigail had left because she loved him.

"You all right, Jock?"

"I thought we should head west when the war is over."

"I like that."

* * *

Only The Leaves Whispering

A week later, Jock and Jim were resting after a raid when the black outline of a man came walking towards the boys.

"Who's that comin'?"

Jim eased a Colt pistol from its holster and cocked the weapon.

"It's Buster. I know his walk," Jock said.

Jim uncocked the Colt and tucked it in the holster.

Buster swayed by the fire. He clutched a jug.

"Evening, boys. This is your birthday, Jock. I brought a jug of refreshment. Tasted it myself. God knows where it's from or who made it, but it'll have to do."

He raised the jug in an awkward toast. "May you survive this war, my young Scots friend. Good luck."

Buster handed the jar to Jim.

"I'll drink to that." Jim held the jug in both hands and took one swallow of what he suspected was Oklahoma moonshine.

"What the Hell is that, Sergeant?"

"Whiskey."

Jim passed the jug to Jock.

He put his forefinger through the neck lug, cradling the vessel on his right elbow and forearm. Jock swallowed twice, suppressed a fit of coughing and passed the jug back to Buster.

"My God, but that's strong medicine."

Jock moved along the slicker covering his bedroll, and Buster sat down next to him. He slugged down a couple of mouthfuls of the raw spirit.

Buster reached inside his shirt and withdrew a square of rolled, clean parchment.

"Borrowed this from the General's headquarters. Wrote it out fair, but from memory. It's a prayer for your birthday. I had a look at your enlistment papers. I wanted to get you something, but there's nothing to be had in the Nations these days. The prayer's in the old way. It's a Cherokee Blessing. Thought you'd like that."

Jim Ellis

Jim caught Jock's eye. Now they understood why Buster had whiskey. Without some drams inside him, he'd never have attempted to read the prayer to Jock.

Buster started quietly, but his voice soon gained confidence.

"May the warm winds of Heaven
Blow softly upon your house,
May the Great Spirit
Bless all who enter here,
Make happy tracks
In many snows,
And may the rainbow touch your shoulders."

"Right kind of you, Sergeant Parris. Thank you." Jock said.

"You're sixteen now, Jock?"

"Yes."

Jock rose and excused himself. He felt the Oklahoma juice, as he headed towards distant bushes to relieve himself.

In the feeble light from the fire, Buster watched Jock. He turned to Jim and smiled.

"You're about eighteen, Jim. Jock's just a lad. He's a waif hiding in that Bushwhacker shirt, that hat sitting on his ears. Them Colts in his belt and the .36 Navy Colt in the shoulder holster are weighing him down. I worry that he'll trip over that sword he carries."

"Never thought I'd have a white man for my best friend," Jim said. "Saved my life down in Galveston." Jim rubbed his right wrist. "Fixed this up well when I broke it a while back. Best goddamned sharpshooter in the Rifles."

"He is, and with a good heart, too. I'd have liked a brother like that young feller," Buster said.

Jock came back into the firelight and sat down on his slicker-covered bedroll. Buster handed him the jug. "Have another drink, Jock. It's your sixteenth birthday."

Only The Leaves Whispering

Jock took two good pulls at the jug. This time, he liked the sensation of the passage of fiery liquor into his gut. He passed the jar back to Buster.

Buster broke the silence. "You're happy now with soldiering and keeping your doctorin' sharp?"

"I am."

Jock thought about his hard life and dire prospects for his future in Westburn – a Catholic orphanage, labouring at best, poverty living in the Old Vennel, a slum. Choosing the sea had shut the door on that black hole.

"I was always for the South. In the Navy, aboard *Alabama*, and the Rifles, reckon I found myself serving the Confederacy and the Cherokee."

Jock touched his heart. "Feel it in here. Don't need to say more."

"That's good, son," Buster said. He passed the jug to Jock.

* * *

The Rifles continued raiding and ambushing Federal forces. Jock was happy assisting Surgeon Adair. The sick and wounded liked him for the kind words he had for them each day.

Jock found the courage to acknowledge to himself that he was glad to have a rest from the strain of raiding and fighting. But he could not silence the serpent of doubt that stung him. Jock was no coward. He meant to see Buster and get back to straight duty. Jock sensed that the last phase of the war had begun. He wanted a part in it.

It was in plain sight that the war was not going well for the South. Even Buster, a pillar of optimism in the Rifles, was gloomy.

Jock left the medical area and went to see Buster and Jim on their return from a raid.

"Couple of wounded. A Minie ball ricochetted. Hit one man in the left leg," Buster said. "Missed the thigh bone and he ain't losing blood. Surgeon Adair'll take care of him."

"Is that all?" Jock said.

Jim Ellis

"Lieutenant's got a head wound," Jim said. "A Yankee cut him with a sabre. The Lieutenant shot him. Bleeding bad. One for you to look at, Jock."

"I'll speak to Surgeon Adair, and I'll get the Lieutenant sutured up."

Later that day, after supper, Buster sat outside his quarters with Jock and Jim. He liked to spend time with 'his boys'. A lighted candle cast shadows as they warmed their hands on cups of acorn coffee.

"Well, at least the food was hot and the biscuits fresh," Buster said.

"I've eaten my share of beans and fatback bacon," Jim said. "Enough to last the rest of my life."

"If I never saw beans or bacon again, it would be too soon," Jock said.

There was an esprit de corps in the Rifles, founded on Stand Watie's exceptional military skills. He led his men to raid and plunder the Yankees.

"We beat the Federals at Cabin Creek. It raised hope down here," Buster said.

"But you don't reckon we can win the war in the Nations?" Jock said.

"That's right. We ain't goin' to drive the Federals out. I've said it before. I recollect the waves of hope coming through the South after Chickamauga. But damned Federals held on to Chatanooga."

"We can surely do it again," Jim said.

"I've prayed that we could. But the Federals got an army twice the size of ours. Their Navy blockades Confederate ports. The Union has more of everything. I wish I could stop reading about it, but I can't."

"Sweet Jesus," Jock said.

"Sweet Jesus, right enough," Buster said. "This General Grant is a goddamned tornado. When Lee and the Army of Northern Virginia mauled the Yankees at The Wilderness, Southern morale shot up, but it didn't last. Any other Yankee general would have pulled back. Grant kept attacking. He can replace men who are lost. Lee can't."

"You're making us miserable," Jim said.

"Well, here's more. Grant has got Lee under siege at St Petersburg."

"Rifles have to keep going," Jock said.

"Right," Jim said.

Only The Leaves Whispering

"Glad to hear you boys say that. The General is goin' to fight on, raiding and ambushing. There's no talk of surrender. Confederate and Cherokee honour means we keep them Blue Bellies down here."

"Sergeant, I have a request," Jock said.

"Go ahead, son."

"I'd like a return to straight duty. I want to be out riding with you and Jim."

Buster grinned. "I'll attend to it right away."

Chapter Nine

The raids stayed with Jock. A set of images that he'd recall throughout his long life. The column of Cherokee Mounted Rifles behind Stand Watie and the flag of the Cherokee Braves. The subdued racket of cavalry getting underway. The rhythmic creak of saddle leather and chafing harness. A discordant chorus of metal fittings adjusting as the men settled in the saddle for the raid.

He would not forget the dead and wounded returning from battle.

The Rifles, dressed in any clothing they could find. They were low supply priority for CSA Quartermasters. The slouch hats, some with CSA badges. Other heads covered by stained, worn butternut kepis. Here and there, the flash of a yellow-striped trouser leg.

These were the memories he'd share only with Jim. To retell it to someone who hadn't been, there was a sacrilege against the regiment. What could an outsider know?

Since 1863, Jock had lived on the frontier between life and death, held there by the war. He'd been afraid for his life more than once, but he'd overcome the terror of combat. By age sixteen, the Rifles had made him hard. But Jock had not shed his humanity. He was glad that Surgeon Adair had encouraged him to treat sick and wounded soldiers. Jock had applied what he'd learned from David Herbert Llewellyn aboard CSS *Alabama*.

Buster was right when he said, "You're never the same after fighting a war. It'll stay with you forever."

Only The Leaves Whispering

They'd lost the war. The fight for Southern independence was winding down. But the Rifles felt vindicated as men and soldiers. In the bleak days of spring 1865, the General was in command not of a broken rabble, but a feared and respected fighting brigade.

And the boys had loved and lost. Jim had suffered a tragedy when Jayhawkers raped and murdered Miss Harriet.

Jock had found first love with Abigail. But Abigail knew prejudice would keep them apart. Yet she had left Jock with hope for the future, and Jim, too.

"Oh, Mr Doc, you special. You an' Mr Jim – great things for you is comin', Ah can see. Not every man goin' to like what you an' Mr Jim goin' do. But you do good. Ah know the truth."

* * *

"Major Pete and Captain Willie – what are they going to do when the war is over?" Jim asked. He thought for a moment. "Whatever it is, there'll be more fighting."

"You're right, Jim," Jock said. "War has a hold on Major Pete and Captain Willie. I reckon it has a hold of what's left of O'Leary's Rangers."

The boys did not have long to wait to have their intuition confirmed. Captain Willie came to see them.

"The Major is askin' for you. Sends compliments and hopes both are well. He'd like to see you. He has an offer. Somethin' for you to consider. Sergeant Buster is with him. You boys free right now?"

"Yessir."

The boys sat with Major Pete, Captain Willie and Buster outside Major Pete's quarters. He described the situation.

"You know about Lee's surrender to Grant?"

"We do," Jock, said.

"Well, Kirby Smith surrendered the Army of Trans-Mississippi back on 26th May. The General wouldn't admit defeat until now."

"We're with the General," Jim said.

"Likewise," Captain Willie said.

Jim Ellis

"I've always been with him, but we have to face facts," Major Pete said. "Week by week, day by day, since Appomattox, the Confederate Army has fallen away. We're the last significant Confederate force still fighting."

"We're with the General until he says it's over," Jock said.

A weary Pete drew his right hand across his eyes.

"The General knows he can count on all his men. The Grand Council of Confederate Indian Chiefs met and decided fighting on is pointless. The war is over for the brigade."

A terrible silence engulfed them. A sadness beyond words.

Pete stood. "I need a drink."

He entered his quarters and emerged with an unopened bottle and a tray with five glasses.

"Mezcal. I sent some boys across the Bravo, and they brought back a couple of bottles. Tell you about that in due course. I wanted, not this, but to celebrate Southern Independence over a bottle of Irish Whiskey."

Pete poured five shots of Mezcal.

"To the memory of the Cherokee Braves and O'Leary's Rangers and to their future." He raised his glass.

"A Union Officer, Lieutenant Colonel Asa C. Matthews, is coming to meet the General here at Doaksville, Fort Towson," Major Pete said. "There's the talk of disbandment and sending the Braves home."

"Mezcal – whew! It takes your breath away," Buster said.

"The Mexicans make it from agave. Sure gives you a jolt," Willie said.

"Now that the war's finished," Major Pete said," what're y'all going to do? Willie and me have a suggestion."

Buster, Jock and Jim exchanged glances and said nothing.

"Let me tell you about Benito Juarez." Major Pete described the leader of the Juaristas and their struggle against French occupation.

"I got relatives down there, my wife's family. I sent a couple of our Mexican Rangers to see them and sound them out about us goin' down to fight alongside them. Well, they're waitin' on us comin'."

"We're takin' what's left of O'Leary's Rangers to help them fellers kick the French out," Willie said.

Only The Leaves Whispering

A tight grin split Willie's face. "I hear the Frenchies brought their Foreign Legion to prop up Emperor Maximilian. We go up against them – see how they'll do against us Rebels."

Pete had brought a hundred men to the Cherokee Rifles. Fifty survived, and many of them had suffered wounds. Jock had patched them up and helped Surgeon Adair with the severe cases.

The Ranger's casualties were higher than fifty percent. Buster reckoned that twenty to twenty-five new recruits had joined. Many of them were dead now, or wounded and unfit for soldiering.

"We were an elite unit within the Rifles, killin' Yankees, Jayhawkers and Red Legs," Pete said. "But we paid a heavy price."

Pete poured another round of Mezcal. "Let's drink to our dead."

Muffled coughing after the company swallowed the second round of Mezcal.

"What do you have in mind, Major Pete?" Buster asked.

"Well, Sergeant Buster, we ain't mercenaries, but I've re-formed the Rangers. We're well-armed freelance troops. Got hold of a twelve-pound light howitzer: deadly at close range. We have a Gunnery Sergeant, just out of the Confederate Army and not ready to go home. The Juaristas can make good use of the Rangers."

"That's impressive, Major Pete," Buster said.

"Well, how about you joinin' us? Keepin' discipline and training Juaristas when we get to Mexico?"

"I thought Palmer Brown was doing most of that?"

"Palmer Brown's dead. Killed on our last raid," Willie said. "Buster, you're the best sergeant in the Rifles."

"I thank y'all kindly for askin' me. Have to say I've had enough of the war. Goin' to see about getting my family back home from Texas." He glanced at Jock. "Abigail is with them. See about the printing shop and ranching I worked at with my father."

"That's good, Sergeant Buster," Major Pete said. "Different for us. I heard Yankees killed my father. He was sixty-seven. Rode with Bedford Forrest."

"That's hard, sir," Buster said.

The boys murmured their regrets.

Pete turned to Jock and Jim. "There's a place for you boys. Jim, you'd be the Scout, and Jock, we need your doctorin' and sharpshootin'. What do you say?"

"Thank you for the offer, Major Pete," Jock said. "Jim and me, we've talked about what to do after the war. We're reckoning on heading west. Set up as wranglers, and one day aimin' on havin' a horse ranch."

"And you, Jim?"

"I'm with Jock. Be nice to forget the war for a while."

"You boys got money for this?"

"Yes, sir. Captain Semmes gave me Sovereigns when I left *Alabama*. I saved them."

Pete dug into his inside jacket pocket and withdrew a bulging wallet. He peeled off a hundred dollars in mixed bills and handed them to Jim.

"Here. Take care of the money. Help you get established out west. Got the dollars from a Yankee payroll."

The boys said thanks. But Pete hadn't finished.

"Wille and me, we're glad to have known you boys and to have served with you. Our trouble is, you can get to like war too much."

"Can't say that, sir," Jock said.

"Jock's right about that," Jim said.

"Out west, there's wild Indians. You boys take care. I understand you want to be through with the war. I have to say it – you fight in a war, you're never the same. It stays with you."

"Sergeant Buster believes that's true," Jim said.

"He's right," Pete said. "All I'm saying is that maybe war ain't finished with you."

* * *

At sunrise, 22nd June 1865, Buster, Jock and Jim waited as the Rangers formed a double column. They saluted as the column passed. Major Pete and Captain Willie returned the salutes.

Only The Leaves Whispering

Brigadier General Stand Watie and members of his staff waited and watched. With Pete and Willie leading, the Rangers passed, and the General saluted with his sword. Pete unsheathed his sword, wheeled his mount and saluted his old commander, lowering the sword point to the toe of his boot. Officers waved their hats, and the surviving Mexican trumpeter played *Dixie.*

Pete O'Leary and Willie Sullivan led O'Leary's Rangers out of Fort Towson, near Doaksville in the Choctaw Nations. They rode for Mexico, all the men lost to the war.

* * *

The boys stood, hands in pockets, disconsolate at the loss of old comrades. They gazed at the dwindling tail end of O'Leary's Rangers.

"Jock, Jim," Surgeon Adair called. The boys turned.

"General would like a word."

"Something wrong, sir?" Jock asked.

"No, no. The General has something to say to you both."

The General wore dress uniform displaying a Brigadier General's badges of rank. The coat collar showed the three stars set in an open wreath pattern. The buttons of his uniform coat carried an embossed eagle. He wore a holstered cavalry pistol and sabre.

Jock and Jim came to attention and saluted.

"Stand easy, boys."

The General cared for all of his men, but given the collapse of the South, he thought more about the young Cherokee and his Scots friend.

"Well, Jim, you rode across half the country to join the Rifles. A veteran at eighteen. You did well. And you, Jock MacNeil, my young Scots friend from the Confederate Navy, crossed the ocean aboard CSS *Alabama.* You save Jim's life in Galveston and came with him to join the Rifles. Saving life and limb, working with Surgeon Adair. My best goddamned sharpshooter."

Stand Watie approached the boys and shook their hands. "Right proud to have served with you, boys."

Jim Ellis

"Yessir!" Jim said.

"Thank you, General," Jock said.

The General explained that the Yankees were coming to Fort Towson the next day.

"You should leave by noon today. Stay clear of Yankees asking questions about an Eastern Cherokee and a Scot serving in the Rifles. Some Bluebelly meddler might want to send you back to Scotland, Jock."

"You boys have plans?" Surgeon Adair asked.

"Set up as horse wranglers, out west," Jim said.

"One day we reckon on having a horse ranch," Jock said.

"You have money for this?" the General asked.

"Yes, sir. I saved some of the sovereigns given me by Captin Semmes when I left *Alabama*. Major Pete helped, too."

The General stroked his chin, and a sly grin escaped.

"We heard the Major laid hands on a Yankee payroll."

"Well, Jock," Surgeon Adair said, "I think you should stay. When things settle down, you could study medicine, become a doctor. You have the gift. You have healing hands."

"Doc Merriweather down in Galveston said that too, sir. I quit school at thirteen and went to sea. Can't see me as a doctor.

"Think about it, son. I'll help you."

Jim frowned, and a wan look enveloped his face. He worried that their plans for the future were about to vanish.

"I thank you for the kind offer, sir. But Jim and me, we gave our word and he's my best friend. Reckon we'll stay together and head west."

Jim's colour returned, and a smile creased his face.

The General talked about the negotiations with the Federals.

"I'll try to get agreement on the disbandment of the Rifles. Let the men get home. There'll be much work with the Yankees on a postwar settlement. And we need to meet the Cherokee who sided with the Union."

"You still have that Confederate Navy medical kit, Jock?" Surgeon Adair asked.

"Yes, sir. But it's short of supplies."

Only The Leaves Whispering

"I'll send a man for it and see what supplies I can let you have. You can set up as a medical man. A useful skill for your travels west. Pick it up before you leave. And you can have a packhorse."

* * *

Jock set his worn, damaged, plumed slouch hat with the CSA badge given him by Doc Merriweather, on his head, with the brim tipped over his eyes. He rubbed at a stain on his soiled Bushwhacker shirt adorned with several colours of silk ribbons, worn over a Cherokee war shirt. He wiped the skid of grease off his forefinger and thumb after he rubbed his dirty red hair, which was hanging below his shoulders. Removal and trimming of the copper-hued, unkempt fuzz covering his face would have to wait until they were well away from Fort Towson.

He grinned at his futile attempt at elegance, adjusting his long blue silk neckerchief, knotted in Navy fashion learned aboard *Alabama*. The romance of the Southern Cavaliers had ended in defeat.

"We're a sorry-looking pair going to say farewell to the General. But it's the best we can do."

The defeat of the South depressed Jim as much as it got Jock down. Low spirits showed in his troubled face. Jim's outer clothing was a mixture of half-leggings, grey uniform jacket and a dirty red waistcoat. He wore a soiled white shirt over a buckskin Cherokee war shirt. A long black neckerchief added a sinister air. The black hat he wore, with a CSA badge and feathers stuck in the band, made him look like a killer.

"What the hell are we going to do?" Jim said. "You keep wearin' that damned shirt and the Yankees'll find us and think we're bushwhackers. We're Cherokee Mounted Rifles."

"Take a look at yourself. You're straight from Hell."

Jim glanced down at himself and smiled. "Reckon I am."

* * *

Stand Watie handed them discharge papers and letters of recommendation.

Jim Ellis

"I hope these documents will help you."

The boys dismounted. Jim held their mounts and Jock secured the replenished medical kit to the pack animal.

"Fresh bandages, lint, iodine, arnica, black salve," Surgeon Adair said. "The Chevalier forceps for tooth extraction. I showed you how to use that. Scalpels, probes and the like. A small bottle of ether. I included a few rations. It was all we could spare."

"Thank you, sir.

The General walked round. "You boys are well set. Wish I had some clean kit for you."

He cast an approving eye over their weapons. Jock carried four pistols. A Navy Colt tucked in a shoulder holster brought from *Alabama*, a holstered cap and ball cavalry pistol, a Bowie knife and two Navy Colts tucked into his belt. The Hawken gun, a sawed-off shotgun, and his sabre hung from the saddle.

Jim was likewise armed, but carried an Arkansaw Toothpick and a Henry Repeating rifle.

"You boys can look after yourselves. Don't go starting any wars now. How do you go?"

"Well, sir, reckon we'll go by the Staked Plains, the Llano Estacado," Jim said. "Keep well back from settlements and cross into New Mexico."

"Good. Take care in New Mexico. That's Apache country. You're welcome back here anytime."

Jock and Jim exchanged salutes with the General and Surgeon Adair. They flourished their hats in farewell and rode out of Fort Towson.

* * *

Dear reader,

We hope you enjoyed reading *Only The Leaves Whispering*. Please take a moment to leave a review, even if it's a short one. Your opinion is important to us.

Discover more books by Jim Ellis at
https://www.nextchapter.pub/authors/author-jim-ellis

Want to know when one of our books is free or discounted? Join the newsletter at http://eepurl.com/bqqB3H

Best regards,

Jim Ellis and the Next Chapter Team

The story continues in:

The Last Hundred by Jim Ellis

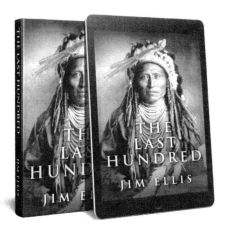

To read the first chapter for free, please head to:
https://www.nextchapter.pub/books/the-last-hundred

Manufactured by Amazon.ca
Acheson, AB